A CROSSBOW CHRISTMAS

A CROSSBOW CHRISTMAS

ANN SWANN

5 PRINCE PUBLISHING

Published by 5 PRINCE PUBLISHING & BOOKS, LLC

PO Box 865, Arvada, CO 80001

www.5PrinceBooks.com

ISBN digital: 978-1-63112-294-1

ISBN print: 978-1-63112-295-8

Cover Credit: Marianne Nowicki

To strays everywhere

ACKNOWLEDGMENTS

I would like to acknowledge my lovely editor, Cate Byers, for tidying up my words and visions. And for putting up with me in general.

I would also like to acknowledge Bernadette Soehner, C.E.O. and magician of the whole shebang, for allowing me to remain on the team.

And as always, I must acknowledge Dude, my partner in crime. He's my Alfred.

A CROSSBOW CHRISTMAS

CHAPTER 1

THE JOURNAL

You know how it is, life breaks your heart, but you survive. You work at stitching things back together and after a while it begins to seem better. Until sometime in the quiet curve of the day or in the middle stretch of a lonely night, you realize blood is still seeping. Just a little. Seeping out between the stitches. Drowning you in sorrow.

Carina read what she had written, frowned, then closed the journal. Geez. Talk about a pity party. Even my teenage journal wasn't this bad.

Turning the page, she wrote, "Dear Lord, please direct me back to my happiness. This pity stuff is *pathetic.*"

She underlined the word pathetic three times for emphasis, then she pushed the pen into the little elastic holder on the side of the journal and stared out the picture window at the still-green grass of the front lawn.

There had been very little winter in West Texas this year. January, that's when the freeze will hit. Maybe even February, but not December. Nope, not December. No white Christmas for us. Not in Landon.

Setting the journal aside, Carina strolled to the kitchen where she ran a sink full of dishwater and sipped the last bit of cooling coffee from her favorite Christmas mug, the one with the image of a rustic cabin on a snow-covered hill.

The mug was a long-ago gift from her husband, Alfred, the first year she'd taught fifth grade. She'd been nearing thirty by then, having postponed her degree until all her children were in school.

"Your first Christmas coffee mug," he'd said. "All the best teachers have them." Later, at the classroom party, she'd received several more mugs from students along with small stuffed animals, lovely jewelry—the kids knew by then how she loved quirky necklaces and earrings—and tiny cellophane bags of cookies and chocolates bearing words like #1Teacher or #BestTeacherEver.

She treasured every single gift, every year.

But Al's mug was different. He was the one who had convinced her to go back and finish her teaching degree even though their finances had been short.

The colorful cup held a special place in her heart. She only used it at Christmas time. The note that had been curled up inside it on that long ago day—*Best Teacher-Wife Ever*, in Alfred's spiky cursive—now resided in the bottom of her dresser drawer with all her other irreplaceable possessions.

She slipped the treasured mug into the warm, soapy water, wondering if the quaint cabin resembled the one in her friend Max's vacation village. He'd told her the place looked just like a Thomas Kinkade (*Painter of Light!*) painting when it snowed. "You're welcome to use the cabin for the holidays," he'd said, "you and your family."

Carina had been dumbfounded at the generous offer. Winter

in a ski resort meant high dollar rent and yet here he was offering it to her for free.

She'd also been impressed he knew about Thomas Kinkade, at his young age. He said his late wife had been a budding artist who knew everything there was to know about art.

Carina tried to think of the best way to tell him she didn't know if she would have a family Christmas this year. Everything was still up in the air where the kids were concerned. Grown and flown described them perfectly. All four of them. Even her husband, Alfred, seemed more intent on work than on celebrating.

Drying the precious coffee mug on a fluffy dishtowel decorated with sprigs of holly, Carina inhaled deeply. Her cozy kitchen was fragrant with nutmeg and ginger, the spices necessary for the pumpkin pie she'd put together earlier.

She washed the coffee pot and various dishes she'd used in making the pie, and then peeked into the oven to check its progress.

It needed a few more minutes.

Carina continued to let her mind wander to the upcoming holiday. She was doing her best to infuse some Christmas cheer into the house with the seasonal smells. The pumpkin pie would go to the senior center down the street. Her mom had loved playing cards there. Carina still visited, even though it had been a few years since her mother's passing.

Peeking in through the oven door glass again, Carina twirled the simple gold band on her ring finger. It was a habit she often found herself doing when waiting for something. Seems I've spent the last few years waiting on one thing or another, she thought. Waiting two more minutes for the pie, waiting for nurses and doctors, waiting for medicines to be delivered, to kick in, to help with the pain … waiting to see if anyone can make it home for Christmas.

She twirled the thin gold band again. Alfred used to ask if he could replace it with something more extravagant, but she'd always said no. They both came from humble backgrounds.

He had grown up in true poverty, living out of his family's car after his dad died and his mom suffered what he called "a nervous breakdown." His childhood sounded much more desperate than her own lower-income upbringing. Perhaps that's the reason he always wanted to buy her a nice diamond wedding ring now that they had good credit and a wallet full of plastic.

But Carina didn't believe in buying on time as her dad had called it, so she just always smiled, twirled her simple gold band, and said it was all she would ever need. They'd both worked hard to give their children easier, more secure, childhoods. Then Alfred had gone all mid-life crisis on her.

The timer dinged and she cleared her head of her husband's odd behavior of late. She slid an oven mitt onto her hand, removed the pie, and carefully placed it on the ancient wrought iron butterfly trivet her grandmother had given her. So many memories, she muttered. Every moment of every day is stuffed with them. I should be *making* memories, not reliving them. I'm not *that* old.

She turned off the oven and went to touch up her hair and lipstick before walking the pie down to the senior center. Giving to others was her way of forcing herself out of the house, to keep from becoming a hermit, to work up some actual holiday spirit, perhaps. Maybe it's time for me to go back to the classroom, she thought for the millionth time. At least on a part-time basis.

It had been a tough three years, and with Christmas on the horizon, and no certainty about the kids and grandkids, she did feel a little down. Blue, her Gran would've said, you've just got the blues. Hard work will cure them. Good old Gran, nothing ever seemed to get her down. Or, if it did, she had never let on.

Lately, Carina decided the latter was more likely the truth.

By the time she combed her white-streaked hair, clipped it up on top of her head, touched up her lips, and pulled on her walking shoes, the pie had cooled enough to go into the carrier with the convenient rubber carrying handle.

She donned a light jacket and started out, admiring the neighbor's twinkly Christmas decorations along the way. Alfred hadn't made time to put up their outdoor lights this year. Busy, busy, busy, he said. This year more than ever. Probably one of the reasons she felt so blue.

The other reason had to do with Romy, her eldest daughter, the one who had moved to Dallas with her own four kids and her current husband, Sean.

Carina had been shocked the day Romy called her from Vegas to tell her she and Sean had eloped. She'd only had three children then. The youngest, Little Sean, came along six months after the wedding.

She had flown to Dallas for the birth—that was before Covid hit—but since she'd been looking after her ailing mom battling lung cancer, Carina was only able to stay a couple of days. Overnight sitters for adults were astronomically expensive, and Carina's lone sibling, who stayed during the day, had begun having health problems of her own.

That had been three years ago.

Romy and Sean brought the kids down twice over those three years. The summer after Little Sean's birth when the older kids were out of school, they stopped by on their way to the mountains. "It's like the family vacays you and Dad took us on as children," Romy told Carina, eyes shining. And Carina had been thrilled, hoping her girl had found her soulmate at last.

The next time they came had been for her mom's memorial. A few months later, Carina's father suffered his first stroke, then her sister crashed her car in a fatal accident, and to add to the sudden horrific turn of events, Covid came around.

No one could come for her sister's memorial service, and even after her father suffered two more strokes, and lost his own battle with Covid, still no one could come. All visits had been curtailed.

She and Alfred soldiered on, leaning on each other in a way they never had before. But the virus didn't care how brave or self-sacrificing you were ... Carina made it through her father's memorial, and then a week later she found herself in the hospital on a ventilator. There was no vaccine in the early days of the virus, and at first, Carina assumed she was simply exhausted. The shortness of breath finally convinced her otherwise. It had been an absolute tsunami of grief and sickness and her poor old body had almost given up.

She'd fought hard to survive.

After two and a half months of isolation in the hospital, she had emerged a different person. Only then did she learn Alfred had caught the virus, too. He hadn't gone into the hospital; he'd beaten the pneumonia at home with prescriptions delivered by a cousin, and meals delivered by friends and neighbors.

Carina thanked God daily for bringing them through it. Later, she learned that Romy and the children had prayed the Rosary every night for her and Alfred to recover. Romy had even convinced a nurse to ask her own husband, a deacon, to baptize Carina right there in her ICU bed. Few people knew she'd never been baptized as a child.

Then the nurse had draped her personal rosary beads over Carina's head and within a couple of days, she was off the ventilator and being transferred to a private room. Carina still wore the rosary like a necklace, only removing it to shower or bathe.

It had taken six more months of at-home rehabilitation to build up the strength to walk again. At first, she could barely raise her head off the pillow, but finally Carina began to feel stronger. After all, Alfred had done it. Nothing seemed to knock him down for long. But for her, it felt as if she'd barely survived the virus and now, she had to relive the loss of her parents and her sister. Everything had happened so quickly, like dominoes falling one after the other, she'd had no time to grieve.

That's when one of her physical therapists had mentioned the Facebook grief group, *Holding On*. That's where she'd connected with Max Paper. They'd been texting ever since.

~

CARINA STEPPED OUT ONTO THE COVERED PORCH AND LOCKED THE door behind her. Even in this neighborhood, where they'd lived for twenty years, things had changed. No one went out without locking up anymore.

The Barton's house, down the block, was now a rental. After Jim had passed away, June had moved in with her daughter.

Carina hadn't even met the family who'd rented their house before they'd been evicted, and a second family had moved in. But this bunch was impossible to miss, with their loud dogs and louder vehicles. And the broken lawnmower standing in a patch of weeds where Jim's roses had once thrived.

Hurrying past the near-unrecognizable house, Carina tried not to recall drinking coffee right there in the bay window breakfast nook with June two or three times a week. Even though Junie had been older, by a decade at least, the two of them had shared a love of books and photography that had made them instant friends.

If any of the kids came down this year, they would be surprised at the state of that house. Childless Junie had loved baking cookies for them during the holidays. If the kids did come for Christmas this year, it would be the first big family get-together in *forever*.

At the end of the block, Carina looked both ways, crossed the street, and turned left. The red brick senior center sat smack dab in the center of the next block.

She tried a smile, made certain it fit, then forced her mind to turn off the memories. It's just transition, she told herself. Everything changes. Just like the old adages proclaim, the only thing certain, except for death and taxes, is change. Things cannot remain the same. It isn't how the world works.

She walked up the sidewalk, careful not to swing the carrier lest the perfect edges of the pie crash against the inside of the carrier.

Stopping in front of the main doors, Carina pulled an ever-present face mask from her pocket and looped the slim elastic bands around her ears. Masks were no longer required everywhere, but out of respect for the ages of the seniors—and their various chronic ailments—visitors to the center were still expected to wear them. Carina certainly didn't mind. After her own battle, a mask was never far from her hand. Especially in public.

She straightened her back and stepped inside.

Half a dozen wizened faces greeted her with waves and blown kisses. "Air hugs," several called out. They even offered to restart their card game so she could sit in. Hearts was the current favorite, with Spades and Gin-Rummy a close second and third. "Keeps us sharp," her mom's old pal Sara said, tapping her temple with her forefinger.

But Carina bowed out, offering to cut the pie and serve it instead. She hated that she'd forgotten the can of whipped cream she'd bought to top off each slice. Memory glitches were just another Covid leftover, but lack of whipped cream was a minor thing, so she wouldn't worry about it.

The card-playing crew claimed the pie a hit, even without the whipped cream, but Carina didn't linger. Every time she visited, another regular seemed to be missing. This time it was Mary, one of her mom's oldest friends.

After wishing them all a Merry Christmas, Carina left the center and walked back home. The center usually improved her mood, she just felt out of sorts because of Mary. "Yes, she's gone," one of the group members had said in answer to her inquiry. "Congestive heart failure," another had murmured. "A blessing, if you ask me," someone else offered. "Swelled up, she did. Forty pounds of fluid, I heard."

Thankfully, Mrs. Davenport, the woman in charge of the building, hurried over and changed the topic of conversation by pulling out her smartphone and showing Carina pictures of her new great granddaughter.

Carina had taken her leave shortly after that, relishing the short walk back home. The weather stayed mild, so she removed her jacket and tied it around her waist.

Trying not to think about poor Mary swelling up with so much fluid, Carina walked the other side of the street on the way home, to avoid the loud barking from Jim and Junie's old place.

At home, she hung up her jacket, sat in her chair beside the picture window, and picked up her journal. But instead of more pathetic musings, she wrote a prayer.

"Dear Lord," it read, "please let all the Senior Center friends have a happy and healthy Christmas. And please, Lord, if it be your will, let Romy and her family make a safe trip home for the holidays." Then she added three more prayers. One for her eldest son, Heath, and his wife, Gia. One for sweet Aaron, the oldest middle child, a super laid-back athlete, and lastly, one for the youngest, Annabelle, the free spirit. Wherever she might be.

Eyelids growing heavy, Carina felt herself begin to doze.

When her chin hit her chest, she awoke with a start. She'd been dreaming of standing at a picture window watching snow fall on a piney hill. A fire burned in the fireplace nearby.

Loneliness lent an air of melancholy to the scene. A log crackled and fell apart. That's the sound that woke me, she thought. Then she laughed at herself. *It's a dream, dummy, just a dream.*

But she knew where it originated. Between her Christmas mug and Max and his offer of the cabin in Colorado, her brain had decided she needed to think more about that. Max had said the cabin had its own snowy hill just perfect for sledding.

"My wife inherited it from her grandfather. Then we poured all our energy into renovating."

Carina thought it sounded perfect. Wouldn't it be nice if the whole scattered family could meet there for the holiday? Max said there was plenty of room.

But no. That was silly. If the kids couldn't even make it home to Landon for Christmas, they certainly wouldn't be able to travel to the mountains of Colorado.

It might be another quiet holiday. Last year Alfred said the quiet holidays were fine with him. But he said that about everything. Besides, she'd still been recovering then. Things were different this year.

Not to Alfred, though. At least it didn't seem so.

When he wasn't out of town for his job as an independent financial auditor, he golfed or hunted. After the kids had all left home, he sometimes golfed even on Christmas morning. Of course, that had been before Covid when she'd been caring for her mom. Or her dad. It was sometimes difficult to remember which had happened first.

Carina sat up, forced herself from her dream and her reverie. Back to reality, she thought, touching her crazy-wavy hair springing out of its clip. She reached to close the still-open journal, her eye catching on her written prayers. If it be Your will, Lord, she thought. If it be Your will.

When the children called last Sunday, she'd told them the only thing she wanted for Christmas this year was to have everyone at home for a couple of days. It can be after Christmas or before, I don't care, she'd said. I just want a family celebration like we used to have when you all were younger.

Even as she'd said it, Carina had realized how needy it sounded. Who knew needy would be a side effect of facing down mortality? She sighed and rubbed her neck.

Her phone dinged.

She clicked the icon and read a message from Max. "Hey, there," he typed. "How are you today?"

She still marveled at the way she and Max had connected. He was just about the same age as her own children. The only difference was, he shared her deep and near-debilitating grief. He had recently lost his young wife to ovarian cancer. They'd only had three years together and like Carina, he seemed to be searching for a deeper meaning behind the suffering.

"I'm okay," she typed back. "How's my favorite doc-in-training today?"

"I'm having a good day," he wrote.

Carina plunged ahead. "Hey, Max, I wondered something after we spoke earlier … if the cabin belonged to your wife's granddad, are you certain my family should be there?"

"Oh, sure," he replied. "It was a simple hunting cabin when she inherited it. We renovated it, thinking the rent would be like a small income. It was our thing while I was getting my undergrad degree." He'd sent that sentence but kept typing. Carina watched his cursor dots pulse as he finished his thought. "Then she got cancer and it became sort of a goal. Something to hold on to. Something to finish. You know?"

Carina did know. She knew all about finding things to hold on to when everything seemed to be slipping away. That's one reason she had agreed to join the group. The title made so much sense.

She settled back and put up the footrest on her recliner. One of her most vivid recollections from the months she'd spent lying immobile in her hospital bed, trying to understand how she'd become so debilitated so quickly, had been an image of this chair, with a blanket for her knees.

Outside the window beside her chair, a couple of sparrows pecked at the remains of bird seed that had fallen from the feeder.

Still so incredibly grateful to be home, she couldn't quite understand this growing pocket of emptiness inside her chest. But she wouldn't tell Max that. Not right now. Not at Christmas. "Well, okay," she told him. "I'm still thinking about it. And I'm glad things are going well for you. It's been a nice day here, too."

"A couple of hopefuls have inquired about renting the cabin for Christmas," he wrote. "But I told the caretakers it wasn't available because I wanted to check it out for myself."

Carina's heart thumped. She glanced down at the prayer she'd written in her journal, about letting the kids come home for Christmas. "I wish I could say I will accept your generous offer," she wrote. "But to be honest, I'm still waiting for the phone to ring. Holding out hope that this year will be different than last."

A cabin in the mountains. Would it work? Was it possible? Her hand moved over the journal page, voicing her questions to herself. *There's no way of knowing unless you call them. Or at least text them. Make the leap.*

Make the leap, she thought. Very funny. She didn't even like asking if they were coming home to Landon for Christmas, she sure didn't want to ask if they'd be willing to drive or fly all the way to Colorado. She hated to sound ... needy.

But we never know what life has in store. I'd love to think it wouldn't matter if we weren't together this year, that there's always next year. But if there's anything I've learned from losing every member of my nuclear childhood family, it's that grief is always waiting. Seemingly around every corner.

The cursor blinked, begging her to respond to Max.

"It sounds like a dream," she replied. "You are so generous to offer. But to be honest, I don't know if the kids are coming for Christmas—here—or anywhere."

Max sent back a smiley face. "It's okay. No problem. I've got some days off so I'm going up to check that all the renovations are complete. We've rented it out a couple of times, but the garage apartment wasn't completed so I want to see that for myself." He sent that message and continued, "If you and your family want to come, you're more than welcome." He inserted a Santa emoji. "But if you do decide to make the trip, I'm hoping to wrangle a Christmas dinner invitation for myself. Fly in, fly out. That way I don't spend another Christmas alone, either."

Carina felt a tug on her heartstrings. There it was. That last tacked on sentence. *That way I don't spend another Christmas alone.*

She blinked back tears and wrote, "Even if we don't come to the cabin, you are more than welcome to share our Christmas dinner here in Landon."

"Did I just invite myself?"

"Yes, you did," she wrote. "And it was the best idea you've had yet. I don't know why I never thought of it. Houston is a non-stop flight to Landon."

Her phone rang.

It was Heath, calling from North Dakota where he worked on a pipeline. "Mom?"

She felt her heart lighten in her chest. "Hey, my first born, it's so good to hear your voice."

"You, too, Mom. How are you doing?"

Before she could answer, he spoke again, obviously nervous. "I'm sorry. I don't think we can make it for the holiday."

Carina felt her holiday spirit sink. "Oh, no? Is it work? Do you have to work *all* of Christmas?" She knew it wasn't a question of money to fly home, he probably earned more than all her other children combined.

"No," he admitted. "It's not work, it's Gia."

CHAPTER 2

NO CHRISTMAS

"GIA, WHY?" CARINA PICTURED THE YOUNG WOMAN IN HER MIND. A tiny little thing, very animated, from a large, close-knit family. Carina had liked her immediately. A reader like herself, Gia also confessed to keeping a poetry journal. Carina had been thrilled.

"I've seen some of your photos on Facebook," Gia had said at their first meeting. "The landscapes inspire my poetry sometimes."

Carina remembered how special that had made her feel. How thrilled she was to have such a kind, creative daughter-in-law. Why wouldn't she want to come home for Christmas? "Is it her folks? Do they want y'all at their house? I mean that's understandabl—"

"Sorry, Mom, it isn't that."

Carina could imagine him rubbing his large right hand across his eyes as he held the phone in his left. He'd been her lefty-child. An independent soul from the start. "It's just ... she just doesn't feel like coming."

Carina sucked in a breath.

Heath must've realized how it sounded. He hurried on. "I

don't mean she doesn't *want* to come for a visit. She really doesn't—"

His voice grew more and more exasperated.

Finally, he said, "She's afraid to fly. That's all."

That took Carina completely by surprise. "Oh. Well." She'd heard of people who didn't fly, she just didn't know any of them. "I guess it's too far to drive."

Heath laughed. It was the short, unexpected chuckle of someone stuck between the proverbial rock and a hard place.

"It's okay," she reassured him. "We'll miss you, but if it can't happen, it can't happen. There's always next year." Even as she said it, she crossed her fingers against Fate. They all knew holidays weren't promised. The past few years had certainly taught them that much.

"Mom?" Heath's voice brought her out of her reverie.

She turned up the volume on the phone's speaker. "What is it, honey?"

"Gia's pregnant," he blurted. "She's not afraid to fly, she's afraid of getting sick on the plane."

Carina stood and walked to the kitchen. "Pregnant? That's *wonderful*." She immediately began to smile. She couldn't *wait* to be a grandma—again. But then she realized she had no idea if they wanted to be parents or not. "It is wonderful, isn't it?"

Heath laughed. "It sure is, Mom. I wanted to make a big production at Christmas, not throw it out this way." He chuckled again. "I was going to at least wrap up a baby blanket or something for you."

"That would've tickled me to death. I'm sorry if I ruined your surprise."

"It's okay, my little sis probably would've been so jealous she'd ruin it anyway."

Carina laughed. The sibling rivalry between Heath and Romy was legendary. "Well, she has a houseful of kids, so I'm sure she wouldn't begrudge the two of you at least one." She didn't want to agree or disagree about the jealousy part. It was true, Romy liked to be the center of attention, but Carina had learned long ago not to even appear to side with one or the other. Nothing good ever came of that. They thought nothing of using their mom as ammunition in their ongoing battles.

"So, is Gia excited?"

"She's over the moon. I've wanted to call and tell you ever since we found out last week, but she's been so sick she made me promise not to tell a soul until we make certain everything's okay." He chuckled again. "Guess I let the cat out of the bag anyway."

The plot seemed to thicken. "Sick? Like morning sickness?"

"That's what she thinks. Her doctor's appointment is this afternoon. Maybe we'll know more then."

"Good. Good. That's good. Call me when you know more, okay?"

"I will, Mom. And hey, can we keep it between us for now?"

"Of course, honey. Give Gia my love."

"Sure thing. We love you, too."

Her dear, sweet, giant of a boy. She missed him and was proud of him and couldn't wait to get another call telling her everything would be all right. She hoped the baby would be a lanky, freckled guy just like his dad. One he could play ball with, take fishing and camping, all the things he'd loved as a kid.

There I go, getting ahead of myself. She swiped beneath her eyes with the tail of her soft, flannel shirt.

Since she'd entered her middle years, comfort had taken over her closet. Or maybe it was a result of her long recovery. Whatever the reason, knit and flannel had become her winter wardrobe staples.

Alfred still attended work dinners and functions where formal dress was required, but her presence was no longer required. Covid had brought about a million little unseen changes. At least she thought that was the reason.

After ending the call with Heath, Carina noticed the message icon had a little red number one beside it. "Oh, Max. Oops." She opened the message.

"Don't worry about the offer. I don't mean to pressure. I'm going up to check out the renovations no matter what."

Dear, dear boy, she thought, I'd love the change of scenery, but it really isn't up to me. "You are so kind," she typed. "I'll speak to the kids, and Alfred, and get back to you ASAP. And even if we don't make it there, perhaps you could stop here on your way back."

He didn't reply right away, but she knew he'd probably been on a break earlier. Being in med school, his days were not really his own.

After talking to Heath and texting with Max, Carina rattled around the house, dusting, watering plants, rearranging her collection of snow people and snow globes—Christmas décor from years past—then finally gave up, grabbed her jacket, and stepped outside again.

This time she strolled the neighborhood in the other direction, enjoying the cool air and clear skies. She thought about doing a little retail therapy, but before she could decide, her phone dinged with another message telling her the refill for one of her daily medications was ready to be picked up at the pharmacy.

She turned and headed back home for her Subaru.

At the drug store she accepted the small white sack containing her blood pressure medicine, then gravitated toward the children's toys and books. Of course, she picked up a small gift for each grandchild. Just in case they got to come.

Then she paid for her purchases and made her way back to the car.

The small keepsake snow globes near the checkout stand had caught her eye. They could go into the kids' stockings. If they didn't get them this year, she could always save them for next year. Along with the other doodads she might pick up during the clearance sale the day after Christmas.

Shopping on half-price day had been a fun holiday ritual she'd shared with her mom and sister. The three of them would meet at one of their homes, then they would hit Walgreens and Hobby Lobby to take advantage of the huge sales on Christmas items for the following year. Sometimes they would even get brave and go to the mall, but usually the crowds there were too daunting.

Carina always joked that she hadn't paid full price for Christmas cards or wrapping paper in twenty years. After shopping, the three of them would go to lunch. They almost always chose Mexican, sometimes even splurging on Sangria Swirls or Margaritas if it was late in the day.

They had often gone in her sister Jodie's car, a brandywine colored '68 Mustang Fastback she called her baby. Her husband, Curt, had restored it especially for her. He'd always given her the most extravagant gifts. Carina and her mom thought it was to compensate for their inability to have children.

Jodie had loved driving.

Carina steered her mind away from those old memories. They always culminated in the news video of the brandywine Mustang crashed into the concrete abutment on the highway. The front end of the small car looked like a bright abstract accordion, the white leather seats barely visible, window glass glittering sharply in the high, Texas sun.

The accident had been after they'd lost their mom. Their dad had suffered his second stroke and Jodie had been helping with his care. But then she'd begun to have incidents of fainting, and her doctor had recommended not driving until they figured it out. Jodie had been convinced she had some horrible disease. And not driving was literally driving her insane.

Or so it seemed.

Carina remembered telling Max about the accident that took her sister's life. He was the one who finally spoke the words she'd tamped down in the back of her mind. "Was it an accident? Could it have been something more? I thought she wasn't supposed to be driving…"

Back at home, Carina tuned the radio to the Christmas music station, and tried to find joy in wrapping the little gifts in the colorful—discounted—wrapping paper. After affixing decorative name tags to the inexpensive gifts, her *Linus and Lucy* ringtone from "A Charlie Brown Christmas" began to play on her phone.

It was Heath, calling back to tell her Gia and the baby were fine, but they definitely couldn't make the long trip home for Christmas. Gia had to be given intravenous fluids while at the clinic because the constant vomiting had caused her to be dehydrated.

"Poor Gia. Hot ginger tea with three or four crackers. Got me through all my pregnancies. Now, if she can't tolerate ginger, then mint or even the old standby, chamomile, first thing in the mor—"

Heath chuckled softly. "It's okay, Mom. The doc gave her a prescription and I brought her home and tucked her into bed. For the first time in days, she is finally getting some rest. I'm sure the fluids helped, too."

Carina laughed self-deprecatingly. "That's wonderful. I'm so glad everything looks good. Do you have a due date?"

"Yes," he said. "Right around my birthday."

"Oh, wouldn't that be wonderful?" The news made her so happy she let him hang up without telling her if they'd learned the baby's gender.

When Alfred called to say he was on his way home, she was

nearly bursting with excitement. Her words tumbled out before she could stop them.

Alfred agreed it was the best news they'd had in ages. He relished being Gampa at least as much as she relished her role of Gan.

CHAPTER 3

THERAPY

THAT NIGHT, AFTER SHE AND ALFRED SHARED A SIMPLE CHICKEN casserole dish that had become one of her go-to meals, they cleaned up the kitchen and watched the ten o'clock news.

Alfred showered and went to bed first, citing his early tee time with a client, then Carina took a leisurely bath, read a new Jeffery Deaver on her Kindle for a bit, and then quietly crawled into bed and set her phone alarm for eight.

She had an appointment, too. But there was no need to tell anyone about that. Alfred was already snoring, anyway. He would be up and at 'em before the sun rose. Wednesday was his standing early time even when there were no clients to woo.

He often remarked that watching the sun rise from the clubhouse deck over Irish coffee made life worth living. It hurt her feelings, a little, but true to her nature she hadn't said anything. She was certain he didn't mean that was the *only* thing that made life worth living.

Alfred made his living working freelance. He often talked in grandiose terms delivered in a big, booming voice. "I'm my own business," he told her once. "I have to be my own cheering section, too." Sometimes she wondered if he even stopped to think how his statements sounded.

"I say what the customer needs to hear," he often said. "Or what they want to hear at least, within reason of course." He favored her with one of his wide grins when he said it. One of those grins that reminded her of the boy who'd won her heart as easily as he'd won her the giant teddy bear at the county fair.

This year would be their thirty-fourth anniversary. They'd married right out of high school, attended college one right after the other—him first so he could get his degree and start earning for their first home—and it was right for him to have a hobby— or hobbies. He liked to go hunting every now and then, too.

But that was a thorny thing between them. One they rarely talked about since she was very anti-hunting. Killing animals for sport or entertainment seemed the lowest type of hobby one could do. Especially after she'd seen the high electric fencing that surrounded the hunting ranches around the state.

"Why, those animals don't have a chance, do they?" she'd asked in astonishment. "And you tell me they feed them in certain areas on a regular basis so they will return to that spot over and over?" Carina had been sickened and appalled. "Why not just go and shoot a few pets down at the pet store? It amounts to the same thing."

She recalled how Alfred had rolled his eyes. One of the few times she'd ever seen him do that in relation to something she'd said. They'd been driving to Houston to visit Romy and Jake—her daughter's first husband—because Romy was already in the delivery room. That's when they'd passed several large hunting ranches. After the first one, Carina could spot them easily by the tall fencing and tidy roads running along the inside border.

"You didn't hunt when we were first married." It was the first thing either of them had said in fifty miles.

"I didn't have time," he replied. "Back then it was all work and kids, remember?"

"Of course, I do." Carina had crossed her arms over her chest. "I worked, too, remember? Hospital switchboard on the night shift." She huffed. "Night shift paid well so that's what I worked." Even though it was no fun, downright uncomfortable much of the time, she done it for years while he completed his degree.

And though she'd never really enjoyed that shift, it had taken on a whole other meaning once she'd found herself pregnant with Heath. That's when real life had reared up and kicked both her and Alfred right in the teeth. But that was ages ago, she remembered thinking. Another lifetime it had seemed.

By the time they'd arrived at Romy's hospital that day, the atmosphere in the car had felt like mid-winter. The chill between them fierce.

Baby Heather, their first grandchild, had thawed it like magic. They had both turned to mush when the nurse placed the swaddled girl in Carina's arms. Romy beamed from her hospital bed, a box of chocolates from her little sis by her side. It had seemed some sort of omen that her husband, Jake, had gone somewhere to smoke a cigarette. Carina thought a first-time father would be nervous before, or maybe during the birth, not after.

He finally showed up a couple hours later, saying he'd needed some air. Fatherhood had not seemed to sit well with him. Or maybe it was married life that didn't sit well. He seemed intent on sowing his wild oats regardless of his new responsibilities.

Now, Carina smiled to herself as she snuggled in with the memory of that tiny baby nestled in her arms. She'd always thought love at first sight was the top of the Ferris wheel with Alfred. Or the sight and feel of each of her own children as they were placed on her chest in her hospital birthing bed, but those feelings were like candle flames compared to the hot spotlight of first-time grandmother adoration.

She recalled how Heath had sent Romy a basket of flowers that day. "Congrats, little sis! You came in first again." The card alluded to the fact that Romy had not only married first but now had the first grandchild in the family. It had continued to be a running joke when she had the second grandchild, then the first divorce, then the third grandchild and later, the first remarriage.

Heath never let her live any of it down.

Carina drifted to sleep after saying her nightly prayers, asking God to look after all her children and their children, and Alfred, of course. She also added prayers for Max and Curt, her brother-in-law, who had both suffered such terrible—and similar—losses.

WHEN SHE ROSE THE NEXT MORNING, THE COFFEE WAS MADE, AND Alfred had gone. She'd been almost awake when he got up, but as she hadn't slept well—waking up every couple of hours as if someone unseen needed her—she'd dozed off again while he dressed.

In the kitchen, a rolled-up note stuck out of her Christmas coffee cup. "Roses are red, the sun is yellow, I'm off to the golf course to meet up with a fellow." He'd signed it with an elegant letter A inside a heart, just like he used to do.

She loved the note. Maybe they would get back to the way it used to be, eventually. Carina drank a cup of coffee, ate a cup of yogurt with granola, and got dressed. She'd scheduled her appointment for ten o'clock. At the last moment, she grabbed her Kindle from the nightstand and stuck it in her purse.

It was a short drive to the clinic, but the wait could be long. Dr. Patel gave each patient as much time as necessary, even if it did put her behind schedule.

Carina donned her mask and went inside, signing in at the window and choosing a spot away from the two other patients in the waiting room. Since Covid, social distancing had become somewhat second nature.

When the nurse opened the door and called her name, Carina

was so lost in her novel she didn't respond. The nurse simply smiled, repeated her name, and waited. They knew her here. She'd been Dr. Patel's patient for nearly twenty years.

Today Carina expected to get the results of the complete physical from the week before. She followed the nurse to the exam room and settled herself in a faux leather chair. After the nurse took her blood pressure and left the room, Carina pulled out her Kindle and picked up with Detective Lincoln Rhyme again.

After a half hour, the door opened, and Dr. Patel swished in carrying Carina's file. "You've got to start taking care of yourself." She looked at Carina over the tops of her reading glasses. "You're already on blood pressure medicine and now your cholesterol is out of control. What happened to walking two miles a day and watching those carbs and sugar?"

Carina looked at her Kindle. She didn't want the doctor to see the guilt she knew would show in her eyes. "I've been so busy. I'll do better. I swear I will."

But Dr. Patel wasn't fooled. "How are you sleeping?"

"Oh," Carina said, "you know. Pretty well."

"Lack of sleep is a major problem, Carina. It disrupts systems—"

Carina pushed a wiry strand of silver behind her ear and shrugged. "I'm okay. I don't have to punch a clock anymore, so I just nap if I don't sleep well at night."

Dr. Patel frowned and made a note on her computer. "Lack of exercise and lack of sleep, poor dietary choices. I think those factors are causing your blood pressure readings and your bad cholesterol numbers. So, in addition to the BP and cholesterol meds, I'm going to write you a prescription for a sleep aid."

"Oh, no," Carina shook her head. "I don't need that. I'll stick with my over-the-counter remedies or chamomile tea. I don't believe in those strong drugs." She smiled. "But thank you anyway."

The doctor closed her file and pulled her rolling stool closer to Carina's chair. "You are one stubborn woman."

Carina smoothed her blouse and looked at her friend. "Too stubborn for my own good?"

Dr. Patel sat very still. "Maybe. Is there anything you'd like to talk about?"

Carina glanced up at the clock. "How much time do you have?"

The doctor tilted her head to one side and peered at her patient in contemplation. "You've been through a lot these past few years. What with the hospitalization for Covid—"

"—Romy's divorce and remarriage, the deaths of my mom and dad, and Jodie, (saying that one almost took her breath away). And then there was the problem with the roof after that hailstorm. The loss of my cats—" Her voice broke, and all the hurt flowed down her cheeks.

The doctor leaned over to pat her shoulder. "I knew you had a lot on your plate, but I had no idea it was a smorgasbord."

Carina dug a wad of tissue from her jacket pocket and dabbed at her face. "Oh, don't mind me, everyone has problems. I'm just a silly old woman—"

"Uh. Carina." The doc's tone of voice changed.

Carina sniffled and looked up.

"We're the same age, remember?"

"That's hard to believe." She allowed her gaze to take in the doc's smooth skin, her walking shoes made for squeaking up and down the halls a million times a day, and her long black hair knotted behind her head with a pencil stuck through it. "You seem so much younger."

The doc shrugged and pointed to a few strands of silver peeking through her locks. "I'm not immune to the passage of time. But I stay healthy doing what I love. I don't answer to anyone except my patients. My husband is a surgeon whose schedule is even more hectic than mine. He practically lives at the hospital when he's on call. My only child lives two hundred miles away. I keep up with her on Skype and Instagram." She pursed her lips. "When I have down time I paint in my little home-studio. It relaxes me. Well, that and the occasional glass of wine." She smiled and inched her doctor's rolling stool back a bit. "Now, I'm going to say something you may not want to hear, but it's for your own good."

Carina waited. She had an idea what her doctor was about to say.

"You need to get away. A good long trip."

Carina was a little taken aback. "Well, I expected you to say I need a rest, or a vacation, but a *good long trip*?" She pressed the toe of her dress shoe against the leg of the chair. "I don't think Alfred can take off right now."

"I didn't mean with Alfred. I'm talking about you. You're my patient."

Carina's ability to speak seemed to leave her.

Dr. Patel stood and tapped a few more keys on the computer. The screen went back to the clinic's screensaver. She picked up Carina's patient folder, made some small notation, wrote out a prescription—for cholesterol medicine no doubt—and handed it to Carina. She seemed all business again, almost as if she regretted speaking so bluntly.

"Doc?"

The physician squared her shoulders. "I shouldn't have said that," she murmured. "I have opinions, but I should keep them to myself and stick to prescribing medicine."

Carina sighed. "You're probably right. I've been so worried about family stuff I've pretty much forgotten about me. I don't eat properly, can't really sleep, can't even drag myself back to the walking trail I once loved." She frowned. "I did walk to the senior center yesterday. That's something … but for the record, I totally respect your opinion." She sniffled. "The thing is, I worry constantly, but I don't have anyone to *physically* look after anymore. Suddenly, it's just Alfie and me. And he's gone most of the time. Doesn't seem to need me at all." She laughed a bit when those words slipped out. "You're right, Doc. I feel sort of, I don't know, used up. Maybe I do need a new outlook."

Dr. Patel shifted her stethoscope to one side and stood, squeezing her patient's shoulder. "Change of scenery," she said. "Do one of those bucket list things with a friend. Let your husband handle things at home for a while."

Carina hesitated as she rose and picked up her purse. "Seriously?"

The doctor nodded. "Especially after what you told me last time, about the suicide note. Did I understand that correctly?"

Carina felt her shoulders slump. She forgot she'd even mentioned it after her father died. Covid had grabbed her by the throat just days after his memorial service and a lot of what she'd said and done in those days was now lost to the void. Only sometimes something would leap out of the darkness like a spawning salmon if someone jogged her memory.

She plopped back down on the patient's chair. "I was straightening up, gathering some of Dad's old clothing, and I found the note in his handwriting." She clenched her teeth together. "It said if he could get out of that bed, he'd take his gun, put an end to it all. He said he hated being a burden."

The doctor leaned down to hug her. "Oh, honey."

"I know. I thought I was doing such a great job taking care of him and come to find out, he was in agony. How could I not have known?"

Dr. Patel shook her head. "He didn't want you to know. It's natural. I'm so sorry you had to find out though. I'm sure he didn't intend that to happen."

Carina shrugged. "I don't know. Why else did he write it?" She wiped her eyes. "I went out for a long walk, had a good cry, then shredded the note and fed the pieces to the wind. I haven't been back to that walking trail since."

"I'm beginning to get the picture." Dr. Patel sat back down, took her hand. "Tell me about your daughter. The one who recently married."

Carina smiled a half-smile. "You mean Romy?"

"Of course. She's the same age as my Prisha. We once compared high school graduation photos of them. Romy is so beautiful."

Carina nodded. "And Prisha, too. She's a physician like her mom, right?"

"Close," Dr. Patel said. "She's going to be a surgeon like her father. She's doing her residency now."

"That's wonderful." Carina stood, tugged her coat off the back of the chair. "I've taken up way too much of your time today—"

The doctor touched her sleeve. "Stop. Sit back down. Tell me about Romy."

Carina sat heavily. "I almost don't want to tell you." She waited for some word of protest, something like 'Oh, that's all right then, you don't have to delve into it,' but none came. The doc simply waited.

"She just got married again." Carina couldn't keep her voice from quaking. "For the fourth time. She married this new guy as soon as her divorce from Jake was final. They married twice, you know, her and Jake I mean." Carina knew she was rambling but couldn't seem to stop the flood of words. "Now she has taken the kids and moved to Dallas with Sean, the new one. He is a paramedic there. I haven't seen the kids in ages. Covid, you know, plus both parents work so they have little time for travel or anything. Even though travel is no longer restricted."

She sucked in a breath. "I shouldn't burden you with this." Her eyes filled. "I just feel like such a failure. Why does my sweet daughter seem unable to settle down, buying a house here, a vehicle there, changing jobs and cities and husbands, never a thought for the future, for the passage of time?" She swiped at her nose. "I thought Alfred and I gave our kids such a strong foundation, such a good home life. What is my girl searching for?"

The doctor shook her head. "First off, you aren't burdening me. But really, I think you need a counselor. Or a therapist. Someone you can talk to. What does Alfred think about all this?"

Carina looked away. "Alfred says stay out of it. The only other person I've told is my friend, Sophie. But she's been awfully busy house hunting. John-Paul, her husband, is retiring. They're looking for a home on the coast."

Dr. Patel smacked her hand against her forehead. "I don't know how you're coping with all this, and now you tell me your best friend is moving away, too?"

Carina laughed softly. "Yeah. She was pretty much my last contact with the outside world."

"What can I do to help?"

"You've done it already. Just listening. Making me acknowledge everything. I think you're right. About the counselor, I mean. Do you have one in mind?"

Dr. Patel nodded and wrote a name on a note pad. "Dena Sealey. Give her a call. She can help. And you, take care of yourself. Think about getting away, even if only for a week or two, promise?"

Carina stood. "I promise." She picked up her handbag, multi-colored cats frolicking on a black background—her last birthday gift from Jodie—and made certain her Kindle was tucked inside. "And thank you. Talking about it helped a lot."

They briefly clasped hands.

Dr. Patel said, "Dena Sealey is an old college friend. She's in Westridge, about an hour away, but she's very kind. I think you will really benefit from her expertise. And by the way ..."

Carina waited.

"You asked why your dad wrote the awful suicide note?"

"Yes—"

"Maybe it made him feel better." She hesitated. "You used to keep a journal, didn't you? Even wrote stories from time to time. Why did you do that?"

"Just like you said, sometimes it makes me feel better."

"You don't do it anymore?"

Carina grinned. "Sometimes …"

"Good girl." The doc laughed, sounding as if they were still the young women who had connected twenty years earlier.

"Thank you." Carina spontaneously hugged her before she opened the door of the exam room. "I will definitely keep all this in mind."

She walked the short distance to the checkout station and paid her copay. The doc was right, of course. Having someone to talk to might be helpful. Her husband was not a talker. He was a doer. Feelings and emotions were her department. Working, playing golf, mowing the lawn, those were his departments.

Sometimes she regretted quitting work to stay home and care for her mother, and later her father. It still amazed her how quickly she had become isolated, even before Covid. Part of it was her own fault, of course. She could have gone back to the classroom after her mom lost her battle with lung cancer. But she'd barely settled back in to being just a wife again when her dad started having problems. Then her sister had been killed.

A thought flashed across her mind like that same salmon breaching upstream. Was that when Dad wrote the note? After Jodie died? He'd been devastated by her death. Children are supposed to outlive their parents he'd said in his halting new way of speaking. *Maybe that was it.*

Somehow that idea made her feel lighter, as if a load had been, maybe not lifted, but lightened at least. Dr. Patel had brought it up, made her think about it after all this time.

In addition to this counselor, maybe I will finally start attending church. Find a priest or pastor to confide in as well.

She had considered it many times, of course. But after Covid,

Carina still found herself hesitant to sit in a crowd of people, anywhere.

Besides, it was one more thing she would be doing alone. Sunday morning always found Alfred on the golf course.

Always.

CHAPTER 4

DECISIONS

Carina settled into the car, replaying parts of their conversation in her head. Dr. Patel had given her plenty to think about. Where *were* all her old book club friends? Her old lunch buddies? She couldn't believe how she'd let everyone fall away. Even her husband—whom she loved so dearly—seemed to consider her little more than a pesky child.

One day they'd been standing side-by-side at the counter. She'd just poured their first cups of coffee and he began stirring Coffee Mate creamer into his with a metal spoon, clanking it side to side, really banging it back and forth, as if to wake the dead.

"Honey, please. Do you have to stir like that?"

Alfred continued incorporating the powdery non-dairy creamer into his World's Best Dad mug. "Like what?" he asked.

"Like that—all clanky—side-to-side."

A tiny smile crossed his lips. "The way I stir my coffee bothers you, sweetie? After all these years?" He stopped stirring and rolled his eyes. "Did you sleep at all last night?"

And of course, she hadn't. But did he just roll his eyes? She thought she'd spared him her tossing and turning by moving to the couch in the den, with the TV on low for company. In repayment, he rolls his eyes and makes her feel like an idiot.

Carina thought about it that night—her feelings were still raw —and the next morning, she made certain to stay clear of the kitchen while Alfred made his coffee. Something about how he made so much noise, and then rolled his eyes, really bothered her. Where was the love, the tenderness, the understanding?

After the clanking stopped, she walked in and took her own Cat's Meow mug off the hook. With a plastic spoon, she stirred the creamer into her own cup. "Good morning," she said, before she sipped.

Alfred raised his mug and his spoon and winked. "Are you proud of me for being careful how I stirred this morning?"

Carina knew it was meant as a joke, to show her how silly she'd been, but that didn't help. And he hadn't been careful at all. She could hear that metal spoon all the way upstairs when she was getting dressed.

Why does it bother me now? Surely, he's always made this much racket in the mornings. He's boisterous in everything he does, the way he speaks, moves, *everything*.

She stopped almost mid-stride as reality hit her. Before Covid, at this time of day, she was either at her folks' home, having spent the night there, or she was already up and out the door, on the way to relieve the nighttime caregiver.

No wonder, she thought. No wonder I've forgotten. This is like starting over. On top of the weakness and forgetfulness lingering from Covid, we grew into old fogies, too. Where did the time go? And I wonder what I do that gets on *his* nerves?

That realization is the one that made her decide to definitely take Dr. Patel's advice and seek out the counselor. Nevertheless, she was still angry at Alfred for making a joke of everything. Why, if one of her students had rolled his eyes at her, he or she would have been writing sentences on the board for the rest of the year.

She couldn't very well make her husband write sentences, but she also did not have to stick around and put up with it. Wasn't she her own person? Didn't she have some interests of her own? To that, she didn't have an answer. It had been so long since she'd thought of only herself.

Taking her coffee into the living room, Carina sat and watched the birds outside the large picture window. Alfred had just left. Did it matter that he was right? That she hadn't slept much? One look at the shadows beneath her eyes and anyone could see she'd had another sleepless night. But not even a peck on the cheek when he left? What was going on? It had been a long time since he'd called her his brown-eyed girl.

Carina showered and dressed and clipped her hair up in a loose knot. Then she put the address of the clinic in her phone and before long she found herself sitting in her car in the parking lot, unsure when she'd actually made the decision to go.

She sighed, dismayed that she didn't even recall what time she'd left the house or how long it had taken to get here. Her clock said it had taken the better part of an hour, just like Dr. Patel had said, but shouldn't Carina have better recall? This was becoming the norm. It occurred to her that the unrelenting insomnia could be making the bouts of forgetfulness even worse.

Maybe the counselor would have some solution to it all. In the back of her mind, Carina was beginning to wonder if she even had the mental ability to go back to work.

She looked at the clock again. Twenty minutes before her appointment. She always had been the early bird—if you're not early, you're late, had been her philosophy—so she clicked on her Facebook icon.

Carina had become quite addicted to Facebook while caring for her parents. During the day she and her mom played Scrabble and Skip-Bo, worked the crossword and cryptoquip in the newspaper, and while her mom napped, Carina plowed through books and scrolled through Facebook. Right up until the day her mother forgot how to hold a pen or a fan of cards. Right up until hospice came.

After the funeral when everyone had gone, Alfred went back to work and to his golf club and Carina was left with Facebook and her Kindle. With the help of the library and Amazon, she reread many of her favorite authors, and discovered a ton of new ones. Then, just when she'd made up her mind to go back to the classroom, her dad had suffered his first stroke.

Carina couldn't think of putting him in a nursing home after she'd devoted so much time to her mom. That would seem a betrayal. Instead, she pulled up her bootstraps and moved in with him, only going back to her home for clean clothes and to check on Alfred. Occasionally she would hire a woman to stay overnight and give her a break. Carina was certain it would be only temporary. And it seemed to free Alfred up to work and play golf as much as he wanted.

After the second and third strokes hit, Carina wound up staying for three years, only visiting her own home on weekends. At her dad's place, she fed the feral cats, fell in love with them, and started writing in her journal again, some entries even wanted to become stories, the same way they'd done in college all those years earlier.

When not writing, she continued to read. From Daphne du Maurier to Debbie Macomber to Jeffery Deaver. Anything to take her out of her own head. She also joined a once-a-week book club.

In addition to all that, Carina began to take photos around the rural property. Her iPhone camera proved almost as good a companion as her beloved books. But then all her feral kitties disappeared, one by one.

Carina had been trying to tame them from day one. They began to disappear about the same time Jodie was killed. Life was cruel. No wonder people wanted to make art and music and write stories to pretty it up, to try and impose some control over it.

That may have been the moment Carina felt herself to be hanging on by a thread. How much grief can one person stand?

When she became friends with Max Paper in *Holding On*, he had asked if her mother—during her struggle with lung cancer—had done all the chemo and radiation and still lost the battle.

Carina told him that she had. "She fought it, hard," she wrote.

"Did she suffer?" he asked.

Carina could sense the pain behind those words. "Yes," she admitted, "she suffered terribly." She couldn't sugarcoat it because she knew his young wife must have suffered, too. Few people escape cancer without suffering.

Carina recalled watching the screen on her phone for a reply. For a moment nothing came through but then it popped up and Carina knew he understood.

"Not everyone knows how it feels to watch a loved one suffer when the medicine has stopped working."

"It is soul-changing," Carina replied.

After that day they corresponded in bits and pieces like a mother and her adult child. He told her of his daily victories, she praised him and encouraged him to keep going. He told her his mother and father had divorced when he was a kid, and his mother had remarried and remarried and remarried, never finding the happiness she craved.

Carina thought of her own Romy but didn't say anything. She hoped the girl wasn't on a path like Max's mother had been. He told her he'd just started college when she died suddenly in, of all things, a car accident. T-boned by a drunk driver.

"I'm so very sorry," she'd written when he told her that.

He'd immediately responded that after watching his young wife linger in pain for months, a sudden death sounded almost idyllic.

"I can't argue with that," she'd replied. But in her mind, she'd *thought* about arguing. After all, she'd lost her only sibling to a car accident. At least she hoped it was an accident.

But she had swallowed those words, for the moment. On one hand, she didn't want to detract from his story, and on the other hand, the parallels between their sorrows seemed almost too much to believe.

No wonder he's glommed on to me, she thought. I feel like his ancient, female, grief twin. Doppel*griefer*, anyone?

They had continued to text each other right through her Covid recovery and his medical school trials and tribulations. He was there when she and Alfred had to come to grips with selling her childhood home and all her parents' possessions. Carina told Max it felt as if she was being forced to put away all her childhood things. Just like it said in the Bible.

But in her mind, the opening line to *Rebecca* kept surfacing. Only instead of dreaming about returning to Manderley, Carina always dreamed about returning to her father's house in the country. Where the feral cats were still alive and waiting patiently near their bowls beside the old cistern.

Sometimes her mom and sister were there, too. On the patio with her dad, waiting. She told Max she often felt as if she—and Alfred—had escaped the grip of the Covid monster but still walked crouched over in its shadow.

The dregs of the ICU-induced hallucinations lingered in her daydreams and sometimes in her nightmares. "How did you avoid contracting it," she'd asked Max. "Working in the hospital day in and day out?"

"We double and triple masked and had lots of gowns and face shields and gloves, you know PPE, personal protective equipment."

"Oh, yes," Carina agreed. "I saw plenty of that while I was there."

Max continued. "Being a student, we were kept away from the Covid floors as much as possible, and of course all healthcare workers were given first stab at the vaccines, no pun intended."

"Right," Carina wrote. "I'd been home several months before I was allowed to take the vaccines. But I was certainly glad when I was able, I'll tell you that." She shuddered just writing those words. "I hope I never have to go on a ventilator again."

Max's ellipsis glowed and pulsed as he wrote.

Carina waited patiently.

Then the dots stopped pulsing, but nothing came through.

"Max?" she wrote. "You okay?" Oh, Lord, they'd talked only about her and her family. What about him. Isolation had been tough on everyone. She recalled waiting and waiting on his response.

Finally, he said, "I enjoy talking to you. But I don't want to put all my worries on you because you've been through so much."

"Please!" Carina wrote. "Tell me everything. I've been way too wrapped up in myself and my own problems for months now."

He sent back a smiley face and began to type again.

"I think Andrea's parents blame me for not saving her."

Not at all what she'd been expecting, but she tried to keep up. "What makes you think that?"

He remained silent for quite some time. This time, Carina remembered giving him all the time he wanted. She felt a little guilty for not asking him sooner, but she hadn't been in her right mind. And she didn't mind admitting it. Unlike what others thought, she knew the drugs and illness had taken a toll on her thinking. But she also knew her thinking was good now, just not as quick as before.

Not yet.

Carina glanced at the text. The dots were pulsing again.

"Today would have been Andrea's twenty-sixth birthday. I messaged her folks, but they haven't replied. I thought we might say a prayer together, or something. Anything."

"Oh, Max," she pictured the bespectacled curly-top young

man in her mind. "I am so sorry. You know everyone grieves in his or her own way—but I can't imagine how painful it must be to lose a child. If I were there, we would take the most beautiful flowers out to Andrea. We would say a prayer, talk to her, tell her how much you miss her, tell her everything you've been doing, and what's next in your life. I think she'd like to hear all that." Carina pushed send and hoped she hadn't said too much. It was simply all the things she did when she visited her mom and dad and sister who were buried side by side in the family plot.

"Yellow roses," Max wrote. "I took her yellow roses first thing this morning. I told her how I did on my first USMLE and how it's almost time to choose my first rotation."

He stopped typing so she jumped in. "USMLE … that's the United States Medical Licensing Exam you told me about, right?"

"Yes," he wrote.

"How did you do?"

"Oh, it was fine. I was well prepared despite everything."

"So, you took roses to Andrea, and you told her how much you missed her and needed her."

"Yes," he immediately sent back. "I told her everything. I needed someone to share it with. But I also needed someone *else* to share it with, someone who can speak back. I thought maybe her parents would be those someones."

"It's all right," Carina said. "They may come around. It hasn't been that long."

He said, "They're angry at me because now they can never have grandchildren. Which is exactly why Andrea put off her treatment at first without telling anyone. She was pregnant."

"Oh, Max. I had no idea."

"She miscarried." His typing became hurried, full of mistakes. "She miscarried and then it was too late, and her folks won't accept that I didn't know about it so now they blame me, and I *don't* blame them."

Wow. Carina sat back and took a breath. Poor kid.

"It makes me think I shouldn't be a doctor after all." He inserted a sad emoticon. "I couldn't even diagnose my own wife. Couldn't save her once I did know."

The message sat there, staring at her, willing her to make it better somehow.

"That's what I really told her this morning," he wrote. "I told her I should be in that grave and she should still be walking the halls of the elementary school where all the kids loved her and called her Pretty Mrs. Paper."

"Oh, you dear boy. I wish I were there so I could give you a big hug. You need a great big Mom-hug."

He sent a smiley face with arms outstretched.

"Exactly," she wrote.

"Thanks," he replied. "You always help with your virtual hugs. That's why I offered the use of the cabin for Christmas."

"It sounds amazing," she replied.

"It is," he'd written. "The beauty of Crossbow, Colorado is unmatched. But to be honest, I'm a little bit scared to go back alone."

"Scared? Why?"

Max typed, but it must've been slowly. Finally, the message appeared. "I'm afraid I'll lose my mind if I try to go by myself. I miss her so much. I thought of not going, just selling it, but that seems cowardly. I know I'd regret it. I want to see it finished, at least once."

Carina was dumbfounded. Several seconds went by. She couldn't think of a thing to say. On the one hand, she thought *what a nice gesture,* on the other hand she had to wonder if he had some ulterior motive, after all, this was a Facebook connection. She hadn't met him in person. Supposedly all the grief group members were vetted, but what did she know? What if he wasn't a young man going to med school? What if he was a stalker or an axe-murderer?

"You're not an axe-murderer, are you?" she typed.

Max Paper sent a whole series of belly laugh emoticons. "You crack me up, Ms. Pinner." He sent more laughing faces. "I'll tell you what, let me call you on FaceTime. I'm just about to leave the dorm. You can go with me, see the campus, and even audit my next class, you know, sit in with me without anyone being wiser. I'll just turn the phone camera around and let you see everything."

Carina sent a laughing face, too. "Okay. Let's do it. But first, tell me you forgive me. I mean, I really do understand about the fear and the need to face it."

He sent back a thumbs up emoji so she gave him her phone number, and then immediately regretted it, until she recalled what he'd said. "Wait, you said you were leaving the dorm?"

Max wrote, "Yes. University of Houston College of Medicine."

"Oh, I knew that. I just have trouble associating you with a dorm ..."

"Yeah," he wrote. "I wouldn't be in a dorm if I still had Andrea. But it's better this way. Not as quiet in the time I do have off."

Carina tried to picture him as a med student. But with all his grief, he seemed much more worldly.

"Anyway," he typed. "Andrea and I stayed at the cabin a few times during the early days, but the trip became harder and harder on her, all the way from Houston. You know we had so many plans." He sent a sad face. "You know we both lived in Crossbow when we were kids. Then I moved away when my folks divorced, but we would still see each other on my court-mandated summers with my dad. We became best friends, and eventually, more. Anyhow, I don't want to be there alone. I want you and your entire family to come up and have a wonderful time."

"Max, this is incredibly sweet of you. Are you certain?"

"Completely," he said. "The only caveat is that you have to feed me."

"Well, of course," she replied. "But what about your dad? Won't *he* expect you for Christmas?"

"Nah," he said. "We don't have much in common anymore. After the divorce, we drifted apart. He usually spends Christmas with his sister and her husband on a beach somewhere." His voice grew quiet. "Oh, don't get me wrong, I'm always invited to go, too. But sunshine and seaweed just don't spell Christmas for me." He stopped typing for a moment. "To be honest, I need to see the cabin one last time before I decide whether to give it back to Andrea's family."

"Oh," Carina wrote. "Sounds like you've got a big decision to make. But the place sounds idyllic. Let me talk it over with Alfred and see what he thinks. Even if the kids can't make it, maybe the two of us will."

"That's what I admire about you, Carina Pinner, you and your husband have such a solid relationship. And your kids, you've told me bits and pieces over the last few months, I hope I get to meet them."

Carina thought back to the things she might have said. Had she told him how upset she'd been over Romy's latest marriage and move? Had she mentioned how she worried that her daughter would never settle down even though she already had a houseful of kids? Or that her eldest son couldn't make it home no matter where they had Christmas? Had she told him her youngest child was so far off the grid Carina didn't know where or when she would surface again? Had she even mentioned her third child, the only one who might jump at the chance for a ski holiday?

And what about Alfred? What in the world had she told him about Alfred? A solid relationship? They barely saw one another anymore.

Maybe going north wasn't such a great idea. She'd been listening to this young man's problems in the grief group, but hadn't she been using him as a sounding board, too? What if things were awkward? After all, real life wasn't Facebook, no matter how much they'd shared in the group.

She shook her head. On the other hand, a *free* week in the mountains at Christmas might be just the thing to bring her errant family together for a nice holiday. The one she craved so badly since suffering so much loss.

Her *Linus and Lucy* ringtone song began to play.

She looked down at the screen and it asked if she would accept a FaceTime call from Maxwell Paper. "Why, yes," she told herself. "I believe I will."

CHAPTER 5

MAX FOR REAL

She touched the green circle to accept the call. "Hello?"

Max's handsome, boyish face appeared on screen. He looked exactly the same as his picture on the group's list of members. And on his thumbnail photo.

"Ms. Carina?"

She touched her hair self-consciously. Her own photo on the member's list was from a while ago, when she'd still been coloring her curls brown. Now, they were streaked with silver. "Max. So good to see you."

"Great to see you, too. And to hear your voice." He sounded as kind as his text words made him seem.

"Thank you." She touched her hair again. "I haven't kept up with my hair appointments like I used to. Before ... everything, you know."

He nodded. "Of course I know. That's the thing we understand about each other. How deep things go when no one is looking."

She couldn't believe he always seemed to put into words how she felt. "You should have been a writer."

He grinned. "Maybe I will. Ever heard of Robin Cook, or Michael Crichton?"

Carina laughed. "Or Sir Arthur Conan Doyle, or Anton Chekov?"

"I knew you'd get it," Max said. "So, now that we've got the introductions out of the way, how about I show you around?" He touched the screen to turn the camera around and she was treated to a beautiful green campus bustling with other students coming and going.

"Lovely!" Carina said. "Where are we headed?"

"We are headed over to my molecular biology lecture."

Carina laughed and agreed to go with him, but she didn't have time to sit through the whole class. It was over her head anyway. What am I doing, she asked herself. Can an old woman really be friends with a young man her *son's* age?

She walked the campus with him—virtually—and went with him into the lecture hall which appeared to be filling quickly.

Carina thanked him for the call, but admitted she felt like a voyeur. "I'll text you after I talk to the family about the cabin," she whispered.

Max grinned, agreed, and they disconnected.

It did not surprise her how light she felt. It had once been her mission in life to make young people smile. Especially in her own classroom all those years ago.

No wonder we get along, she thought. His wife sounds like she was the same sort of teacher I tried to be. And an artist at that.

A sudden ache invaded her chest. An ache for the loss of a bright young woman whose whole life had been stretched out ahead of her, beckoning. Poor Max. He must feel so lost.

Why would a loving God take a young woman and her unborn child and leave a kindhearted husband all alone to grieve? Why not just take me, an old woman who has been through the wringer already? Why?

Carina gave herself a mental scolding, pushed aside the existential malaise trying to creep into her thoughts, and forced herself back to the present.

"Life is short," she murmured. Just like all those silly but truthful memes. *Live it while you can. Stop worrying about what might happen. Hold on and let go.* She had dozens tucked up in her memory from all the countless hours spent scrolling the FB newsfeed between cooking meals and dispensing medications.

She usually pooh-poohed such generalities, but every now and then one slipped through. Buried into her subconscious. Made her stop and think. *What are you waiting for?* One asked. *Time doesn't.*

That out-of-nowhere thought spurred her into action. Time *doesn't* wait. If I haven't learned that by now, I guess I never will.

Christmas would be here, soon. If they were going to Colorado, she had a lot to do. Starting with calling the children.

She took a deep breath, stilled her jangly too-much-coffee nerves, and called Romy first. No doubt, she'd be the toughest sell.

Romy, dew of the sea, conceived on their first cruise. The one that had been paid for by Alfred's company because he'd had such unmitigated success his first three years on the job. Romy had been unexpected, but very welcome, just like their first child, Heath—who had been conceived on their honeymoon in Scotland.

Her eldest daughter was also usually the easiest to get in touch with since her phone always lay on the rolling towel cart inside her hairdresser station. It was never far from her hand. Her clients knew to text her for appointments. Carina took a deep breath as the call went through.

Romy answered right away. Her voice sounded slightly irritated, as always. "H'lo?"

"Hey, Honey, can you talk?" Carina heard the sound of another voice in the background.

"Doing a cut right now, Mom. Can I call you back?"

"Of course," Carina said. "Just be thinking of this ... a white Christmas in a secluded Colorado cabin. Picture it. Our whole family together in the mountains. Doesn't it sound wonderful? Okay, that's all I wanted to say. Call me when you can."

There was a scant moment of silence on Romy's end, and then, "Okay, but geez, Mom, Colorado?"

Carina's finger pressed the END CALL icon. She hadn't meant to hang up without answering, but her finger had already been hovering. She could picture her daughter standing there, scissors in one hand, a strand of hair in the other, phone pressed between her cheek and shoulder, scowling into the wall-width mirror in front of the customer chair.

Oops. Sorry. Carina hated to bother anyone at work, but she was just so excited at the possibility of a white Christmas with the whole family.

Next, she called Alfred.

He didn't answer.

Oh, well, he'll call back when he can. She looked at his itinerary stuck to the fridge. Today he'd flown to San Antonio to begin auditing a large pet food company. Carina touched the words San Antonio. They'd taken vacations to that lovely city over the years. Had taken all four kids to visit The Alamo, even before all the touristy things had popped up around it.

The first year, when Heath and Romy were toddlers, they'd met a security guard in the park who had a pet squirrel riding on his shoulder. He'd been a bit abrasive, but did show the kids how the squirrel would take peanuts from his lips.

Good times, Carina thought. Wonderful times. And then there had been that year they went back at Thanksgiving. Her mom and sister had still been alive then. They'd all met, stayed in the same hotel on the river walk, and watched the parade of lighted boats that night from their adjoining balconies.

Getting away at the holidays was nothing new. In fact, they'd done it on several occasions.

One year they'd rented stone cabins at Lake Brownwood and cooked the turkey in an oven so tiny there was no room for anything else, not even the rolls.

Alfred and Curt, her late sister's husband, had built a fire in the firepit on the patio and they'd cooked all the sides and rolls over the campfire.

It had been the most memorable holiday ever. After the meal, they'd strolled through the lovely weather, singing songs and letting the kids run wild—Annabelle had been the toddler then—scaring the wildlife, and generally acting as if they all enjoyed each other's company which, at least on that day, they really had.

That night, they'd put the turkey carcass on the immense stone patio—one of the best things about the awesome cabins built by the CCC back in the thirties—and watched as raccoons and possums pulled it apart. "Look at their eyes, Mama," Romy had whispered. "See how they glitter?"

It had been a magical time.

Absolutely magical.

Nowadays, *woke* Romy would have a fit if they fed turkey bones to the wildlife.

Carina let her mind wander back to those happy days and was surprised when the ringtone on her phone woke her. Her head had fallen forward on her chest again.

It was Romy. "Mom? Tell me about this cabin. Is Dad on board with it?"

Carina told her about Max and that she hadn't been able to get in touch with Alfred yet. Even through the phone she could hear the wheels in Romy's head turning.

"So, let me get this straight," she brought out her you've-got-to-be-kidding-me voice. "This guy, this Max, is a Facebook acquaintance. You don't really know him in person, right?"

"Well," Carina began.

"And you don't actually know anyone who knows him?"

"Well, no, but—"

"Oh, Mom," Romy punctuated her words with a loud sigh.

Why did I even tell her about Max?

"It's all right," Carina said, cutting her daughter off before she could say anything too hurtful. "It was just an idea, no big deal. He's a nice kid in my grief group, but you're right, it was silly. Never mind."

"Don't get all butt hurt, Mom."

Carina hated when her daughter used that term and she knew it. "Don't worry about it. I've got to go. I'll talk to you soon." She hung up before Romy could say anymore.

Sleep-sweat prickled the back of her neck, tears prickled her eyelids. She hated having her ideas dismissed as foolish. It was just like the morning Alfred had rolled his eyes at her simply because she had never noticed how loudly he stirred his coffee. *They all think I'm nothing but a ridiculous old woman. All because I want to have my family together for Christmas. Why is that such a bad thing?*

Swiping at her eyes and the back of her neck, she strolled to the kitchen, glanced over the pantry and the freezer, waved the door back and forth a few times to cool off her wounded pride, and wondered if she should pick up something for supper. She would be dining alone since Alfred was out of town, but at the moment, she wasn't really hungry. There were plenty of sandwich makings in the fridge and even some homemade chili from the day before.

She tried calling Aaron and Annabelle, leaving messages for both, but she didn't really expect a different response from the one Romy had given. Her idea had been tarnished. Blown out of the water.

Maybe it was time to finish up her Christmas shopping. A little more retail therapy might help her feel better. She might even find something for the old Scrooge who rolled his eyes at her.

Should I get something for the expectant mother, Gia? She could hardly wait until Heath told everyone their good news. Another grandchild was always a welcome thing.

As if on cue, her phone sounded again. She glanced at the screen surprised and delighted to see Heath's name and face.

"Hey, baby," she answered. Heath had always been her sweet little man even though he was huge, imposing, and her first born.

"How ya doin', Mom?"

She could tell by his tone he was worried about something. "I'm okay," she said. "How are you? How's Gia?" No use beating around the bush.

"She's fine," he said. "The puking has let up. The doctor says it will pass completely before long."

"Well, that's good news, right?"

"Yes. It is. I can't believe how sick she's been."

Carina thought back over her four pregnancies. "I think it was Romy that affected me that way. But it might have been you *and* Romy. I lived on toast and tea with the occasional banana thrown in for good measure."

"That sounds right," he said. "And the ginger really helped. She wanted it since you recommended it. But the real reason I'm calling is because ..."

She waited.

"Romy called and said she was afraid she hurt your feelings about the cabin idea."

"Crossbow," Carina said. "Crossbow, Colorado. But hey, it doesn't matter. You guys can't travel, and Romy thought it was stupid, and I can't even get in touch with Annabelle or your dad." She huffed. "It was just a silly old woman thing. I tell you what, though." Another idea had struck her. "I might invite this young man to our house for Christmas. He's a young widower and I

51

think he's looking for a way to avoid being alone. You know he recently lost his wife to cancer—"

"But that's what I'm calling to tell you, Mom," Heath interrupted. "It's not a silly idea. We all love you for your big heart. We'd never hurt you in a million years if we could help it. Hey, maybe next year, huh? I looked it up on Google Maps and it's not *that* far from us. We could definitely hit those slopes after the baby is born."

"Sounds like a good plan," she said. "We will definitely do it next year. Thanks for calling sweetheart. I *was* feeling a little low."

He said something under his breath.

"What, honey? I didn't catch that."

"Sorry, Mom. I was asking Gia if I should tell you what Romy said, or wait until she tells you."

"Go ahead," she began. "No, you don't have to tell me, I can tell by your voice. She's all out of sorts because she's kicked another hubby to the curb."

"Well, not exactly. But I think there is trouble in paradise."

"Oh, no." Carina pictured her daughter's face. Such a gorgeous girl, but flighty. Anytime an idea occurred to her, she followed it. Like a butterfly. "I hate to hear that, but—"

In the background she heard Gia say, "Maybe that's why she questioned your friend, Max. She's trying to be cautious for you. Since she tends to leap first and look later." Gia and Heath had been together for three years. She'd already been witness to one of Romy's divorces and one remarriage.

"Maybe you're right," Carina said. "She might be learning to be cautious. On my behalf."

There was a tiny silence and she imagined Heath trying to decide how much to say. Sometimes it was necessary to walk on eggshells where his sis was concerned. "Anyway," he said into the phone. "Apparently, her and Sean are taking a break. When I asked her what happened she just sighed and said more of the same." He cleared his throat. "I don't really know what that means, and I was afraid to ask."

Carina closed her eyes and said a silent prayer for her headstrong daughter. "Well, if she's on her own again, then I'm sure finances are bad—"

"Flat broke," Heath said. "I told her I'd send her some Christmas cash."

"Oh, I hate that they're going through a rough patch. And right here at the holidays." She sighed. "But you, you're going to make a great dad, you know it?"

In the background, Gia laughed. "Yes, he will Mama, yes he will."

She sounds in fine spirits, Carina thought. Maybe it's the pregnancy making her sound so giddy. "Well," she said. "I'll be glad to send her and the kids some Christmas cash, too. Heaven only knows what will happen next." Carina blew a smooch into the phone and told her son she would talk to them again, soon.

They disconnected and she laid the phone on the counter where Schroeder's piano immediately began to play again, to signal a new call.

Wonder what he forgot to tell me? She pushed the answer icon. "What did you forget, kiddo?"

But it wasn't Heath, it was Alfred.

"Well, hello," she began, pleased to see his picture pop up on the screen.

"We've hit a major roadblock," he said. No greeting, no how are you, he just dove right in as if they'd been in conversation all along. "The firm they had handling their quarterly taxes has gone into bankruptcy and everything is an absolute mess."

He paused and Carina pictured him dragging one hand through his wavy, still-dark hair. Before she could respond, he went on to explain that he was going to be tied up for weeks yet, maybe months.

"I'm thinking of renting a small apartment near the San Antonio office," he said. "Save me hotel bills and cab fares."

Carina put the call on speaker. She couldn't reconcile his words with the man she'd slept with for the past three decades. Especially not right before Christmas. "What do you mean, rent an apartment?" Her mind reeled. "Don't you have to sign a lease, six-months or something like that?"

"Of course." He sounded like a college professor talking to a slow learner. "But as I said, it will save me money in the long ru—"

"Alfred, who do you think you're talking to right now?" She couldn't keep the exasperation from her voice.

"What do you mean, baby? I'm just telling you why—"

"You're not telling me anything. I know the pet food company provides you an expense account, a very *hefty* expense account. It definitely includes cab or Uber fare to and from your *paid* hotel room." In the back of her mind a thought blasted through her brain like neon fired from a paintball gun. *Is this how it starts? The beginning of the end?*

Alfred cleared his throat again. "Sweetie, you haven't really heard what I've been saying. This company is broke, remember all those Chinese pet products that killed and injured so many dogs?"

Carina mumbled, "Yes, so?"

"This company was heavily invested in those products. When the lawsuits started, they didn't take it seriously. Now, they're playing catch up. They've cut all ties with foreign markets and gone back to MADE IN AMERICA, but the books are shredded. No expense account, no frills, they're on a downward slide that I have to stop immediately." He cleared his throat again. "But here's the upside ... they've drawn up a contract that gives me—us—a percentage of the company when I stop the slide."

"Wow," she huffed. "That is something, isn't it?" She was duly impressed. The company was one of the oldest pet food corporations in the country. "But what if you can't save them, then what? You've done all this work for nothing?"

"Honey," his salesman voice came out. "You know I can save them. This is me, Super Al ... Alfred the Great, remember?"

Carina pulled the kitchen desk chair out and sat down heavily. "Sure, I remember. I married him, didn't I?" She closed her eyes and rubbed her forehead with the tips of her fingers. She could feel the pressure building like a storm cloud. "Okay, Superman," she said at last. "Do what you need to do."

"I knew you'd understand, Care." Alfred's tone was back to normal. "You'll see. When I pull this one out, we'll be set for life. I'll retire early and we'll travel just like we planned. Europe, New Zealand, Africa, Australia—"

"Sure," Carina agreed. "Just one thing, though."

"Yes?"

"What about Christmas?"

Alfred assured her he would partake in whatever Christmas plans she made. *Cabin in the woods?* Check.

Only much later did it occur to her that he'd said *he* was going to rent an apartment. He. Not the company. Not the ones who were supposed to be paying him to save them. Was doing all this work for free in hopes of earning part of a hemorrhaging company really such a great idea? She wanted to call him back and grill him, but she didn't want to fight. They never fought, seldom even disagreed, until the last few years, everything they'd done had been easy-peasy. Maybe too easy.

She began to feel selfish. He deserved early retirement. He'd always worked hard for the family. Even when she'd practically moved into her parents' home to care for them one right after the other.

I should return to work. Just in case. Pick up my old life somehow, the one I had before I turned nursemaid. The one where I actually earned a paycheck. She suddenly felt on tenuous ground. Maybe it was just the holiday season, but everyone seemed so busy, everyone *except* for her. No one seemed concerned about a family Christmas at all. It was as if they were all still isolating because of Covid.

Stop whining, old woman, she muttered. *You've got it made.* That thought caused her to laugh at herself, just a little. It was something Alfred's great uncle always said, "Chin up, kid, you've got it made."

In the meantime, she would keep a close eye on their bank account. Make certain Super Al wasn't simply having a little super mid-life fun. She hated being suspicious, but Alfred was a terrible flirt. Always had been. A salesman's personality, she'd always told herself, but every now and then she wondered if there hadn't been indiscretions along the way. She'd been so wrapped up in caring for her ailing parents over the last few years, anything could have happened. Ignorance is bliss, she murmured as she pushed in the desk chair and straightened the kitchen. *It is bliss. Isn't it?*

Her text message alert dinged. "I'm there, Mom! Get some lift tickets. I can't wait to try out those slopes." Aaron. The athlete. Easygoing, a joy to be around.

She tapped a quick reply. "I'm sorry, kiddo. Romy thinks it's a bad idea, and Heath and Gia can't make it so …" She hit send without finishing the thought.

"That's okay," he wrote. "I told her it was a great idea when she messaged me. Hey, just me, you, and Dad? Nothing wrong with that picture." He added a skiing emoji.

Carina stood. Then sat. Then stood again. "You may be on to something," she wrote. A terribly wonderful idea had entered her brain. *I've got GPS. I know how to read a map if that doesn't work. Why should I stay home, alone?* "Well alright," she typed. "I will get the lift tickets. Will you drive or fly?"

He said he would fly in and rent a car so she wouldn't have to worry about picking him up at the Denver airport. "I'll be there

Christmas Eve," he wrote. "I'm getting the flight info now. Will let you know the time … what about Belle? Is she coming?"

Carina smiled. "I haven't heard from her yet."

He sent a happy face. "See you Christmas Eve, Mama." He followed his words with a heart and then he was gone.

Well, at least one will be there. That's the good thing about having four children. The holiday odds were better.

She sent a text to Annabelle, telling her Aaron was on board. But not knowing exactly where she was, Carina couldn't be certain anything was getting through.

CHAPTER 6

LEAVING HOME

CARINA FILLED HER TANK AT THE CONVENIENCE STORE ON THE corner of Parkway and Glen, then she took the loop that would drive her around their smallish city to intersect the highway north of town. In about thirteen hours—750 miles if you don't measure distance in hours the way most Texans do—she would arrive at the tiny town of Crossbow, Colorado. From there, she would simply follow the directions Max had texted to her phone yesterday.

She was quite excited, and truth-be-told, a little nervous. Carina couldn't remember the last time she'd made a lengthy trip on her own. Oh, there had been her best friend's second wedding down in Cancun, but that didn't count. It had been eons ago, and the three bridesmaids had flown down together. Hardly the same as driving all day straight up the middle of the country by herself. What if the car broke down, or God forbid, she had an accident, what would she do?

Deal with it, she told herself. Deal with it and move on the way everyone else in the family does. *Hold on and let go.* Alfred didn't think a thing about renting his own place and living alone in San Antonio. Heath was well able to stand on his own two feet, make decisions day in and day out, for both himself and his expectant wife—though knowing Gia, Carina suspected not many decisions were made without her input. As it should be.

Still, even Aaron, her third child, made all his own decisions about college down there in Galveston. He was going to be a radiologist. "Someday, I'll own my own imaging clinic," he'd told her. "Then I'll just sit back and rake in the dough while the technicians I hire do all the work." He'd treated her to that GQ grin, and she'd melted the way she always had with him.

He was so much like his namesake father she couldn't help but laugh. "Alfred Aaron Pinner, always a head full of the future." But she wasn't scolding him, not at all. She was extremely proud of Aaron. He'd thought he was going to school on a soccer scholarship and did, in fact, have dreams of playing professionally, but a motorcycle accident had wrecked his knee right along with his sports plans.

Aaron hadn't even flinched. He'd simply shifted his focus from sports to medicine and spent all his recovery catching up on credits so he could transfer to radiology. "Doesn't bother me much," he'd said when Carina asked him if he was terribly disappointed. "I'd a lot rather play soccer for fun than for money."

Where had he inherited that sunny, can-do, attitude?

Oh, yeah, his father.

If it had been left up to her, Carina would have worried herself right into an early grave—or at least another ulcer.

And then there was their youngest, Annabelle Carina, the wild child, the rebel. The baby of the family. Always happy, never knew a stranger, thought school should be held outside in all kinds of weather. Took a few classes at the local junior college where she had joined a hiking and climbing group that made regular forays into McKittrick Canyon, down in the Big Bend, then Arizona, New Mexico, California, Nevada. Wherever the wind blew, and the group could afford to go.

Last year, the four kids had coordinated a Zoom chat to wish her happy birthday. They'd also chipped in together and sent her flowers and chocolate-covered fruit.

Carina had been thrilled. "I adore the gifts," she'd said, when she answered the Zoom. "Now tell me all your news." She'd laughed and made herself comfortable in her easy chair, chocolate-dipped fruit, and flowers by her side.

They'd all chimed in with bits and pieces, beginning with Romy. "I love my new job," she said. "The salon is so busy, and everyone shares clients, no one is selfish about directing their overflow your way. And the kids are finally settling into their new Dallas schools." She didn't gush, but she claimed things were going well, nearly perfect. Carina remembered crossing her fingers in her lap, out of sight of the camera.

Heath said he and Gia were working a lot and enjoying tons of live music and camping trips now that the weather had grown warmer. Winter in North Dakota was like another world, he'd said with a grin. "We've been suffering from cabin fever just a bit."

"What? No place to ski?" Aaron asked. Tanned, with sunny blond streaks in his caramel-colored hair, he had leaned back in his recliner—iPad on his lap—and went on to say, to no one's surprise, that he'd been spending all his free time at the beach, learning to surf and play beach volleyball instead of soccer.

"Ogling the bikinis, you mean!" his big brother had yelled.

"You know me too well, Bro," Aaron replied, refusing to be baited.

Carina laughed. "And how about you, baby girl?"

Annabelle had favored her mother with her patented look-at-these-dimples smile that thawed every heart within a two-mile radius. "Oh, I'm working, Mom, no worries."

"By working, you mean, the work study at college, right?"

Annabelle shook her curly head, and then she had dropped her bombshell. "Taking a little break from the books right now."

She flashed the dimples again. "I'm waiting tables at Hooters." As if it were no big deal. "The three of us girls all work the same shift, you know Jerricha and Sendy, my hiking club roommates, and then the Caveman still has his tattoo booth. We're all good. Just living life, having fun. Getting on with it." Another of those dazzling smiles which reminded Carina of the thousands of dollars' worth of orthodontia they'd paid for not so long ago.

"Hooters? Getting on with it?" *Did everyone speak in memes?* Carina had suddenly become aware of how her face must appear on the computer screen, but she couldn't help it. "Not going to school?" She turned to look for help from Alfred, but he'd wandered away, into another room.

At that moment, Carina had felt every one of her fifty-plus years piling up on her bones like extra flesh. In moments, she figured the force of gravity would pull her right down into the floor.

She'd tried to make her voice sound normal, but it had sounded like a squeaky toy. "Why are you waiting tables at Hooters?" Her right hand went to her forehead and her fingertips began to massage the furrow between her eyes. All that money for braces and piano lessons so she could sling hash at a bunch of leering men who wanted nothing more than to see her bend over to pick up one of their dropped napkins or forks.

Annabelle laughed the tinkly laugh that went so well with her dimples, and then she'd blown a kiss to her mother and told her not to worry. "The tips are excellent," she said. "Much better pay than the vet clinic in Arizona—although I really miss the people there, and Dr. Parr. They were awesome—but don't worry, Mom. I don't consider Hooters my *vocation*. It's only while I'm young and carefree." She leaned her head back and stretched her arm out toward the apartment window to illustrate the big world out there, or so Carina assumed. "Besides, we've got a great boss who lets the three of us have every other weekend off to go hiking and climbing."

Carina found herself completely speechless. She'd barely gotten used to the idea of her baby living with three roommates —especially one called Caveman—and now this. *Where did I go wrong?* It felt as if her two daughters had been sent just to test her.

One by one the kids had come back into the conversation to ease the pain so obvious on their mother's face. And then, after singing the birthday song—with the required addends on the tail of it and Aaron's impromptu coffee table drum solo in the middle —they had all clicked out one by one until only Heath was left. "Don't worry, Mom. I'm sure it's just a phase. You know Belle, she always was the adventurous one. She'll figure things out."

Alfred had walked up behind her, laid his hands on her shoulders. "I agree with Heath." He grinned and waved at his eldest son. "Tell Gia hello for me, and be careful up there, you hear?"

Heath nodded. Carina knew how hard he tried to live up to his dad's work ethics. He bore the burden for all of them, it seemed. Always seeing the best in his younger siblings, looking out for them, ready to step in at any time and be the diplomat of the family if needed.

"I sure love that boy," Carina said when Heath disconnected. "But my little Annabelle, oh, Alfred. Hooters!"

"Yeah, I've had to meet clients at those places." He frowned. "Never my first choice, that's for sure. But the younger generation doesn't see things the way we do." He squeezed her shoulders again, then walked away without further comment.

"That's for sure," Carina echoed. She recalled how she could feel the new worry burrowing into her as she'd closed the laptop and went to the kitchen in search of antacid.

Now, she thought of that Zoom call and all the other texts and phone calls she'd had with the kids since that day so many months earlier.

Romy and Heath said they were definitely not going to make it to the cabin, or even home if she decided to stay here, but

Aaron said he'd be in Colorado with bells on. Looking forward to hitting the slopes, he'd said. And she didn't begrudge him that. She was just pleased he could still ski after his surgery and rehab.

She'd finally heard from Annabelle, too. The group members had all saved up their days off and were now climbing in Red Rock, Nevada. She'd sent Carina a brief text in response to the idea of Christmas at the cabin. "Sorry, Mom," her text read. "We're only twenty minutes from Las Vegas." She'd inserted a selfie with Caveman and the girls on the Vegas strip in their hiking gear. "We're seriously considering applying for jobs here. Great pay, and the climbs are *amazing!*"

After she got her heart rate under control—*at least it's not Hooters*—Carina texted her back. "Enjoy your holiday sweet girl." She didn't say *are you crazy?* She often had to swallow her words where both her daughters were concerned.

CARINA FORCED ALL THAT OUT OF HER MIND AND FOCUSED ON enjoying the drive. *It's in your hands, Lord. I give it all to you.* She'd been practicing that prayer, that way of thinking, ever since the ventilator and the following months of gaining back the strength to walk and breathe and dress herself again.

She inhaled deeply, imagining the air circulating through her body until her lungs were filled, then exhaling, letting all the toxic thoughts and fears leave her on the long deep breath.

Giving it all to God.

It worked. Her mind eased. Her nerves settled.

The hardest thing about this trip is going to be choosing which one of my new playlists to play first … well, that and keeping myself from turning around and going back.

Alfred had called and told her he needed to work through Christmas, after all. "We'll have our holiday as soon as I've corralled some signatures."

She didn't even bother to tell him she and Aaron were going on up to the cabin. Oh, she would tell him, after she arrived. But if she told him now, he would only try to talk her out of going. And she was already looking forward to spoiling Aaron by letting him ski to his heart's content and drink cocoa with her by the fire afterward.

Carina thought back over her hasty departure, making certain she hadn't forgotten anything.

After packing her warm clothes—something she seldom had need of in West Texas—and her nearly-new fleecy coat, she'd packed up a Tupperware container full of nuts and berries, and a handful of Cheez-It Duoz, her favorite snack cracker weakness.

She also added a bag of M&M plain candies, hers and Alfred's once-favorite traveling candy. To balance things out, Carina also brought along a couple of apples and bananas. Just in case she broke down somewhere. *Paranoid, much?* She could just hear the voice of her children. They'd always teased her about being over-prepared for everything. *I know I'm not going to get stranded anywhere* she muttered, *but I can always snack on these at the cabin, too.*

She also poured both of her insulated sipping mugs—perfect for traveling—nearly full with fresh, hot coffee, added two teaspoons of powdered Coffee Mate to each, loaded an eight-pack of bottled water into the backseat, and then looked around.

One Diet Coke, she thought. *Or maybe a six pack for the cabin.* She knew it was bad stuff, all the doctors said it was like drinking chemicals, but she'd been addicted to it for years. *My one remaining vice,* she often joked. *If you don't count chocolate or caffeine.*

Carina tried not to think how lonely it had felt when she'd checked her purse, set the lights on timer, turned on the radio—an old habit she used to do for her sweet kitty, Moochi—and finally, went out and locked the door behind her.

Then she'd immediately had to turn around, disable the

alarm, unlock the door and go back in for her jacket and cell phone. "Geez, old woman," she'd chastised herself. "It's going to be some trip if you can't even get out of the driveway."

She grabbed her things, reset the alarm, relocked the door, climbed in the car, and fastened her seat belt. "It's going to be *epic*," she'd said to the universe, and then she backed out of the garage and pointed the car toward Colorado.

"I can't believe I'm doing this," she said aloud, sipping her coffee and giving thanks for a gorgeous sunrise pinking up the car windows and rear-view mirrors.

Carina drove happily, crunching and snacking her way clear across the far edge of Texas—about four hours—and didn't have to stop for gas until hunger for something other than nuts and berries, and the need for a bathroom, had her pulling into a Denny's Restaurant in Roswell, New Mexico.

After stretching her legs, and eating a plateful of surprisingly fluffy flapjacks, she went across to a gas station with attached touristy gift shop and bought all the grandkids alien gifts representing the well-known flying saucer crash of 1947. The tiny alien figures were wearing red and white Santa caps and frolicking around a silvery Christmas tree.

The gift shop windows were painted with flying saucers sporting red and green lights and the giant alien out front was also dressed like Santa. The music playing over the shop's speakers came from the decade of the forties and fifties.

Carina spent fifteen minutes looking through the UFO and alien-themed gifts and cards. Finally, she paid for her tiny Christmas aliens and pulled herself away.

Refreshed, Carina climbed back into the driver's seat. She itched to call the kids, or Alfred, but she knew they were all busy and she didn't want to worry them, so she resisted and cued up another long playlist.

The highway was nice, and it wasn't too long after leaving

Roswell, that she began to notice the dark blue silhouette of mountains in the distance.

Her Bruce Springsteen and Tom Petty playlists had just given way to old time gospel songs when she crossed the border from New Mexico into Colorado. The thirteen-hour timeline had turned out to be a bit wishful. Her plan to see the sunrise in Texas, and the sunset in Colorado wasn't happening. Due to construction and various detours, that timeline had fallen by the wayside.

Snow had arrived in northern New Mexico and the once-silhouetted mountains were now dusted with sugar. The silently falling flakes were beautiful and unhurried, soft, and white. They lit up the near dusk and made Carina feel as if she were driving through one of her own treasured snow globes. She didn't care that it slowed her progress even more, she simply enjoyed the ride.

CHAPTER 7

THE CABIN

MAX CHECKED ON HER THROUGHOUT THE DAY. SHE KNEW SHE WAS exhibiting a tiny act of rebellion in not telling the kids and Alfred she was going up alone, and in the back of her mind, she wondered if she was being stupid, or at the very least, careless. But they all had their lives, she just wanted to have hers.

An adventure, just an adventure. Besides, the phones work both ways. They could just as easily call her as she them.

After the death of her sweet little Moochi, at the age of nineteen, the house had felt completely empty. It was to be expected, of course, she was very old for a housecat, but still no one crawled into her lap every time she sat down. No one curled up on her bed pillow at night. And since Alfred was away on business so often, it felt almost like a different home. *Maybe that's because I spent the last few years at Mom and Dad's house, then went almost straight into the hospital with Covid.*

Come to think of it, maybe little Moochi had simply been waiting on me to get home before she crossed that old rainbow bridge.

Nope. There was nothing to keep her at home this Christmas. Her mom's old circle of card players might miss her, but it was doubtful. She got the idea they only thought of her when she showed up out of the blue with pie.

Max told her to call him when she got to Crossbow, and he would direct her to the cabin a few miles outside town. He seemed as excited as Carina. "I can't wait for you to see it," he said. "I had the company who handles the rentals go by and make sure everything was perfect. It's a husband and wife team, Terry and Cheyenne. They even left the porch light and living room lamp on for you."

"That's so nice," Carina said, excitement causing her foot to press the accelerator a little harder.

He hesitated for a moment. "It will be dark before you get there. Let me call them and have them meet you. Even with the lights on, you shouldn't have to go inside in the darkness."

"No, no, no. That won't be necessary. I don't want to burden anyone. Besides, it won't be dark if the lights are on."

"Still," he said. "It's sort of isolated. I wouldn't feel right—"

"I can keep you on the phone while I walk in," she said. "If you aren't too busy, that is."

"Not busy at all." He chuckled. "When you see The Crossbow Inn, take a right. Eagle's Nest road goes up and up and up, directly behind the Inn. Don't worry, you won't go to the top. Follow it for half a mile and then you'll come to Paper Lane. That's where the cabin is located."

"You have your own Lane?"

His voice held a note of sadness she didn't quite understand. "Yes," he replied. "Even though the land and original cabin belonged to Andrea's granddad, the state allowed us to apply for our own name since it's a private road. Her granddad never named it. In fact, it was little more than a dirt trail, unusable in the winter. He called it his fishing cabin, only went up in good weather. It's surrounded by state park land."

"I noticed that when I Google mapped it," Carina said. "And now her parents want it back?"

"I wonder if I should give it to them. It's sort of got her stamp all over it, you know? Our dream vacation house."

"Oh, Max. Are you sure I should be staying here. I wouldn't want to get in the middle—"

"No, no, don't worry about that. I've been renting it out to complete strangers, remember? Besides, her folks always go to Florida in the winter."

Carina had forgotten that part.

"I can't wait to see it again," he said. "And then I'll make the decision about it. I love it, and I love what it represents, but maybe it does belong to her folks, and not me. I had her for such a short time—"

"I don't know. It was your dream together." Carina rounded a slight curve in the highway and the village was laid out before her. "Oh, wow … I'm here. This town is *adorable*. Every building looks like a ski lodge. All the heavy wood and peaked roofs and Christmas lights everywhere. It's beautiful."

"Didn't I say?"

"Oh—there it is. The Crossbow Inn. I see it's also a restaurant. Isn't that lovely? So quaint, and all the lights strung from every post and under every eave, it's just like something out of a movie. And look at that gigantic tree. How on earth did they get the star on top? A crane?"

"I think they do use a crane, or a manlift perhaps. Do you know why it's called Crossbow?"

"No, I never thought to ask." She laughed self-consciously. "I assumed it was just a catchy name."

"Once upon a time it was a huge hunting ranch, I mean the whole town was owned by this rancher."

"Oh, no," Carina began.

"Right," Max interrupted. "But not anymore. When the original owner, Jessop Cross, got older, he began to mellow. People say it was his first granddaughter who did it. Anyway, he left her everything in his will, and even gave his blessing—in writing—for her to turn the entire property, about five thousand acres, into a family ski resort and hiking area."

"No hunting allowed?"

"Exactly."

"That's amazing," Carina said. "Oops, I went through town quicker than I intended. I think I missed the turn." She stepped on the brake and slowed the car. "I was so busy trying to see inside that beautiful Inn that I forgot what I was doing."

"It's all right," Max said. "I'll bet there's no one on the road. Just back up until you—"

"Actually," she said. "There are a couple of cars out front, and one of them is about to leave. I'd better do this right." She drove on until she spied a convenience store. "Ahh," she said. "Even gorgeous little resort towns must have convenience stores." She pulled into the parking lot of the well-lighted shop and made a U-turn.

"Good for you," Max said. "7-Eleven, right?"

"No, this one is a Circle K." A chill tickled her scalp. For the first time she wondered if she'd made a mistake coming here alone, on a whim, without telling a soul. Although, truth be told, Aaron knew she was meeting him here. He just didn't know she was coming up early.

"I guess it's changed hands since I've been there," Max said. "Are you headed back to the turn?"

Carina maneuvered the car through the parking lot and back onto the road. The digital clock on the dash read 8:20 p.m. "If it wasn't for the reflective snow, it would be awfully dark here."

"Yes," he said. "I think the Inn is the last well-lit place on that end of Main Street. Except for the convenience store. But if you go back the other direction, toward the Alpine Ski Lodge, and take that fork in the road, that's where you will find most of the people."

"Oh, so I came in right on the far edge—"

"Yes," he said. "You came in on the southern fork of the Y, but if you follow the northern fork, you will find yourself in the midst of the skiers and snowboarders. I grew up there until Mom and Dad divorced. The Crossbow Inn is usually quiet, more family oriented, but downtown is a different story."

Carina debated driving on past the turn and exploring the glow of lights further up the northern branch of Main, but she didn't want to keep Max on the phone too long. In fact, after his forgetting about the Circle K store, she was more than eager to find the cabin and see it for herself. Make certain everything was on the up and up. If not, she could always ask for a room at the Inn instead.

She took the turn and the road narrowed quickly into a dark single lane. Patches of snow glimmered through the stands of trees, and the ditches running beside the road were filled to the brim with white. Every now and then the moonlight made its way between the towering trees to shine a spotlight on the larger drifts spilling across the edges of the road all the way to the center.

The world went silent. Carina forgot about the two or three cars on the street outside the Inn. She forgot about being nervous traveling all this way alone, she even forgot about Max on the still-open phone.

"Carina?"

She pulled her eyes away from the soft flakes swirling down through the gaps in the trees. "Sorry, Max, this scenery is so amazing. I just saw little golden eyes glittering beside the road."

"Probably a deer," he said. "Or if they were way down low, a raccoon or a possum."

She laughed. "I think it was the height of a deer."

"Okay, it's been a couple of minutes, you should be coming up on Paper Lane."

"How will I know when I—" she stopped talking and let her foot off the accelerator. "Oh, the lights."

Max chuckled. "Cheyenne said they put up a few extra for you."

"It's beautiful. The entire porch is strung with twinkling lights and way out on the snowy front yard, four squares of gold are shining down from the upstairs windows."

"Like a painting," Max said. "A painting on the snow. That's the loft. That's my favorite spot in the whole cabin, well, that and the couch in front of the fireplace." His voice had grown soft.

She turned into the recently cleared driveway. "The stained glass—"

"In the front door? That was one of Andrea's projects. One of her many projects she did before the chemo."

Carina couldn't speak for the huge lump in her throat. "Should I park in the garage around back?"

"You'll be okay tonight if you just want to leave the car out front. I know it's dark back there, kind of spooky—"

Her voice sounded shaky, even to her ears. "Exactly what I thought."

"I didn't even like parking back there late at night," he said. "But you get used to it later. My next project is to put up a big spotlight between the house and garage, especially now that the guest quarters above it have been renovated. I just haven't taken the time to do it. You are the first one to stay there since the guest quarters were finished. And we didn't think of the lighting until a couple days ago." He chuckled. "I'm wondering if I need to just go ahead and add an attached garage. If I make enough in rentals to pay for it." He sighed. "If I decide to keep it."

"Such a hard decision," Carina said. "Are you certain it's okay to park out front over night? My car won't freeze or anything?"

"Not tonight," Max said. "I checked the weather forecast and it is going to be mild for the next few days. You came at exactly the right time."

Carina tried to keep that in mind as she looked at the open area between her SUV and the front porch. Even though it was beautiful and well lit, she did not feel as brave as she pretended. She gathered her keys and her purse. "I've got my flashlight turned on so I can see the lockbox. 318, correct?"

"Right," he said. "Just a routine combination lock. And the door keys will be inside the box. I'll be with you the whole time. Ready?"

"Ready," she whispered, wishing she'd let the management couple meet her like he had suggested. *Why am I so obstinate sometimes?* She turned off the engine, grabbed her phone, hit the speaker icon. "You still there?"

"Yes," he whispered. "But why are we whispering? Want to FaceTime?"

She opened the car door and put her left foot out into the snow. "Yes, please."

The call disconnected and she immediately got a new call with a FaceTime request.

She pressed accept.

"Hey," he said.

She could see he was still dressed in scrubs. "Are you at the hospital?"

He nodded. "I love it so much I'm thinking of just moving into the doctor's lounge." He grinned and she realized he was making small talk to put her at ease.

Carina took a steadying breath and closed the car door behind her. The thunk of metal on metal was slightly muted beneath the gently falling snow. "This is so beautiful." She couldn't make herself speak above a whisper.

"It is beautiful," he agreed, a touch of melancholy creeping into his tone.

She glanced at his face. "Let me turn you around." She reversed the FaceTime camera.

"Cheyenne and Terry did a great job." His voice cracked. "It looks very inviting."

"Let's get inside," she said. "This has to be hard for you."

"It's all right. The last time I was there, the shutters needed replacing, the chimney leaned, and the driveway was overgrown with weeds. It's so much better since I hired them."

Thanks to the twinkly Christmas lights, the wraparound porch was nearly as light as day. The numbers on the lockbox wheel turned easily. In seconds, she had the keys in her hand and the door wide open. Warmth greeted her. A cheery fire burned low in the stone fireplace, but she could tell there was a central heating system as well. "Oh, my goodness, this is wonderful. I can't believe they even made a fire."

He laughed. "They just left a few minutes ago. Totally their idea. I can't take any credit."

"Wow. Just, wow." She looked around the cozy front room with its comfortable leather couch and brightly colored throw pillows. "The furnishings are perfect. I can't wait to see the rest of it." She headed for the kitchen visible through the adjoining dining area with its rough-hewn table and chairs. A polished bench sat under the dining room window, extra seating if needed.

"The kitchen took the most work," he said. "Well, that and the bathroom. Andrea made all the plans. She actually found the appliances online. One of those vintage reproduction places."

Carina skirted the table and entered the spacious kitchen with its narrow island. Turquoise antique-replica refrigerator and stove stood out in the soft lighting coming through the many windows.

"The light switch is right there, beside the doorway."

She flipped it and the delicate antler-chandelier glowed. "Oh, that is unique." She reached up and touched it gently.

"Yep. Takes a good anchor bolt for that guy. Andrea and I gathered the antlers the first time we stayed there. We made certain to get smaller ones. She fashioned the fixture and I wired it."

"How can you stand it?" Carina said, as if talking to one of her own children.

She glanced at the screen just in time to see him swipe at his eyes. "It's okay," he said. "I like the thought of someone nice being there, enjoying it. Andrea would have liked that."

"And you'll be coming, too, right? Coming for Christmas? I've brought decorations, not too many, just a few favorites. I'll find a small tree in town."

"Yes," he breathed. "I plan on coming for Christmas. I will stay at my dad's place, though. He's going to Hawaii, last I heard. I won't stay at the cabin, not yet. I will come for Christmas dinner, though."

She tried to sound jolly. "Okay, then. We've got a plan." She touched the fridge and the stove and admired the beautiful stoneware canisters on the counter. "Let's head upstairs."

Together they went up the stairs to the wide loft. It had been divided into two separate sleeping areas with two full beds on one side and two sets of bunks on the other. A small bathroom sat just off the landing. "Don't worry," he said. "The master suite is downstairs, we skipped it completely." He laughed. "And tomorrow you can explore the guest quarters above the garage."

Carina uncrossed her fingers. Even if all four kids and the grandkids had been able to come, there would have been plenty of room. With just her and Aaron, it would be downright spacious.

"It's just wonderful," she told Max. "And plenty of room if you decide to stay here, too. It will only be my Aaron and me. Now, on with the tour." She sensed he wanted to ask something, probably why no one else was coming, but he was too polite to dig.

Back downstairs, she stepped into the master suite. It wasn't large, but the bed was a hand-hewn four-poster with an authentic crazy quilt for a spread. A rugged chest of drawers and dresser completed the décor. Through the wide doorway she could see the spa-like bathroom. "Ahhh," she sighed. "I can hardly wait to try out that jetted tub."

Max laughed. "And when you get tired of that, head on out back to the hot tub."

"What? Are you kidding me? Max Paper, this is not a mountain cabin, this is a resort all on its own." She couldn't believe her luck at being offered this place free of charge.

"That's why it's almost paid for itself already," he said. "Also another reason I've held on to it. Before Andrea and I put all our work and savings into renovations, it really *was* little more than a dilapidated shack with a loft."

"I swear," she said. "You are so young. The two of you had so many plans."

"Yeah," he agreed. "Who said that about the best laid plans of mice and men? Steinbeck?"

"Hmmm," she said. "Robert Burns first, I think."

He chuckled. "I figured you were going to say The Bible. It seems as if it's a biblical thing."

"Should be," she said. "Heaven knows we can plan, and plan then watch those plans go out the window in the blink of an eye—"

"Right," he agreed. "That's why we should learn to appreciate every moment while we can."

Carina nodded. She was thinking of her husband down there in San Antonio. It suddenly struck her as odd that he had never even asked if she would like to visit him. She wondered what he would think if she popped in on him unexpectedly. Oh well, too late now.

"This place is amazing," she said to her FaceTime buddy. "And a hot tub, too? Will wonders never cease?"

CHAPTER 8

FIRST NIGHT

Max stayed on the phone with her while she brought in her luggage and made herself comfortable.

"I can't thank you enough," she told him over and over again. "You didn't have to do all this for an old woman you barely met."

The young man shook his head. "First of all, you aren't old. Secondly, I think you know me better than anyone since my wife. I know it probably seems selfish on my part, but yeah, I have come to think of you as family."

Carina smiled. "Thank you, that is such a sweet thing to say. To be perfectly honest, I can't believe I've done this. Jumped up and drove across country without really knowing—"

"Nah! Don't say it. Don't even think it." He shook his head again. "Now, make yourself comfortable, get some good rest, and head into town tomorrow. Check things out, stock up on the basics, and get ready for a phenomenal Christmas." He grinned. "Doctor's orders."

"I will," she smiled back. "You get some rest, too."

Max gave her a quick salute. "Yes, ma'am. I'll check in on you tomorrow. Enjoy your evening."

They ended the lengthy call and Carina locked the doors and

went through every room again. She felt like a little ghost, or a made-up character waiting to come to life in someone's story. That's what I've always been, she thought. A character in someone else's story.

She sighed and put away her clothes and her toiletries, took a short, soothing soak in the jetted tub, changed into warm knit pajamas, and then turned on the big TV mounted opposite the fireplace. Max told her they had satellite TV and for once, she was glad. The sound of an old movie made her feel comfortable. She immediately recognized Jimmy Stewart's voice in the holiday classic *It's a Wonderful Life*. It was one of those movies she couldn't pass up when it came on.

But she couldn't make herself go to bed in the master bedroom. The house was too strange, too empty, too different. She made a cup of chamomile tea, which had been left on the counter by the realtors in a lovely basket with a *Welcome to Crossbow* mug.

She took her tea, gathered a pillow and blanket, and settled into the leather sofa. At the last second, she hurried back to the bedroom to retrieve her phone charger—proud of herself for remembering it—and plugged it into the nearby outlet. Then she curled herself into a ball facing the black and white drama playing out in the snowy town onscreen. From the corner of her eye, she could see the Christmas lights illuminating the wide front porch.

She reached over the end of the couch, dug around in her tote bag, and pulled out her well-worn journal. Sipping her tea, she pulled her favorite pen out of the attached elastic holder, found a blank page, and wrote the date at the top.

"What a long, strange, trip it's been," she quoted the old Grateful Dead song. "I left Landon pre-dawn, now it's well past midnight and no one even knows I'm not at home, tucked up in my little bed like a bunny in her burrow."

Carina looked at what she'd written and it brought tears to

her eyes. Several times throughout the day she had almost called Alfred, or Romy, even Heath, just to tell them where she was, and what she was doing. But something always stayed her hand.

She felt a bit of moisture tickle her bottom lid. No one even knows where I am at this moment except for Max Paper, a boy I've never met, a boy as lonely as me.

When the moisture spilled over onto her cheeks, she attributed it to Jimmy Stewart's troubles. After all, look at her blessings. Look at this beautiful place. What did she have to be sad about? Nothing. Absolutely nothing. Silly old woman. She swiped a finger across her cheek as she thought of Alfred eating his Christmas dinner on the Riverwalk.

Silly, she thought again. Just silly.

She touched her favorite pen to the thick, soft paper. I'll write myself a happy Christmas. A happy Christmas for my boy Aaron, my friend Max, and me. Then I won't be sad, I won't feel sorry for myself, and I certainly won't dwell on this dream of a large family around a long table.

She crossed her fingers. *Be like Aaron.*

On the top of the page, she wrote: *Christmas Adventure*

She tapped the end of the pen against her teeth. Adventure. I like the sound of that. Tomorrow I'll drive into town and see what's what. It's never too late to have an adventure. I'm not old. I've just had a hard year. Or three. She wrote a few lines, watched a few minutes of the movie, and drifted off to sleep.

When she awoke the next morning, the journal lay open on the floor and the TV still played on low. This time the movie was *Miracle on 34th Street.*

Struggling out of her nest—thankful for the central heat since the fire had died down—Carina slid her sock-clad feet into her slippers and padded to the kitchen to start the coffee. She'd turned the sound up so she could hear the movie as she spooned grounds into the filter and ran water for the machine.

Twice she heard something she couldn't quite identify. It

sounded like a kitten, meowing feebly. That's not in the movie, she thought.

She stopped moving and listened carefully.

Mew-w-w

Carina moved to the back door and opened it slowly, trying to be as quiet as possible. The sky hung overcast and low, but the snow shone bright and clean, piled in new drifts all around the deck, and there on the one dry spot on the inside corner of the rough sisal door mat, a small ginger kitten crouched into a pitiful little ball of bedraggled fluff.

Shocked, Carina stepped out in her slippers and scooped it up in one hand before it could run away. But there was no chance of that. It felt frozen, as if the feeble *mew-w-w* had taken the very last of its strength and warmth. "Oh, you poor little thing."

The kitten was so light it felt like holding a cold drop of nothing. She snuggled the baby into the hollow of her throat and stepped back inside the warm kitchen. "Where on earth did you come from?" She heated a fluffy dish towel in the microwave.

Holding the towel to her own face for a few moments to make certain it wasn't too warm—or wouldn't become too warm—Carina carefully wrapped it around the freezing baby and tried to think what to do about food.

She crossed her fingers that the realtor had left milk in the fridge, they'd thought of so many things to make her stay more comfortable, but alas, when she popped open the door, milk wasn't one of them.

"Sorry, baby," she murmured to the tiny bundle she carried next to her heart. "It looks like we are going to find a vet or at the very least, a pet store. They will have that replacement milk for orphaned kitties."

She wondered what had happened to the rest of the litter, and to the mama cat. She took her keys and started the Subaru's engine remotely so that it would be warm, then chastised herself for doing that without honking the horn first. Everyone knows feral cats will climb up into warm car engine compartments in cold weather. And while it wasn't warm now, it certainly was last night when she'd parked it there.

Praying there had been nothing sleeping under the hood, Carina scanned the front and back yards for any sign of another kitten or cat. There was nothing. Neither were there any tracks.

"I've got to check the garage," she said aloud, talking to herself as she pulled on fleecy clothes, jacket, and snow boots. She poured a cup of coffee and took a few hurried sips while looking at the pristine landscape. "I can't imagine how you got on the porch without leaving any tracks."

She snuggled the baby close again. "You must've been out there so long the snow covered your path." The idea of it there all night in the wet cold made Carina cringe. "I'll just tuck you into the front seat when it's warm, then I'll take a quick peek in that garage." She hadn't seen another shed or barn where a cat might live.

After a few more sips of coffee, she nestled the baby down inside her tote bag, still in the warm towel, zipped her jacket, and pulled up her hood. Tucking her cell phone and wallet into her pocket, she stuck her key fob into her other pocket and made her way to the car.

After a couple of bangs on the hood with her fist, mostly to make herself feel better, Carina opened the door and placed her tote bag in the passenger seat, making certain the baby was still wrapped and warm, but not suffocating.

She closed the car door gently, left the engine running, and counted twenty snowy, knee-deep steps from the car to the garage before she remembered the remote opener she'd seen lying on the kitchen counter.

"There has to be another door," she muttered. "Not just the overhead." She walked carefully around the corner of the reddish colored barn-siding garage. It had obviously been built on the property much later than the original cabin. A couple of times snow fell over the tops of her fur-lined boots and went down inside them, but she barely noticed.

The east side of the garage sported a regular sized door with a regular lock. Steps went up to a small balcony and another door that had to be the entrance to the guest quarters. That makes sense, she thought. I'll go up and check it out when we get back, right now looking for kitties. Don't think they'd be up there.

She pulled out the cabin keys—glad she'd slid them onto her own key fob—and looked for labels. Sure enough, one had an ornate F, one had an ornate B, and the third and fourth had ornate letters G1 and G2 inscribed on them.

G for garage, she surmised, fitting G1 into the lock.

Carina opened the door and stepped inside, using her cellphone flashlight to find the overhead light switch.

But in the bright light, she could see it was all for naught.

The garage was as clean as the proverbial whistle, nary a cat nor a kitten in sight. Oh well, she thought. I had to rule it out. Now on to Plan B.

She went out, locked the door behind her, and made her way back to the SUV. Thank goodness the realtors had salted all the porch steps and the short drive from the cabin to the road. Carina prayed the road into town wouldn't be slippery. She had very little experience driving on ice, but even to her untrained eye the snow appeared loose and fluffy, not packed and icy.

Onward, she told herself as she crawled into the warm vehicle. She typed veterinarian into Google Maps and up popped three possibilities. Two were for large animals, horses, cows, and sheep she assumed, but the third listing was a small animal clinic on the far side of town.

She touched the phone link to call the clinic. It went to voice mail. "Our hours are eight to five," the voice said. "Please leave a message if you have an emergency after hours. Doc will get back to you."

Carina looked at the car clock. 7:50. Here we come, she

thought, pulling away from the picturesque cabin with her tiny, too-quiet, bundle. "Hang on little one. They should be open when we get there." She put one hand inside the tote bag to stroke and comfort the baby. "Hang on little ginger kitty."

With her GPS guiding her, Carina drove straight through town, taking the north fork of Main when prompted to do so, barely noticing the quaint Christmas décor in every shop front, and made her way straight to where the Crossbow Small Animal Clinic should be.

But the lot was vacant. The only thing she found was a fenced off area that appeared to be under construction. It seemed the clinic was undergoing a renovation or an overall rebuild but so far all they'd done were the survey lines.

Disappointed, but determined to find help for the kitty, Carina took out her phone to call one of the large animal clinics when she spied the snow-crusted sign wired to the chain link fence.

Sorry for the inconvenience
We'll be back to normal in the Spring
Meanwhile, visit us at 223 West Main in the
Village Shopping Center

Carina clapped her hand to her forehead. She recalled driving right past the Village Shopping Center, a little strip mall, on the way through town. It hadn't appeared open, though. No cars in the parking lot.

She pulled into the empty lot and made a careful turn around. "Hold on, baby, we'll find this place yet." The word ADVENTURE appeared in her mind like a little sign. Ha, she thought. Who said "be careful what you wish for?" *I'll have to keep that in mind from now on. I could be at home beside the fire with a book and a cup of coffee.*

Turning out of the empty lot onto North Main Street, headed

back the way she'd come, Carina stuck her hand into the tote bag. The kitten was dry now, but it still shivered a bit.

She stroked it gently as they drove back through the sleepy, snowy town. This time, when she spied the shopping center, a couple of vehicles were parked in front. One was a Jeep and the other an ancient Land Rover, both were equipped with big snow tires that made her green with envy. The Jeep even had a snow plow attachment on the front.

CHAPTER 9

DOCTOR LANCE

CARINA PULLED UP NEXT TO THE JEEP JUST AS A YOUNG WOMAN appeared inside a thick glass door and fiddled with the lock. She then turned a CLOSED sign to OPEN. The plastic sign was in the shape of a giant dog bone.

This must be the place. She parked, gathered up the tote bag, and stepped out of the car very carefully in case of ice. The girl smiled and waited until she was near, then opened the door and held it for her.

"Hello," the girl said. "Looking for Dr. Lance?"

Carina nodded. "I think so. Is he the small animal vet?"

"Yes, ma'am," the girl replied. "Best one in town."

Carina glanced at the girl's nametag. She wanted to say *isn't he the only one in town?* But didn't want to sound rude. Instead, she glanced at the nametag again and placed her tote bag gently on the counter. "Well, Bonnie, somehow this little guy wound up on my back porch this morning. He was wet and freezing and I have nothing to feed him." She pulled the towel-wrapped kitten out and held it to her chest. "He's still shivering," she said. "And so thin."

Bonnie reached across and took the bundle. "Let me get a look at this little dude. Follow me, please."

She led Carina to a small exam room off the waiting area. "Dr. Lance is giving medicine to a patient recovering from surgery in the kennel," she said. "But he will be here as soon as possible." She unwrapped the kitten on the exam table but left it on the warm towel. "Let's just get your weight and temp," she cooed. "Then we will wrap you right back up. It's too cold for little ones today, isn't it?"

Carina loved the way the young woman focused completely on the kitten and treated it as if it belonged to her. She watched as Bonnie weighed the baby—less than a pound—and carefully took its temperature.

She wrapped it back in the towel and handed the bundle back to Carina. Then she took a heating pad from under the counter and plugged it into the socket at the end of the exam table. Setting it on medium, she held her hand flat on the pad until it was warm, then she took the bundle back and placed the whole thing on the heating pad. "Hold him here," she told Carina, "and hold your other hand on the pad itself so we don't let it get too hot. In a few minutes we will turn it down to low. Remember that for when you get back home."

Carina nodded and did as instructed.

"I'm going to warm some formula," Bonnie said. "I'll be right back."

Knowing she had come to the right place, Carina pulled the heating pad and towel-wrapped kitten closer to where she leaned against the side of the silver exam table. The kitten hardly moved but Carina pressed it against her middle and said a little prayer for it to be all right.

In moments, Bonnie was back with the tiniest bottle Carina had ever seen. "Let's see if it is able to nurse." She pulled the bundle gently toward herself on the opposite side of the table, then fashioned an opening around the kitten's face and made certain the rest of its body remained nestled into the towel. Then she squeezed a drop of the milky substance onto the nipple of the doll-sized bottle and held it to the baby's mouth.

For a moment, nothing happened. She smeared the warm drop of liquid across the kitten's closed mouth and squeezed the bottle to bring another drop onto the rubber nipple.

Suddenly, the kitty's eyes popped open, its little mouth popped open, and a raspy *me-e-w-w-w* issued from its throat.

"Starving, aren't you, baby?" Bonnie whispered. She held the nipple gently against the kitten's mouth as it struggled to get another drop of milk. "Squeeze the bottle ever so gently at first," she said, showing Carina what she meant. "Just place the drop of formula on kitty's mouth—one drop at a time—until it gets strong enough to suckle."

Carina realized she was standing there with her mouth open. She'd had cats all her life, but she'd never had one so tiny and so alone. The only litters she'd been acquainted with had been in the care of their mothers. She'd never hand fed one.

By now the kitten was doing its best to grasp the bottle with its tiny paws. But it still couldn't seem to nurse. Bonnie patiently continued squeezing one drop after another onto the nipple and eventually the kitten would bite and chew and lick until its little mouth was soaked with milky formula.

"Is it actually getting any?" Carina asked. The feeding looked like a battle more than a meal.

Bonnie laughed. "Oh, yes. But we will also supplement with this," she held up something that looked like a toothpaste tube, "when it gets a little stronger." She grinned at Carina. "Don't worry, it's kitten paste, not toothpaste." Handing the baby back to Carina, she said, "Ready to try?"

Carina nodded. Live and learn, she thought, attempting to squeeze only one drop at a time onto the nipple. She heard the door open, but assumed it was Bonnie going out to deal with the next patient.

"I think I'm doing okay, don't you, baby cat?"

"You're doing just fine," a deep, warm voice said.

Carina glanced over her shoulder, surprised to see a tall, white-haired man leaning against the door jamb with his shoulder. He had a half smile on his face and his reading glasses were perched precariously on the tip of his nose.

"Looks like he's doing fine, too," he went on. "Bonnie told me you found him on your back porch, wet and starving." The name, Dr. Lance, was embroidered onto the pocket of his white lab coat.

"Oh, hello," she said. "You're the vet?"

"Guilty as charged." His voice smiled when he did. "I think your new pal is going to do great. I'll get Bonnie back in here to show you how to help the baby go to the bathroom—"

"Wait," she said. "What?" She ducked her head, somehow as shy as a schoolgirl. "Show it how to go to the bathroom? Don't they do that automatically?"

"Oh, it's no big deal, really. You have to take the mother's place, you know. But you won't have any trouble after a bit of practice."

Carina nodded. "I'll need to buy some supplies—"

"We've got everything you need." He pulled a business card out of his pocket and laid it on the table. "And if you have any trouble, just give me a call."

"Thanks." Carina took the card, still holding the bottle with her other hand.

Dr. Lance stepped up to the table, took his stethoscope from his jacket pocket, and listened to the tiny little side-chest. "Good breath sounds," he said. "Is he learning to nurse yet?"

Carina shook her head. "Mostly just licking and allowing it to dribble in his mouth." She smiled. "I have to kind of make sure it gets in the right spot so he can get it."

"Probably only a few days old," he said. "No telling what

happened to the mom." He looked up at Carina. "Did you check for the rest of the litter?"

Carina nodded. "I did. Even checked the garage. Nothing."

He put his stethoscope away and leaned against the table, read the notes in the chart. "Body temperature's a little low, need to keep it on the warmer the rest of tonight, offer it the formula every two to three hours if you can. The little thing seems on the edge of starvation."

"I will," she said. "Thank you, Dr. Lance."

He touched the brim of an imaginary hat and ducked out through the doorway into the hall.

Bonnie came back in bearing a can of formula and a snug little bed that plugged into the wall. "It's heated," she said. "If you don't want it, that's all right, but I wanted you to see it."

"I love it," she said. "It's perfect."

Bonnie took the kitten and turned it over in her hands so she could teach Carina how to help the little thing go to the bathroom. "You'll need to do this after every feeding." She stroked the baby's tummy with a warm, damp cloth. "Are you up to that?"

Carina nodded. "Sure. It's sort of like the mom licking and cleaning him. I didn't realize that's why, though. The poor little guy—it is a boy, right?"

Bonnie laughed. "Hard to tell for certain at this age, but I will say that since 80% of ginger kitties are male, the chances are good." She rewrapped the kitten in the towel and gave it back to Carina. Picking up the chart, she made a few more notes. "I'll meet you at the front desk."

Carina tucked the baby back into her tote bag where he promptly went to sleep.

When she got to the front, Bonnie had her kitty bed, formula, and three small bottles all sacked up and ready to go. "Oh, can't forget this." She added the tube of protein paste, then went on to describe to

Carina how to let the baby lick the paste right off her just-washed finger when he was stronger. "It will be a few days before he wants that probably, but if you aren't sure, just let him try it." She smiled.

"Thank you," Carina said. "80% are male, huh? That's so interesting. I've got to read about that ... do you know why?"

"Oh, yes," Bonnie said. "It's the ginger gene. It occurs on the X chromosome. That means male cats only need one copy of the gene to become a ginger while female cats have two X chromosomes and thus require two copies of the gene." She grinned as if that made it all clear.

Carina felt herself matching Bonnie's wide, sincere grin. "Thank you. I had no idea."

Bonnie shrugged. "Did you know most solid white cats are deaf if they have blue eyes?"

"Now that one I *did* know." She laughed as she handed over her credit card. "But only because we had a white, blue-eyed tom when I was a girl."

"Aww," Bonnie ran the card through the machine. "What was his name?"

Carina glanced up. "Teaken," she said. "Ol' Teak." She cast about in her memory. "But for the life of me, I can't recall where he got such a strange name."

Bonnie handed her card back. "I'm sure it made perfect sense at the time."

"I suppose. I haven't thought of that dear old tom in years." She put her card inside her wallet and tucked the wallet carefully back into the tote with the kitten. "Oh, well, I'm sure it'll come to me on the drive back to the cabin."

"I know what you mean," Bonnie agreed. "When you least expect it, that's when it will appear."

"Yep, just as soon as I stop trying to remember it, there it will be."

Bonnie smiled and went to open the door. "Thank you for

coming in, Ms. Pinner," she said, having seen the name on her card.

"Oh, thank you for all your assistance." She made her way to the door. "And please convey my appreciation to Dr. Lance as well."

Bonnie said she would, and then she helped Carina get out to the car with her purchases and her sleeping kitten. "You'll need a litter box in a few days," Bonnie said. "Once he starts eating the paste and taking more of the bottle." She glanced down the length of the parking lot. "There's a dollar store just down the way. They'll have a box and litter, too."

Carina nodded and sat back in her driver's seat. She thanked Bonnie again, took a deep breath, and started the SUV. She could almost smell the pot of coffee on the counter back at the cabin. Her belly growled in response.

Lifting the edge of the tote to peer inside at the sleeping baby, Carina thought, not exactly the way I envisioned the vacation starting out.

She glanced around, amazed at the pristine, white surroundings, put the car in reverse, and backed slowly away from the clinic. The long, narrow parking lot was nearly vacant, the blanket of white virtually unmarked by cars, except for the tracks of her vehicle and the two others leading from the road to the clinic.

Carina drove the length of the little row of storefronts, watching her tracks unroll behind her in the rearview mirror, checking her new surroundings, wondering if she needed to stop for bread so she could at least have a slice of toast for breakfast.

Dollar Chain. Just like Bonnie said. A good place to pick up the rest of my supplies for when the little guy is bigger. They might have milk and bread, too. But it wasn't open yet. Maybe someone was running late.

She drove slowly on through the parking lot reading the colorful signs. The line of stores would have been nondescript if not for the wooden chalet type architecture and the colorful, hand painted signs and Christmas lights.

Ari's Hair and Nail Salon, Puffy's Pizza, Crossbow Candles, Bronworth's Books-n-More. And on the very end, A-1 Auto Parts.

An auto parts store, Carina thought. Always good to know. One end of the strip was anchored by the small animal clinic, and the other was anchored by A-1 Auto Parts.

Touching the tote bag to make sure the kitty still slept comfortably, Carina turned out of the parking lot and went back through the town. She traveled more slowly this time, taking in the sights and the businesses rather than simply focusing on what the GPS told her.

The village was completely decked out in its Christmas finery. Pine bough wreaths tied up with snow-crusted red ribbons decorated every ornate wrought iron streetlight on every corner. Festive winter displays adorned store windows up and down the sidewalk, and in front of several businesses cheerful snow people smiled and waved. No fear of melting in this clime.

Carina slowed to look at the life-sized nativity scene set up in the town gazebo. A large sign described how the statues would be replaced with live actors and animals at 6 p.m. tonight, and again on Christmas Eve, for the village-wide reading of *The Animals' Christmas Eve* by Dr. Lance and his buddies Dunko the Donkey, Sammy the Sheep, and Blitzen, the reindeer.

Imagining the tall white-haired man sitting on the gazebo with a live donkey and sheep, reading aloud to children gave her a warm feeling. "I will have to make it a point to attend," she told the kitten as she drove slowly past.

Up ahead she spied what she thought she had seen earlier, the good old golden arches of a McDonald's Restaurant with a drive-through so she didn't have to get out of the car. The building's windows were painted with snow scenes and Christmas ornaments and the words Merry Christmas and Happy Holidays!

In front of the fast-food eatery, between the fenced off play area and the sidewalk, stood a massive evergreen tree bedecked with the iconic yellow and red ribbons and tons of McDonald's toys.

Wow, Carina thought. They go all out in Crossbow. I think I like this place.

She pulled into the drive-through and was delighted to find only three cars ahead of her. Although she could smell fresh coffee through the drive-through window, she didn't need coffee; she had a pot of that waiting at the cabin. What she needed was food. Pure and simple. A breakfast burrito with a side of picante. Her mouth watered at the thought.

The line moved quickly, the snow fell softly, and the ginger kitten slept on. Carina tuned the radio and found a station out of Denver playing Christmas music, her favorite. The DJ led with snow and ski reports from all the surrounding resorts and she began to smile.

Carina had been snow skiing exactly one time and that had been as a teen with her best friend, Tonya and her elder sister, Connie. She had never graduated from the bunny slope, but had enjoyed riding the lift and sitting around the massive lodge fireplace drinking hot chocolate and watching the ski instructor —Lars—hold court. Every girl in the place seemed to have eyes for the tall, blond Swede.

Carina put her ancient memories away, paid for her burrito, and headed back through town toward the cabin. It was just after ten o'clock now, but most of the village still seemed to be dozing. She liked that.

CHAPTER 10

THE VILLAGE

CARINA WAS GLAD THE SMALL VILLAGE HAD BEEN LAID OUT geometrically. Main Street ran through the center of town with a north branch and a south branch along with three or four other prominent streets intersecting it along the way.

There's the grocery. She made a mental note of the large store sitting far back on a paved lot just past the Y in the center of town. "Turn south on Redbud," she told herself as a way to fix the location in her mind. "Have to make a grocery run soon. Turkey for Aaron and Max. Hope the grocery has one left."

The Crossbow Inn was the last major business on the west end of South Main Street. It was so beautiful, a true resort-style Inn with snow-draped porches and humpy white landscaping outlining the massive front lawn. She hoped she would have a chance to visit again in spring or summer. Max had said the tourists in summer were mostly families or hikers and backpackers. That would probably be more her style of vacation, but oh weren't these winter wonderland scenes amazing?

She turned beside the Inn and traveled the short distance up Eagle's Nest to the turn off on Paper Lane. Maybe the snow will let up soon. Even with the all-wheel drive on her Subaru

Outback, she was not an expert at actual winter weather driving. Where she lived in Texas, snow was a fleeting thing that came one day—if it came at all—and melted away the next. There were seldom drifts higher than the curb much less higher than the cars.

She smiled to herself, then spoke to the kitten. "Hey, little gingerbread man. I feel like Dorothy. Not in Texas anymore, that's for sure." Then she realized how much she didn't really miss it. Right now, with her husband off in another city doing God-only-knew-what for breakfast, she would have been having a solitary muffin or cup of yogurt beside the radio with the thin daily newspaper spread out before her.

Yep. She was old school. She loved the newspaper not only for the headlines she'd already read on the internet, but because there was a whole page of puzzles, wordy jumbles, and cryptoquips. And true to her nerdy nature, she loved the distinct feel of a ballpoint pen on newsprint as she worked the crossword. There was no smoother writing surface in the world. Not even in her journal.

Sometimes, if she had nothing pressing, breakfast could wind up being a two-hour affair. While that was often pleasant, it could also feel somewhat empty.

"Oh, well, kitty," she murmured, "we're back now. Our temporary home away from home, well, mine anyway. It probably was your first home, which makes no sense—"

When Carina realized she was prattling on and on to a sleeping kitten, she cut off the narrative and pulled into the drive. When it warms up a bit this afternoon, she thought, I'm going out to that garage with the remote and I'm going to park there. Just in case it snows overnight. Wouldn't want to get trapped and end up living on old packets of taco sauce like that poor guy in Oregon who got stuck in his car.

She thought of all the food she would buy at the store later today. Being alone made one think of all the ways things could go wrong. At least it did her. She glanced down at her phone's weather app. Before leaving home, she'd added Crossbow, Colorado as a location and now she could pull up the current forecast anytime she wanted.

No new snow was predicted.

Good, she thought. This is enough for me, enough to make everything shiny and bright and pretty, but not enough to be icy and scary and dangerous.

She gathered her pet purchases and took them up onto the wide porch. A glider sat near the door, so she piled everything there while she fished out the key and unlocked the door.

Moving her things inside, she pulled the door closed and hurried back to the car for the tote bag and kitten. Inside, she took a laundry basket from atop the washer, lined it with a fluffy bath towel, and placed the kitten—still in the tote bag—into its new nest. The kitten was so content it made no sound at all.

"You'll be okay there for a bit," she said. Then she plucked the garage door opener off the counter, went back out to the SUV, slipped into the driver's seat, and moved it the short distance to the detached garage. Along the way, she watched carefully for any sign of tracks in the new snow. There were still none.

The remote opener rolled the overhead up with barely a sound.

Carina drove the SUV inside, delighted to see that the light came on automatically. The garage wasn't exactly warm, but it would keep her vehicle protected from the elements. She locked the Subaru's doors and thought about the Christmas gift in the back seat, a new journal for Max. She would get Aaron's lift tickets soon and she'd sent cash to Annabelle via her Venmo account. She'd mailed all the other gifts to Romy and the grandkids in Dallas, and to Heath and Gia in North Dakota. She hadn't sent anything to Alfred because she didn't have his new mailing address.

When she realized that fact, her stomach dropped as if she'd just come off the tallest hill on The Texas Giant roller coaster at Six Flags. Wow. I don't even know where he lives. The only way I have of reaching him is by phone. A tenuous connection at best. Sort of like the connection I have with Annabelle. She supposed they didn't think of their connection as tenuous because everyone always knew where to find her. At home.

Carina gathered as many bags as she could carry and closed the hatch, determined to put the nagging thoughts out of her head. She and Alfred had been married so long it had probably just slipped his mind not to text her his new address. That's it. That's all. Nothing nefarious, or sneaky. Just forgetfulness.

In one of her gift bags, she had packed some of her favorite ornaments. She had tons at home. Her own tree in the den wouldn't miss these few. This afternoon she would go back into town and do her grocery shopping and look for a small tree for the cabin. But first, she intended to scour the property. In her mind she had a horrible image of a coyote or fox carrying the other kittens away one by one while little Gingerbread, as she had come to think of him, crept away in fear.

She shook her head, strolled out of the garage, and pushed the CLOSE button on the remote before slipping it into her jacket pocket. If there were any more kittens out here, she was determined to find them. Her McDonald's sack sat, forgotten, on the kitchen counter. She'd also forgotten about exploring the guest quarters above the garage.

Ten minutes later, Carina had a good idea of the layout of the entire property from the garage to the hot tub on the deck, to the stone firepit in the center of the backyard and the short walk back around to the front.

There were no more kittens anywhere.

As she once again mounted the four steps to the porch, Carina was reminded of her sweet Moochi, the tabby who had been her companion for close to twenty years. The fierce grief she'd experienced after losing Mooch had taken her completely by surprise. She was a pet, she kept telling herself through the tears. Just a stray she'd taken in off the street.

Not off the street, her subconscious whispered. Right off the doorstep, just like the ginger kitten. Just like that.

She opened the door and stepped into the cozy cabin. The first thing that caught her eye was *not* the McDonald's sack with the breakfast burrito she'd forgotten about. The first thing that caught her eye was the open journal still lying on the floor in front of the couch where she'd fallen asleep last night. The Adventure headline nearly leapt off the page.

Carina picked up the journal and closed it. Adventure, indeed.

She slid the pen back into the elastic holder and placed the book on the coffee table. I'll write about today later on tonight. Write myself a happy Christmas, she thought. That's what I'm doing. Exactly.

She didn't allow herself to look at the prologue to the story she'd started in the journal a few days earlier. The one she'd deemed ridiculous and pathetic. It was intended for Max, and possibly for the group. Not for her son. Not for Aaron.

Her eye fell on her breakfast sack and her belly grumbled like before.

After heating her burrito in the microwave for a few seconds, she devoured it along with two cups of coffee, then finished unpacking her suitcases and hanging up the few outfits she'd brought. Then it was time to feed the baby again.

The little thing still seemed so weak. Bonnie had told her not to let him go more than two or three hours without eating, at least for the first couple of days.

Carina prepared the warm kitten formula and poured it into the tiny bottle. She also took the tube of protein paste and placed it within easy reach of the couch. Once she had everything ready, she wrapped the baby in another warm towel. She also placed her hand in the warmer bed she'd plugged in a few moments earlier, to make certain it was heating. "Come on, little one. Let's get some food in you so I can go downtown and find a Christmas tree."

The baby showed no interest in the formula until Carina put a bit of the paste on her fingertip and touched it to his mouth. That seemed to whet his appetite. Once he got a taste of that protein-rich goodness, his little mouth opened, and Carina was able to drip a bit of formula on his tiny pink tongue. She knew it was important to give him as much liquid as he would drink so he wouldn't get dehydrated.

In seconds, the kitten was licking at the nipple of the bottle just like he'd done in the vet's office. *I wonder if he will ever learn to suckle?* She squeezed the little bottle again and watched the tiny rough tongue lap at the drop. *Maybe he will.*

After she finished feeding and cleaning him, Carina put the kitten back in his tote bag and into the warming bed on low. Then she placed the whole thing into the laundry basket near the hearth. She didn't want the baby to get out and get stuck behind furniture or the fridge, and the nighttime fire had burned to nearly nothing so she knew it wouldn't get too hot.

Okay, she thought as she washed out the bottle and set it to dry. *Now it's time to go downtown.* The fact that it was close to noon, and no one had called to check on her tried to creep into her thoughts, but she wouldn't let it. She thought of the kitten instead. Thought of the way it had appeared out of nowhere just when she'd begun to feel alone. She also thought of how much she loved the cozy feel of the cabin, how much she was looking forward to building up the fire in the fireplace when she returned.

Carina dried her hands, found her coat and purse, stuck her wallet back into her purse, and made certain she had her mobile phone. *I'll build a cheery fire, make a cup of hot chocolate with a peppermint stick in it, and then I'll put on that Christmas movie channel again.*

Maybe they'll be showing A Christmas Carol, the one with

George C. Scott. The idea made her shiver. That last spirit, the one of Christmas Future, really gave her the creeps. Especially when it screeched and pointed that long, bony, finger for Scrooge to follow.

Yes, she thought, I may even substitute a little eggnog or wine in place of that hot chocolate. Then I'll be ready to put up my tree, my very own Charlie Brown tree.

Where'd that come from? She shook her head. Not a Charlie Brown tree, I'm going to get a beautiful little tree. I won't get a big one because I didn't bring that many decorations, nevertheless, it will be fine. It will be perfect. I won't mind putting it up by myself. I was alone last year when I put it up. And the year before that, it had been just Dad and me, the last one before he passed.

The one before that had been hard, too. She'd not only lost her sister, but it was also the year Annabelle, the last kiddo, had gone off to school.

That year, she'd wanted to get them all together to decorate, the way they'd done when they were children. She'd told Alfred her idea of waiting until Christmas Eve to decorate a tree at her dad's house so that the kids and grandkids could help. "I'm afraid it will be the last one we will have with him." But Alfred had pooh-poohed the idea.

"It'll be pure chaos," he'd said. "You know how Romy always arrives at the last possible moment, with the kids all grumpy. And Heath will be impatient, trying to hurry everyone along, and if you aren't careful Annabelle will just sneak in and do it all without asking."

He had glanced up from his phone after telling her his expert opinion, but he hadn't been quite finished. He'd had to add a bit of icing to his negativity cake. "Besides, you know Aaron and your Dad won't care one way or the other as long as there's food." He'd laughed and popped a few peanuts in his mouth. "Truthfully, neither will I."

Carina remembered nodding and turning away so he couldn't see the sudden tears that had stung her eyes. How could she argue? He was probably right. So, she'd gone ahead and put up the tree and decorated it by herself with her dad sitting in his recliner, watching a movie.

Then the night girl she'd hired had come, and she'd gone home and decorated the artificial tree at her own house. Alfred had come home halfway through and gone straight in to change his clothes and make some notes on his phone.

She would've waited on him to help, but as he'd said, he didn't really care as long as there was food. Pompous ass she'd thought, as she'd pulled the foot stool over to place the tiny homemade angel on top of the tree.

CHAPTER 11

CABIN TREE

CARINA PUT HER BOOTS BACK ON AND WENT OUT THE DOOR, locking it behind her. The snow had been falling off and on ever since she first arrived. She wondered if it would do so the whole time she was here. I hope it does, she thought. As long as it doesn't turn into a blizzard. Funny, her phone forecast hadn't shown more snow, but when she pulled it out and looked at it now, it showed up just as if it had been predicted all along.

Walking back to the garage, she half-wished she had simply parked in the circle drive like before. Oh well, she thought. At least it's out of the weather. She was about to open the overhead door remotely when she remembered the guest quarters. Bypassing the entrance door, Carina climbed the white-painted stairs to the small landing. Thank goodness it isn't icy, she murmured as she fit the G2 key into the cold lock. Those steps could be treacherous if they froze.

The door, fitted with a thick, four-paned window, swung open on well-oiled hinges. Carina found the light switch beside the door, and flipped it up, illuminating the room in soft white light.

She was delighted to see a studio-type apartment, one large

room with a rustic, peeled-branch queen bedstead covered with a Native American inspired blanket, a stack of fat pillows, and a sitting area—complete with two comfy-looking armchairs flanking a matching peeled-branch coffee table—snugged up catty-corner to a black pot-bellied stove. A small bundle of firewood filled a metal basket on the stove's brick hearth.

They thought of everything, Carina thought. *Kudos to Max's late wife. Her designer's touch made everything cozy and colorful.* She also noticed a microwave and coffee maker in a tiny kitchenette in the corner. Peeking into the cupboard above it, Carina was not surprised to find a red container of coffee, two heavy white mugs, two thick matching plates, bowls, and a couple of hefty drinking glasses. There were also cans of soup, chili, and an unopened box of Saltine crackers. A playhouse-sized sink completed the tiny kitchen.

She glanced into the small, fully equipped bathroom, and smiled at the thoughtfulness of cellophane wrapped toothbrushes and a fresh tube of unopened Crest beside the sink.

Luxurious towels hung from decorative hooks. It looked like the perfect set up for a couple coming in from a day on the slopes. Since there was no fire in the pot-belly stove, she had to assume the wall panel heater was on a thermostat.

Backing out of the inviting space, Carina closed and locked the door. She made a mental note to ask Max if they should salt the steps—in case Aaron preferred to stay there rather than up in the loft—then she went carefully back down.

She opened the overhead garage door with the remote in her pocket, banged on the hood of the SUV, then climbed into the cold driver's seat before starting the Subaru and backing out to head into town. Her spirits were higher than they'd been in a while, just knowing she had someone—even if it was a tiny kitten—depending on her to get back within a certain time.

Unmoored, she thought. *That's what I've been. Unmoored, unneeded. All afloat. But now I'm needed again. Tied to* something. Could it really be that simple? Her naysayer side spoke up ... *seriously, is anything ever that simple?*

As she reversed down the drive, she kept her eyes peeled for any new tracks in the snow.

Just before the door closed, she noticed a snow shovel and some other implements hanging on the back wall. Good to know those are there. If this snow keeps up, they may be useful.

As she left the driveway and drove down Paper Lane to Eagle's Nest and back to Main, she once again made mental notes of all the businesses she passed. There was the Crossbow Inn first, of course, and then she took the fork in the road and the retail shops began in earnest.

Rental cabins, lodges, and small inns dotted each side of the road. In between were retail shops and restaurants. There were several ski shops for buying and renting equipment, and a large shop bearing a swanky sign proclaiming it to be Ski Crossbow T-Shirts and Gifts.

Finally, near the village green, she spied a small Christmas tree lot. Scott's Christmas Trees. There were only a handful of firs left. The kind growing in buckets so they could be planted in the yard after the holidays. Carina liked that. It meant the trees were still green and fresh, but should she buy something that needed planting? It wasn't her property.

She pulled out her phone and sent Max a message asking permission.

He said it would be fine and he would ask Terry and Cheyenne to plant it in the spring.

"Great!" she wrote. "And only two more days until Christmas."

"I'll see you on Christmas morning," he wrote back. "Give you Christmas Eve with your own family."

"Looking forward to meeting in person," Carina replied, trying to recall if she'd told him it would be only her and Aaron. *Surely, I did ... I think I did ... not that it matters.*

She parked and strolled through the tree lot. "I love this one," she told the young man running the operation. "How much is it?"

He told her the price and then said he'd be happy to load it for her. Carina looked back at her Subaru. She'd originally thought she would just attach a free-standing tree to the luggage rack on top. But this one was upright, in a large container. "Oh, gosh," she muttered. "This isn't going to work at all."

From behind her a deep voice said, "How's that kitten?"

She turned and found Dr. Lance standing off to her right on the sidewalk. "Well, hello," she said. "He seems to be doing great. I left him back at the cabin, sleeping peacefully."

"Good, that's good to hear."

Carina smiled. She wondered what the vet was doing on the village green during business hours. Surely, he was needed at the clinic.

The silver haired veterinarian echoed her smile. "I couldn't help overhearing your plight," he said.

Carina nodded. "Guess I'll look for a small artificial one instead. I think I saw some at the dollar store."

He nodded but his large hand crept to the back of his neck, and he squinted at the horizon. The snow had let up, for the moment. "Or I could carry it to your cabin in Kel's truck." He indicated the vehicle at the curb. "If he doesn't mind." He glanced at the young man who ran the lot.

"Of course," the kid said, handing over his keys as if they did this all the time.

"That's very kind of you, but I'm surprised to see you here," Carina said. She didn't mean to sound ungrateful, but she truly was surprised.

"I had a patient who couldn't make it to the clinic, but I've got nothing urgent at the moment."

"You mean you make house calls?"

Dr. Lance let his gaze wander to her face. "Only for emergencies."

"That's very kind of you—" she repeated, feeling foolish.

He toyed with the needles of the little tree she'd been admiring. "Is this the one?"

Carina nodded. "But the cabin is on the other side of town. Are you certain you have time?"

Dr. Lance grinned. "Of course. What's a home away from home without a Christmas tree?"

Carina thanked him, dug out her wallet, and paid the young man for the tree. He scooped it onto a small mover's dolly and rolled it to his truck. The doc helped him lift it into the bed.

He told the young man, Kel, he would be back soon, and then pointed toward Main. "You lead and I'll follow," he said to Carina.

She got behind the wheel of her Subaru and pulled away from the curb, driving slowly so the vet could keep up. All the way back to the cabin she kept marveling at how nice it was of him to go out of his way like this. If she wasn't an old married woman, she might worry he had an ulterior motive.

She didn't notice a thing driving back through town, concentrating solely on her route and watching the top of the Christmas tree barely visible over the cab of the truck behind her.

In moments she turned beside the Inn, drove up Eagle's Nest and turned onto Paper Lane. Soon they were pulling into the circle drive. Carina stepped out and hurried to unlock the cabin's door.

Dr. Lance got out, stood with his hands in his pants pockets for a moment, looking around, seemingly lost in thought, and then he began trying to unload the sweet little tree.

Carina ran to help him get it down from the bed of the pickup to the ground. "We need a dolly, don't we?"

He nodded. "We should have borrowed one from Kel." He glanced toward the garage. "I wonder if there might be one in there."

Carina recalled the implements on the back wall. "Maybe. I

saw some things hanging on the back wall." She opened the door with the remote, and he headed that way with her beside him.

They entered together. He took a quick glance around and walked straight across to the opposite wall where a red hand truck hung on a peg. "There it is," he said, taking it down.

Carina said, "Well, how about that?"

He smiled. "I have mine hanging in the exact same spot in my garage at home." He pushed it out the door and waited for her. "You've got a regular trail from the house to the garage now. I can see where you've been coming and going, looking for the rest of the kitties, right?"

She ducked her head, embarrassed a little. "You nailed it." She laughed at her myriad footprints in the snow. "I searched and searched. Never found a trace."

The doc shook his head. "That does seem odd. I wonder if Mama Cat was in the process of moving them and lost that little one. I've heard of that happening."

"Sounds logical to me. I've also wondered if there's an opening under the cabin that I just haven't found yet. It wouldn't have to be very large for that little guy to fit through."

"That's a possibility, too," he said as they reached the truck. He positioned the tree's container on the blade of the hand truck. "Here we go." He grasped the handles and tilted the whole thing backward on its two wheels. "Now if it doesn't roll off the side, we'll be in good shape."

"I'm glad the caretakers salted the walkway, aren't you?"

He nodded. "Better safe than sorry."

Together, they got the tree up the steps and onto the porch. Carina opened the door and the doc turned around backward, tilted the hand truck back a little more, and gently pulled it over the threshold and into the living room.

"I'd better grab something to set that on," she said. "I wouldn't want it to damage the hardwood."

"How about the door mat?" Doc said. "It's flat but dense. Should be good protection."

Carina grabbed the wide mat and placed it under the front window so the tree would be visible from outside. "Right here," she said. "Once I get the lights on, it will look pretty when you drive up."

The vet positioned the tree just right, then stood and made a show of wiping his brow.

Laughing, Carina started toward the kitchen. "How about a glass of water or—"

Her sentence was interrupted by the chime of his phone.

He put it to his ear. "H'lo?"

From across the room Carina could hear Bonnie's voice raised in urgency.

"I'll be right there." His voice wasn't hurried, or raised, it was simply matter of fact.

Carina admired that.

"Gotta go," he said. "Emergency at the clinic. Dog vs car." He glanced around the cabin. "Looks great in here. Is the tree in the right place?"

"It's perfect, thank you so much."

He was moving toward the door, still pushing the hand truck. "I'll just put this back—"

"Oh, no," Carina reached out and stopped his forward motion. "Please. Go see about your patient. I'll take care of this, no problem."

"Okay. But if I can be of any more assistance, please don't hesitate to call."

"Thank you, thank you very much." *Oh, brother. I sound like Elvis getting ready to leave the building.* She smiled to cover her embarrassment.

He was almost down the steps when he said, "I really wanted to see the kitten. But you can let me know if he isn't doing well."

He stepped off the last step and gave a tiny goodbye wave as if his mind was already miles ahead at the clinic.

Standing on the porch, still wearing her jacket, Carina watched the tall man climb into his borrowed truck. She said a small prayer for the injured dog. That would be the worst part of a career as a veterinarian, seeing animals in pain.

CHAPTER 12

DECORATIONS

Back inside, one hand on her chest in response to her inexplicably pit-pattering heart, Carina unpacked the Christmas lights, bulbs, and other decorations she'd brought from home.

Most of the ornaments were those that had been made by the kids and grandkids over the years. There were cookie-dough wreaths, popsicle-stick reindeer, and pipe-cleaner candy canes. She'd also brought hers and Aaron's stockings to hang from the mantle, and the kindergarten-made paper-angel topper. A long rope of red and silver tinsel and a double length of old-fashioned lights completed the decorations.

She would need to feed the kitten soon, but maybe she could at least get the lights on. First though, she wanted a fire in the fireplace and a glass of wine. Then it occurred to her she'd never made it to the grocery store. She laughed at herself. *No wine for me.*

Should I go all the way back to town now, or wait until tomorrow? Have to go now, she thought. Unless I want to go to McDonald's for breakfast again. The thought made her smile. What would Alfred think if he knew how things were going? How *unplanned* everything had become.

That thought made her a little sad and a little angry at the same time. Where was he eating his meals? Was he sharing them with someone else? After all these years, was her Alfred finding it easier to be with someone younger, prettier, less needy?

He'd never been so out of touch before. Of course, he'd never been promised a deal like this before either.

Should I call him, see what's going on? We've been married nearly thirty-four years. Shouldn't I be able to call him and see what's going on?

Carina shoved those thoughts away as she carefully stacked logs in the fireplace. She stacked them in a triangle fashion just as Alfred had taught her on the second day of their honeymoon in Italy.

They hadn't had that much money so they weren't in Rome or Venice, but in a cozy private rental in Vicenza, a small city known for its gold jewelry, fantastic Palladian architecture, and ancestral home of the *original* author of *Romeo & Juliet*.

What a wonderful honeymoon we had. Vicenza had turned out to be the perfect start to their new life together. The view from their second story had been spectacular. Early spring, still cold, and the whole valley outside the window had been green and sparkling with dew. She'd snapped picture after picture just looking down from that second-story window.

"Stop," Alfred had laughed, "or we'll find ourselves standing outside the Coliseum in Rome without any film in that camera." *So long ago, before iPhones or digital cameras.*

She remembered taking his handsome face between her palms and directing his gaze toward the view. "Look how the dew sparkles like a handful of diamonds flung out across the valley. That beautiful green grass could be the satin lining in a fancy lady's jewel box—"

"Ahh," he'd said, "A jewel box full of diamond dew."

She'd been pleased that he saw what she was seeing. "Exactly," she said. But when she glanced his way, he was staring not at the valley, but at her.

His voice was tender when he said, "You'll be that fancy lady someday."

Carina remembered smiling at his teasing. Surely, he knew she didn't care about diamonds. She'd just wanted to capture the beauty outside that window with her camera. Take it home and put it in a honeymoon photo album so she could look at it and remember.

No wonder the kids call me sentimental, she thought. I guess I always have been. Silly and sentimental. Now, she found it funny to think how she'd carried that small camera all over Italy, guarding it jealously along with the tiny rolls of film it required. Every now and then, even as she enjoyed it, she'd caught Alfred looking at her indulgently, as if the photography, what he referred to as her picture-taking, was just another one of her quirks.

In all these years she'd never confided to him how she'd hoped to one day be able to take professional photos. She'd daydreamed of having her landscapes made into calendars to hang on office walls. It was so easy to imagine walking into the bank or medical clinic and seeing one of her photos hanging behind the receptionist's desk.

Instead, she'd finished her teaching degree and secured a position as a fifth-grade teacher at the children's elementary school. When you come up hardscrabble, the way she and Alfred had done, daydreams didn't pay bills. Paychecks paid bills. Regular paychecks with attached perks like sick days and health insurance.

So, Carina had put aside her photography dreams and concentrated on creating a career in the classroom. And she wrote in her journal in the evenings or early morning drinking-coffee hour. It seemed that creative spark needed an outlet of some sort, and a journal was much easier than trying to catch the perfect shot with a camera. For one thing, it was often dark by the time she had a moment to herself, either bedtime, or before the sun rose.

Those two intervals became her times. Before the sunrise, and after the sunset and the kids were in bed. They became precious times. Between teaching and trying to keep up with the children, Carina came to cherish those quiet times. She called them her prayer times because she often did write little prayers giving thanks or asking for help with day-to-day problems.

That's how she got through the working years. When her four children moved through elementary and on into middle and high school and beyond, each one had felt like a little heartbreak, like losing them, one by one.

Even then she'd known it was a stupid way to feel so she'd never told Alfred that, either. She'd just gone to work every day until she was in her late forties and she'd been forced to transfer her teaching and caregiving skills from her students and children to her parents.

It wasn't the way she'd thought things would turn out.

But as she had always done, Carina picked herself up and tried to do the right thing. After her mom passed, and her father had suffered his second stroke, she had moved in with him, thinking it would be only a short time. Then her sister had been killed. They were all stunned, but her father seemed to accept it, seemed to be attempting to battle back to where he'd been before. The fact that he never complained made Carina think there was hope, that she was doing a good job.

But then Covid hit.

Within days of burying her dad, Carina had found the suicide note he'd scrawled after his second stroke and the death of her sister, Jodie. It had almost finished her right there on the spot.

She would always think it was the combination of those stressors that had lowered her resistance—damaged her immune system—and allowed Covid to take over her body and land her in the hospital for so long.

Carina shook her head to dispel the memories. Even after she had begun to walk again, she'd haunted her own home like an empty husk, missing her dad's home, missing him and the others. Finally admitting to herself that even at the age of fifty, she now felt like an orphan, or a stray.

SHE WATCHED THE FIRE A MOMENT—TO MAKE CERTAIN IT WOULD draw after she'd opened the flue—and then peeked into the basket to check on the kitten. It was still tucked into the tote bag, sound asleep. "You've had a hard day, haven't you, little one?" She decided to let the baby sleep a bit longer, recalling how she used to snap photo after photo of Moochi stalking a mockingbird or red-winged blackbird, hidden among the wildflowers she'd planted along the back fence, or peering down from a branch of the desert willow whose pastel blossoms smelled like fine French soap.

"My God," she murmured, prayer-like, "save me from my maudlin self." Then she laughed. "And deliver me from these blasted, tangled lights. I know I didn't put them away like this. Must be that mischievous elf I'm always hearing about."

She finally got the string of tiny, multi-colored lights untangled and looped around the tree. "I'm nothing but an old fool, talking to myself all the time. No wonder the kids would rather spend Christmas anywhere else. No wonder Alfred is happier working than being with me."

She couldn't believe she'd said it out loud, but there it was.

There it was.

Thoroughly self-chastised, Carina hurriedly finished decorating by looping the shiny red and silver tinsel around the tree and placing each precious ornament just so. "All we need now are a few presents to go under it."

Picking up her iPhone, she snapped several pictures of the twinkly tree with the rustic stone fireplace in the foreground and the large window framing the snowy yard beyond.

She sent the best shot to Max Paper. "Thank you," she captioned it. "This place is absolutely amazing." She thought about sending one to each of the kids and Alfred, but in her heart, she was afraid they would think she was trying to guilt them into coming. Not Aaron, he'd already said he would be here. But should she send a pic to the others?

A text came in from Max. "Can't wait to see the real thing," he wrote. Then he'd followed it up with a row of Christmas tree emojis. "I can almost smell the wood smoke from that old fireplace."

Carina smiled and sent back a thumbs-up icon. She didn't want to engage him in a lengthy conversation while he was at work, but his enthusiasm gave her the courage to throw caution to the wind and send a picture to Alfred and each of the kids, even Aaron.

She thought about putting it all on one group message, but she detested those things so she sent each one separately with the same message. "I just got the tree up. The Colorado cabin is beautiful, and it looks like it will be a white Christmas."

Since they were all in her favorites list, it took only a matter of minutes to send each one the same photo and message. Technology, she thought. Gotta love it. Her iPhone took amazing photos and she could crop and edit and do all sorts of things with them. She'd even printed some of the ones she'd taken out on the walking trail back in the day. *Photography has certainly come a long way since I lugged that 35 mm camera all over Italy.*

Of course, she wasn't kidding herself. A smart phone was not a real photographer's tool. Sometimes, she thought of going back to college and taking a few photography classes just for fun, to learn about all the new tools. But she'd never done it. She would have felt ridiculous being the oldest student in the class.

I'm a teacher, she would tell herself, not a student and certainly not a photographer. And then she would think of going back to work in the classroom with all those precious little kiddos she loved so much. She tried to imagine how it would be after so many years away.

Maybe I'll do that when the holidays are over.

She went about cleaning up the boxes that had held the decorations. Maybe that's what I need to do. Just go back to work and get out of my own head. After all, Alfred had never chased his dreams, if he had any, so why should I be allowed that luxury? Nope. Not the time to chase reluctant dreams.

Retirement would be along in another decade—they should both work—and save, until then. That would be the sensible thing. And she could start by subbing—substitute teaching—a couple days a week. It was something to think about.

CHAPTER 13

SECOND GUESSING

After clearing away the empty boxes, Carina went to the kitchen to warm the kitten's formula. She turned on the small radio that sat on the windowsill. It was an old-fashioned Bakelite with the large tuning dial on the front. Must be a replica, she thought. No way it would be original and still work. Especially in these mountains.

To her delight it came on right away, already tuned to a classic country and western station. An old George Jones song came on and transported Carina back to her childhood. Her parents had loved George Jones.

She sang along with "The Grand Tour," and it made her feel sad for all the years that had passed and all the people she had lost. Without another thought, she reached over and clicked it off.

I want to pull myself out of the dumps, not lie down and wallow in them. The kitten had brought her out of herself a little bit, she sure didn't want to fall back into the nobody-loves-me blues.

Max, the near stranger, had immediately replied to the picture she'd sent. None of her family members had said a word.

Oh, well, she thought. Nothing more to be done. The ball is in their court. She immediately wished she hadn't sent the darn pics at all. Now if they come, I will think it's because of guilt. *Yeah, but you knew that was a possibility. If you weren't prepared for that, then why did you send them? Silly woman.*

Carina turned off her inner conscience-voice. "I always do that," she told the kitty as she gently woke it. "I always second guess everything, even myself. Especially myself. Ugh. You'd think I would learn. Especially since I'd already said I *wasn't* going to send the pics." *Idiot!*

Oops, there was that voice again.

"C'mon, baby," she cooed as the kitten yawned and stretched. When he started to root around as if looking for a meal, she cuddled it close and sat on the couch. "Sweet little thing. Let's get you fed."

The baby began to lick the tip of the bottle as soon as Carina squeezed out the first drop. She felt like a proud mom. "Well, aren't you a fast learner?"

Carina leaned back into the cushions and sighed. We've both been orphaned, she thought. But then she realized what a ridiculous thing that was, to feel she'd been orphaned when she had a husband, four children, and four grandchildren—soon to have a fifth.

Maybe I do need professional help, she thought. Just like Dr. Patel said.

She looked down at the tiny orange kitten attacking the bottle, fighting to live despite such a cold and terrifying night outside, alone, and she said, "I think it's going to be all right. I think you are going to make it. In fact, I think we both are."

She thought of the long drive home after the holidays with the kitty in its tote bag. *I'll have to stop every few hours for feeding. But that's okay. At my age the rule is not to sit for long stretches anyway.*

All at once, a horrible thought occurred to her. *I still haven't bought a Christmas turkey or ham or anything.* Her heart began to pound and the kitten opened its eyes as if in response.

"It's okay." She stroked the tiny head. "I'll go this afternoon." She chuckled and rubbed its head again.

That's when her phone began to blow up with messages.

She almost dropped the kitten trying to read them all.

"MOM!" Romy shouted in all caps. "YOU'RE AT THE CABIN? I can't believe you went alone. I thought we decided NEXT YEAR?"

"Oh," Carina replied. "Maybe we can do it again next year. This year it will be Max, Aaron, and me. Hug the kiddos for me!"

Romy sent back a heart emoji and Carina clicked on the next message. It was from Aaron. "Great tree, Mom. Love the fireplace, too. I'll be there Christmas Eve with bells on!"

"Sweet boy," she replied. "I can't wait to see you."

"See ya soon, Mom. I hope Santa knows how to buy lift tickets." He sent a wide-eyed-open-mouthed emoji with that one. It reminded Carina of the kid in *Home Alone*, one of the Christmas movies they would always watch together when they were small.

"I'll bet Santa does know about lift tickets," she replied. "You just be careful getting here, okay?"

"I will," he wrote. "Can't wait to see you."

Sweet Aaron. He'd always been mama's little man. It tickled Carina the way he always looked for joy in everything he did. The kid should be a public speaker. Or a life coach. It made her heart soar.

"Okay, my little tow-headed boy, I can't wait to see you."

He sent back the blowing-a-kiss smiley and Carina felt lighter than she had in days. *I know I'm not supposed to let others control my emotions but how does one go about doing that? Or not doing that as the case may be?*

On the heels of that she thought, *why didn't I just call Aaron to begin with? He always makes things better.* Then she chuckled.

"Ginger-kitty," she said, "as soon as you're finished, I'd better go to town and see about buying that turkey and some lift tickets." She thought about trying to purchase them on her phone but since she'd never bought any before, she was afraid she would make a mistake.

The third text message she received was from Heath. "I'm so sorry we can't make it, Mom. The tree is beautiful. You and Aaron will have a wonderful Christmas."

"Take care of Gia and that little sprout," she wrote. "Next Christmas I'll be buying baby toys again."

Carina was let down, but it wasn't unexpected. Romy and Heath had already said they couldn't make it. But there was still no word from Annabelle. In the back of her mind a little worry began to grow. It's getting awfully close now. Shouldn't she be calling or texting soon?

The message alert chirped again, and she thought it would be Annabelle, conjured by her own worry, perhaps, but it was Alfred instead.

Carina's heart began to race. It felt as if she were on the brink of something, as if just hearing from her husband was a big deal. As if he'd been off in war. But then she realized it was only a text, she wouldn't be hearing that deep, sometimes-impatient voice at all.

She clicked the message. "Hi sweetheart," it read. "Sorry so out of touch. Extremely busy. Look for me tomorrow evening. I'll rent a car at the airport. I'm extremely impressed you went alone. Way to go, Mama! Enjoy your time away. You deserve it. I'll TTYS." He ended the message with a heart.

Carina clutched the kitty closer. He was coming. He was coming after all, and the fact that he was impressed she'd traveled without him eased her mind and made her mad at the same time. He wasn't even worried about her. Did he always have more faith in her than she had in herself? Up until that moment, she had been certain he would be shocked. *Is that why I did it?*

She dismissed that idea, sent back an I Heart You message, and told him not to work too hard. Then she began to make a grocery list in her head.

The kitten had fallen asleep as soon as it finished eating. Carina did all the things Bonnie had instructed her to do to make sure the baby was comfortable, then she tucked it back into the tote bag, cleaned up the feeding things, and pressed the horn button on her Subaru key fob, waited a moment, then pressed the remote start.

She saw her journal on the coffee table and recalled the words of loneliness she had written there. Now that she had heard from Alfred, and learned that Aaron was practically on his way, everything seemed better. Lighter. Brighter.

What a difference a few messages can make, she thought. Then she grabbed the Bic pen and wrote LIFT TIX on top of her left hand. Alfred always laughed at her for making reminders that way, but it was much quicker than typing something into her phone. She was much more likely to see it there, too.

Gathering her phone, wallet, and the keys, Carina slipped on her jacket and boots, made certain the fire screen was in place and the back door was locked, then she made her way out to the already warming vehicle.

She'd decided to leave the lamp on since darkness came early to the mountains. Besides, the baby might wake up while she was gone.

THE DRIVE TO TOWN WAS UNEVENTFUL, ALREADY BECOMING second nature. When she passed the village square with its quaint gazebo and nativity scene, she recalled the sign saying Dr. Lance would be reading Christmas stories to children from six to seven p.m. each evening right through Christmas Eve.

Just thinking of the kind, white haired veterinarian gave

Carina a warm feeling. As if she had an actual friend in a town where she knew basically no one.

She pulled into the grocery store parking lot and found a spot near the edge. The store was busy.

Taking a deep breath, Carina made her way across the lot to the entrance. She was always a bit apprehensive when she didn't know her way around a place. This may take a while, she thought, feeling her jacket pocket to make certain she had her wallet. Inside the store, she grabbed a shopping cart and pulled out her hastily scribbled list.

She started with the bakery section and then made her way up and down every aisle finally winding up in the frozen food area where she chose a small turkey. There were very few left. At the last second, she grabbed a package of thick ham slices, too. Aaron loved both.

Standing in the checkout line, she surveyed her cart. It wasn't overflowing but it was full. In addition to her fresh veggies, she had all the makings for her mom's cornbread dressing, her late sister's green beans amandine, her own candied yam recipe, mashed potatoes, broccoli-rice casserole, ingredients for turkey gravy and two packages of brown-n-serve rolls. She'd always read there was some trick to making bread rise at high altitudes, so she wasn't even going to attempt it this time. Just play it safe. She also had the ingredients for a pecan pie and a chocolate pie.

She laughed and mentally slapped her forehead.

"Something funny?" The voice came from beside her.

CHAPTER 14

DINNER?

CARINA GLANCED UP INTO THE EYES OF DR. LANCE. "WELL, hello," she said. "This is a nice surprise."

He smiled. "You were laughing at your groceries," he teased.

She felt heat rise to her cheeks. "Was I?" She glanced back into her basket. "I was just wondering why I bought so much—I mean I have four kids and four grandkids, but only one of the children has said he will be able to make it to the cabin." She hurried on. "Of course, I haven't heard from Annabelle, my youngest. I'm getting a bit worried about her, though I'm sure she's fine. Just off rock-climbing."

"Don't ever get in a serious poker game," the doc said.

Carina cocked her head.

"You ramble and everything you say comes across your face as an emotion." He grinned. "An emoticon come to life."

Feeling foolish, Carina looked down into her basket again. Just when she thought she'd found a friend, he says something that makes her feel foolish. Just like Alfred always did.

"I'm sorry," Dr. Lance touched her shoulder. "That was rude of me, wasn't it?" He shook his leonine head. "I'm too used to dealing with critters who don't talk back. To them I can say anything. With pretty young women, I'm not quite so smooth."

Carina laughed in spite of herself. "It's okay." She looked at all the food again. "I was scolding myself for buying so much, but I do love to cook. And seeing people eat always makes me happy."

He smiled. "My wife loved to cook, too." This time his face was the one that revealed his emotions.

Carina heard the past tense. "I'm sorry, is she ... did she ..."

The doc rescued her stumbling inquiry. "Yes. We were divorced before she passed, but I still miss the woman I married. Sometimes. Like on holidays." His line began to move ahead.

"Grief seems always just around the corner," Carina murmured.

Dr. Lance nodded. "Doesn't it, though?" His line stopped and hers moved up.

Carina suddenly remembered why the doc had left her cabin so quickly. "By the way," she said. "How was your emergency patient?"

He gave her a thumbs up. "Looked much worse than it actually was. A cast, a few stitches, and he was good to go. His owner brought him in. She saw the whole thing. Just an accident, car going too fast, dog slipped out the gate. You can imagine the rest."

Carina nodded and glanced at the vet's basket. All he had were several cartons of instant hot chocolate mix with marshmallows.

He saw where she was looking. "It's extra for the reading tonight. At the gazebo."

She smiled. "I saw the sign. Very impressive."

"I don't have the luxury of grandkids," he said. "So I improvise."

To her surprise, his voice sounded serious.

"I'm sorry. Maybe you will have grands one day. You're right, they are very special." *Now if only I could be with them for the holidays.* That thought ran through her mind, unbidden. She wondered if it showed on her face the way he'd said.

"What on earth is going through your head?" Dr. Lance asked. "It appears to be something very solemn."

He's right, Carina thought. He doesn't make small talk very well. It was actually a rather endearing trait. If her emotions showed on her face—which they obviously must—then his popped right out of his mouth. She laughed. "That obvious?"

He nodded as his line moved forward a half-step.

"I was thinking how much I will miss my own grandchildren this holiday," she said. "They belong to my eldest daughter, but due to circumstances, they wouldn't be coming for Christmas even if I were back at home." She sighed a little. "Nor will my eldest son. His wife is pregnant and having terrible morning sickness."

"That is too bad," he said. "Holidays can be a lonely time."

Carina detected an ache in his voice. Without letting herself think it over, she said, "Why don't you join us for Christmas dinner? It will only be my husband, my youngest son and possibly our youngest daughter—if she ever checks in. Oh, and the wonderful young man who owns that lovely cabin. Can you believe he gifted it to me for the holiday?"

Dr. Lance's head popped up. His hand stopped placing the boxes of instant hot chocolate mix on the conveyor. "What did you say?"

Carina laughed. "That will only mean five of us at the most. Six if you come." She dipped her chin toward her basket. "As you can see, I've got plenty. Besides, I'm used to feeding a small army at Christmas."

He nodded. "Yes, yes. I see what you mean. That's very generous of you." He set the last carton of hot chocolate mix on the conveyor belt and the cashier scanned them quickly. The doc seemed preoccupied now.

"I see you're getting ready for tonight," the young woman said.

Dr. Lance smiled. "Perfect weather, isn't it?"

The girl with the bright turquoise hair smiled back and handed him his receipt. "Josh and I will be right there in the front row." She looked at the vet kindly. "He has talked about it all day."

"I look forward to seeing you." He reached across and patted her arm. "And your little man, too."

Carina watched as he took his bags and headed toward the door. He suddenly seemed a lot older than he had only minutes earlier. At least until he turned and gave her a brief smile and a wave. She found herself waving back like an old friend.

"He's been reading to kids since I was little," the cashier told the next customer. "Even if you don't have children, you should come out tonight and hear him read. It's just …" Her eyes looked off toward the plate glass window where the doc could be seen walking across the parking lot. "It's just magical."

Wow, Carina thought as her own cashier scanned her purchases and sacked them up, I will definitely be there tonight.

When she got outside, she could see Dr. Lance leaning against her Subaru. "Hey there," she called. "Everything all right?"

He nodded and continued eating a handful of peanuts. As she approached, he finished the nuts and dusted the salt off his palms.

Carina clicked the unlock button.

"Want to put them in the back?" he asked.

She shook her head and parked her basket parallel to the vehicle. "I've got the cargo area loaded with empty boxes. These will have to go in the back seat."

He opened the SUV's back door and began to stow her bags inside.

"This is awfully nice," she said. "To what do I owe the honor?" Carina knew she was being extremely formal, but she wasn't used to near-strangers helping her with every little thing.

"Oh, I just wanted to say thanks for inviting me to Christmas." He jerked his thumb over his shoulder toward the grocery store. "We sort of got interrupted before I could accept."

"Well, that's wonderful. I'll look forward to having you meet everyone."

He must've sensed something in her tone, or more likely, in her expression. "Holiday not going the way you hoped?"

"Well," Carina said, "I thought it would be different, you know a good old fashioned white Christmas with the kids and grandkids, sledding down the hill by the cabin, building snowmen, drinking hot chocolate in front of the fireplace."

Dr. Lance chuckled. "The best laid plans."

"Yes," she said. "That's *exactly* what I keep telling myself." She closed the back door and he opened the driver's side for her. Before she slid into the seat, she turned to him. "Speaking of winter fun, could you tell me the best place to buy lift tickets for my son?"

"The only one who *can* make it?"

She laughed. "Yes, that one." She was getting used to Dr. Lance saying whatever came into his head. "The light of my life."

"You can pick up the tickets at Crossbow Skis and Things. It's right there on Main just past The Brewery."

"Brewery?"

"Right. Live music, craft beer, and great food. The best of everything."

"You sound like a commercial."

"That was the commercial, or at least the motto. I believe it's printed on the menu."

"Sounds great, thank you. I'll stop and get the tickets right now, on my way back to the cabin." She thought that would let him know it was time to close the door so she could go, but Dr. Lance didn't take her subtle hint.

"You know, The Brewery cooks a mighty fine steak."

"Is that right?"

He nodded. "I eat there quite often."

"Good to know."

"Perhaps you could join me tonight, after I read to the kids on the village green."

"That sounds inviting," she said. "I was planning on coming in for the reading anyway."

Dr. Lance stood up straighter. "You were?"

"After hearing the cashier talk about how magical it is—"

"Oh," he wrapped his big hand around the back of his neck. "I wish you hadn't heard that. I'll flub up for sure now."

Carina shook her head and reached for the door. He got the message and closed it gently. She rolled down the window and said, "I'll see you tonight, then."

He nodded and wandered back toward his own vehicle a few slots away.

I hope he makes it back to the office, she thought. His mind certainly seems to be elsewhere. She put the Subaru in gear and checked her backup camera, but she didn't take her foot off the brake. She was too busy watching the lanky vet climb into his Jeep. There was something boyish about him, something endearing and boyish and somehow, oddly enough, familiar.

After backing out, she drove slowly across the lot with a wave in his direction. I just accepted a dinner invitation. Did I make a date? Nah. Dinner with a new friend is not a date. What a silly thought.

Her *Linus and Lucy* ringtone began to play, and she looked down to see Alfred's name staring back at her. Perfect timing.

She pushed the button on the steering wheel to answer. "Hey, honey, how's it going?"

"Have you seen the news?"

"News? Well, no. I've been in town grocery shopping. What is it?"

"The company just got hit with another multimillion-dollar lawsuit by a group of veterinarians who had been prescribing their dogfood for their sensitive patients. It killed them, Cari.

Killed the already sick dogs and now I have to try and do even more damage control." He sighed and she could imagine him throwing back a stiff drink the way he often did at home when he encountered a problem.

"Oh, Alfred, I don't know what to say except, how can you do any damage control? I mean, you're the financial auditor, not the public relations guy." Sheesh. Carina really didn't understand.

"Well, they've got PR people, too. In spades. That's who I'm working with. They're counting on me to find the revenue to pay them all. To save them, as it were."

As it were, huh? "So, what does that mean for our holiday?" She hated the plaintiveness in her voice, and she hated even having to question him, but she couldn't help it. He sounded so distant. As if he were talking to her but his mind was a million miles away. Overseas, maybe, where the killer dog food was made. Dr. Lance's kind face popped into her head. *Killer dog food. What would he think? Had he prescribed it?*

Anger clouded her thoughts. "The company tried to cut corners by buying those cheap products and now it's blown up in their faces, yet they expect you to pull off a miracle and get them back on track?"

"That's exactly right. Now they regret their actions."

"Can't you celebrate Christmas and *then* go back to your grindstone?"

His silence told her the answer.

"But why?" she asked. "What can possibly be done on Christmas day? I mean, seriously?"

"Chinese reps are on their way. They don't really celebrate our Christmas. To this particular bunch, it's just a commercial holiday. We'll be working things out with their attorneys." He laughed sharply, more like a bark. "I'm lucky I don't have to go to China, truth be told."

Carina's finger hovered over the END icon.

"Hon?" Now Alfred's voice sounded uncertain.

"I'm kind of in shock, Alfred. It's Christmas. I'm in this beautiful cabin, alone, trying to make a memorable holiday for all of us and you don't even seem to think it's important."

"I know it's important, hon, but this is my career. It's a huge deal. If I pull this off, we'll be set for the rest of our lives." He made a noise in his throat. "But I told you all of that before. Surely you understand, it's only one holiday out of many—"

"Out of all the many we have already shared because we've been married for a hundred years. Yeah. Got it. I understand. Good luck, *hon*. Oh, and Merry Christmas." She hit the end button and immediately felt like a heel. Was she asking too much? He *was* nearing retirement, after all. That had to be why he was pushing so hard. Damn. She pushed RECALL and waited for him to come on. Instead, she got voicemail instructing her to leave a message.

"Of all the *nerve*." She hit the Sirius radio symbol on the dash and blasted 60s rock into the car at full volume. "I see where I fit into his important schedule." Tears of anger, frustration, and hurt flooded her eyes and she swiped them away with a wadded tissue from the cup holder. *Seems like enough concessions have been made for that shoddy company who makes the pet-killing products. Now they have to take over Christmas, too?*

From the passenger window she caught an image of a giant, old-fashioned beer barrel. The Brewery. She glanced around for the ski shop and there it was, Crossbow Skis and Things.

She glanced in her rearview, saw no one, and guided her car into a slanted parking slot. She checked her face in the mirror, got out and went into the shop. Ten minutes later she had red lift tickets for two days in a festive envelope. She'd also discovered a rack of hand thrown coffee mugs that were rather intriguing.

Hurrying home to the cabin, Carina carried in the groceries, put them away, checked on the kitten, then—still feeling out of sorts—took a long walk around the property to calm her nerves. Along the way she checked out several small animal footprints to see if they belonged to a cat or kitten, but according to google they were more likely skunks, raccoons, or even field mice.

In one spot, there were two sets of tracks that alarmed her. Taking another pic and searching google, she determined them to be the tracks of a fox. Google also said foxes would be more than happy to dine on any small mammals like mice, voles, or *kittens*. Her belly clenched. That could explain what happened to the rest of the litter, and why the mama cat would want to move them.

Carina could easily imagine the panic and terror of such a horrible scene. A feral cat trying to save her babies, maybe succeeding, maybe only able to save one or two, maybe losing her own life in the process.

The tears that had surprised her after her conversation with Alfred came flooding back as she poked through the underbrush blindly searching for little frozen bodies or, in the best of worlds, another live one or two.

"This is stupid," she muttered. "The others are long gone. Wilderness. Nature. Life. Death. Just deal with it." She retraced her steps back to the cabin, amazed at how far down the hill she had wandered.

As she worked her way back up, she thought again what an awesome sledding hill this would be if any of the grands had been able to come. *Oh, well, maybe next year.*

She went in, made a small pot of coffee to warm herself, fed and snuggled the baby, ate a banana, and then sat down with her journal. Write it out, she thought. Get rid of all that negativity. She touched pen to paper and didn't look up again until she'd filled two pages, front and back.

CHAPTER 15

THE READING

CARINA EXHALED AND LEANED BACK, RUBBING HER ACHING NECK with one hand. It made her think of Dr. Lance. He always rubbed his neck that way.

She went to the bathroom, took a quick, soothing bath, and touched up her hair and makeup. The idea of a fun evening had fallen by the wayside after her conversation with her husband. Now she was moving on autopilot. She wondered if she should just cancel the whole evening thing and stick around the cabin. *And do what, watch TV? Read? Roast marshmallows and make s'mores alone?* She remembered dreaming about cozying up with Alfred in front of the roaring fireplace, snow falling softly outside the picture window.

I refuse to sit here feeling sorry for myself.

She thought of the tiny kitten that had appeared like magic that first morning. Like magic, exactly. *And maybe Dr. Lance is another magical apparition, another sign that I'm supposed to have a life, too. Not sit around waiting on my family to bring me joy—to find space for me in their important schedules—I've got all day tomorrow to prep the food, bake the pies, make the sides. Then, on Christmas day, I'll get up early and put the turkey in the oven like I've always done. For a hundred years.*

This year, I'll do it for me, for myself. And for Aaron and Max and even Dr. Lance, if he actually comes. It's time to stop basing my happiness and well-being on the whims and schedules of others.

Tears threatened to fall again so she cut off that train of thought and picked up her jacket. She'd placed her boots on the mat in front of the hearth and now she took them to the sofa and pulled them back on. Thank goodness I had these, she thought. They've already seen more snow here than in all the years I've owned them.

She turned the knit top of her sock back down over the top of her boot to keep snow from going inside, pulled the laces taut to make certain they were snug—two things she'd learned after that first wet foray to the garage—and she was ready to go. The kitten had only wanted a few mouthfuls this time when she'd offered. It made Carina think he was already beginning to catch up from his night of near starvation.

She climbed back into the Subaru determined to go and have a good time. But on the way into town, she began to feel like an idiot. Here she was, alone in a strange place. All because her family was scattered. She could have stayed home, served Christmas dinner to Aaron, talked him into helping serve dinner at a soup kitchen, or they could have both rung a bell next to a red bucket.

If nothing else, they would've made cookies and visited nursing homes the way she'd done in other years.

Instead, she'd chosen the selfish way. Trying to relive the days when she'd been the center of the family. The glue.

She sighed and clicked the radio on, but Christmas music was just too jolly. She tried her favorite oldies station on Sirius. Every song seemed to remind her of her youth and her late sister. *Is that why I wanted to come here so badly?* To find things which can *never* be recovered? All the insights were hitting Carina hard.

They all made sense in a self-absorbed sort of way. She heard the desperation in her own thoughts even as they ran through her head. *Not too self-absorbed to try and understand my own feelings, at least. Sort of a wandering in the forest sabbatical moment. Maybe I'll come out of all this with a new name the way some Native Americans did after they'd been on a vision quest. Instead of Carina I could be She Who Makes Herself Miserable.*

When Tracy Chapman came on, singing about driving in a "Fast Car," Carina turned the radio off completely. That had been one of Jodie's favorite songs. "I hear ya, Sis," she said aloud. "I hear ya." But she took no comfort from the song or the memory.

Carina missed her sister terribly. After the deaths of her parents, and her only sibling, Carina had no one else with whom she shared her most treasured childhood memories. She'd inherited all the photo albums, even her sister's baby album, which would've gone to Jodie's own children, if she'd been blessed to have any. Carina sometimes felt she had fallen into one of those existential novels they'd read in college. The ones she'd never quite understood.

Feeling a trickle of moisture on her cheeks, Carina cracked open the window to blow away the sorrow. She missed her old life, her childhood when Jodie caused ruckus all the time, and her young adult years, babies and all the wonder that accompanies babies.

Time has such a way of slipping past. One day you're a kid playing in the yard, then you're in school trying to figure out who you are, and what you want to be, then out-of-the-blue you meet the love of your life, begin your career, have children and before you know it entire decades have flown by while you're busy working, raising the kids, and teaching them how to be adults, how to live a good life. Hopefully even a bit about how to save for the future.

Then one day *BAM* you wake up one morning and you're on the cusp of retirement, or retirement age anyway, and suddenly you discover you are now living life with a stranger, someone who has forgotten everything about you, especially the tenderness of your still beating heart.

When should I have made time for my spouse, the heartthrob I fell in love with? When should he have made time for me, the heartthrob I once was?

Carina sighed and opened the window even wider. Tears clogged her nose and salted her lashes. *Silly old woman.* Is this why so many of her peers got on those antidepressants? *Am I depressed?* She thought of a conversation she'd had with a similarly aged Facebook friend. *Why do so many feel the need for mood altering drugs?*

Carina had wondered the same thing. "Is it our age, or is it our society?"

The other woman, Serena Moon (Carina thought it a fake name, so she was careful what she shared), agreed maybe it was societal influence, but then she said, "Nevertheless, every woman I know is on them after a certain age."

That idea wouldn't leave her mind. Finally, she'd begun to research the topic of depression in middle aged women and found, lo and behold, it wasn't a new thing, and it wasn't relegated to women. Oh, yeah, she'd mentally slapped her forehead in disbelief, middle aged men in red sports cars with younger women, usually blonde. Jeez. How could I have forgotten that old saw?

Carina wiped her cheeks and paid more attention to the road. Her research had also convinced her that back in the olden days, as the kids always called the past, women had so much more to do they probably didn't have time to dwell on their feelings the way she'd been doing.

Washing and hanging clothes on a clothesline, ironing, mending, actually preparing and cooking two or three meals a day—no fast food or frozen veggies to pop in a pan or microwave

—and maybe even a home garden like her grandmother had grown. Wow. Talk about feeling needed.

I don't have to do a fraction of that, she thought. Maybe I'm the one with the problem, not Alfred, not the kids. Me. Always expecting others to make me happy. Selfish. Selfish. Selfish.

Get a grip, Carina. For goodness sakes, get a grip. She drove on toward town feeling a bit lighter even though nothing had been resolved. Maybe I can figure this out, she thought. If not, I won't mess around, when I get home, to the counselor I go, post haste.

CHAPTER 16

STORYTIME

THE DRIVE TO TOWN SEEMED SHORTER EVERY TIME. AS IF HER Subaru actually knew the way. She got a bit of a surprise when she approached the downtown area this time, though. Cars were parked in the slanted spaces up and down Main as far as she could see.

It's not even near six o'clock yet.

She drove all the way to the other end of the business area—where it would Y off into North Main—without seeing an open spot. *Good thing I've got my hiking boots on.* She parked outside Crossbow T-Shirts and Gifts, wrapped her scarf around her neck, and took off toward the gazebo. Thankfully, downtown Main Street wasn't that long.

Feathery snowflakes began to drift down again as she walked. Carina couldn't resist sticking out her tongue to catch a few. She pulled her hood up and relished the crisp air and soft snow. Back home in West Texas, according to her phone's weather app, it was almost seventy degrees.

She stuck out her tongue once more as she approached the crowded seating area. Strung beneath the eaves of the white hexagonal gazebo, twinkling Christmas lights pushed back the coming night. Folding chairs had been placed around the front of the gazebo in curved rows. The seats were all taken so Carina found a convenient tree to lean against. A few more stragglers were coming from the other direction but they were obviously locals. They were carrying their own camp chairs.

A table to the right of the gazebo was manned by a group of young people handing out mugs of what Carina assumed was hot chocolate.

She made her way over, surprised to see a sign proclaiming this to be a service sponsored by The Brewery, Dr. Lance's Small Animal Clinic, Crossbow Skis and Things, and the county library.

At the table, she accepted a real mug of hot chocolate from Bonnie, the vet tech she'd met at the clinic. "There's also coffee if you'd rather—"

Carina sipped. "Oh, no, this is great. I'm surprised at the real mugs, though."

Bonnie grinned. "Our little village banned one-time-use styrofoam and plastic a couple of years ago." She pointed her chin toward a burly man with neck tats and a long, braided beard. "That's Elston, my hubs. He owns The Brewery." A smile turned up one corner of her mouth. "He was the driving force behind the ban, well, him and Dr. Lance. And me." She added herself as an afterthought.

"So, the mugs come from The Brewery?"

Bonnie nodded and indicated the large trays. "When people bring them back, we put them there, in the stackable trays which we load onto that small hand cart. Then we just pull them across the street and slide them right into the industrial dishwasher."

"That's wonderful," Carina said. "I *love* this place."

Bonnie grinned and sipped from her own mug. "You know what else is really cool?"

Carina shook her head.

"Lots of folks bring their own mugs from home."

"Wow—" Carina would have said more but she could see Dr. Lance making his way to a comfy reading throne in the wide opening of the gazebo-stage. The little faces in the crowd were turned toward him in anticipation.

Dr. Lance wore a red Santa hat and a soft flannel jacket. "Hey, kids," he waved his long fingered hand. "It's beginning to snow." He glanced upward and they all followed suit. "Should we call off the reading?"

"Nooo!" the little voices shouted.

He grinned and held up his book, *The Animals' Christmas Eve.* He showed them the beautifully illustrated cover, and then opened to the first page. "Once upon a time ..." He leaned slightly forward. "All books should begin with once upon a time, right?"

The children nodded and murmured their agreement.

"The animals gathered in the barn ..."

Carina found herself leaning forward to capture every syllable of every word. The gentle veterinarian seemed transformed. He was no longer the awkward, lanky man who blurted out whatever crossed his mind, now he was the kindly grandfather every child in the world should be so fortunate to have.

She listened raptly. And when a young woman brought her a canvas camp chair, Carina was not surprised to see The Brewery stamped on the back of it. She glanced over at the table and caught Bonnie's eye. Bonnie gave her a thumbs up and Carina felt as if she'd just been adopted into a wonderful club.

The Animals' Christmas Eve was a Little Golden Book, it wasn't a long read. When Dr. Lance closed it, the children immediately began to chant, "The poem, the poem, the poem!"

He laughed. "But it isn't Christmas Eve until tomorrow."

"The poem, the poem," they chanted, clapping their mittened hands.

Dr. Lance laughed and stood. His deep voice blanketed the colorful crowd of hooded, bundled children and the adults who had brought them. "'Twas the night before Christmas, when all through the house, not a creature was stirring—"

"Not even a mouse!" the children finished.

The doc grinned and looked out over the crowd. "The stockings were hung by the chimney—"

"With care!"

"In hopes that St. Nicholas—"

"Soon would be there!"

Dr. Lance continued. "The children were nestled—"

"All snug in their beds!"

"While visions of sugarplums—"

"Danced in their heads!"

When they chanted that line, Dr. Lance's assistants appeared with buckets of sugarplums and began walking through the children handing them out, one by one. When he came to the part naming the reindeer, "Now Dasher, now Dancer, now Prancer, and Vixen! On Comet, on Cupid, on Donner and ..." He put a finger across his lips and the children whispered, "*Blitzen.*"

Like magic, Bonnie appeared around the edge of the gazebo with a small reindeer dressed out in bright harness and sleigh bells.

"Shhh," Dr. Lance cautioned again, "let's not frighten Blitzen."

Bonnie led the gentle pet around the crowd so the children could lean forward and run their little hands across his fur. Mittens were removed and dropped and retrieved again as Bonnie and her pal made the rounds and disappeared around the other side of the gazebo.

Dr. Lance continued reciting the poem from memory, "He sprang to his sleigh—" The doc looked up and down the street. "To his team gave a whistle—" He cupped a palm around his ear, and from afar we all heard a faint whistle. "And away they all flew like the down of a thistle." Hesitating, he raised his chin and looked up to the heavens from whence the feathery snow still fell.

Then he looked back at the children and murmured, "But I heard him exclaim, 'ere he drove out of sight—"

The children yelled, "Happy Christmas to all, and to all a good night!"

As one organism, they stood and began to clap. But Dr. Lance appeared to not even be paying attention. Instead, he was on tiptoe, gazing down the street, one hand shielding his eyes, scanning the distance, searching for something.

One by one the kids followed his lead and stood on tiptoe to peer down the street through the gentle snow. "Is it him?" a little voice asked.

"Is it?" another echoed.

"It is! It is! I see him, I see—"

"Santa!" they all breathed.

I stood on my tiptoes just in time to see the snow-blurry image of a plump red figure leading the little reindeer away from us down the street. In another instant, both man and beast were lost to the weathery night.

A collective sigh went up from the crowd.

Dr. Lance waved his hand at the back of the retreating figure. "Tomorrow's Christmas Eve, kiddos." He looked out over the restless crowd. "And I will see you all right back here, same time, same—"

"Station!" they yelled, obviously having been indoctrinated to the old saying from years past.

Joyfully, kids and parents alike waved at the good doctor as they stood and gathered their chairs. Many had brought their own but those who hadn't took it upon themselves to gather the chair they'd been occupying and stack it on a specially made cart as they made their way past.

Dr. Lance appeared at Carina's side. "Did you enjoy the show?"

She nodded. "Very much. I'm in awe, actually. Not a single piece of trash litters the ground, everyone put up his or her own chair. And they were all polite and well behaved. Even the adults." She laughed. "What is this, Utopia?"

He smiled. "Come back in the daylight tomorrow and you'll see sugar plums here and there but yes, you're correct. It is Utopia." He slipped his hand under her elbow and led her toward the table Bonnie and her husband were clearing. "I've got to do a little work here, and then we can walk over to The Brewery for dinner." He rubbed his midsection. "I'm famished!"

"I'm not surprised you're starving after such an amazing performance."

He laughed as he helped Elston fold up the big table and stack it on the trailer with the chairs. Together they spread a large waterproof canvas cover across the trailer and fastened it down with bungee cords. "There," he said, "all ready for the final performance tomorrow night."

Elston held out his hand and introduced himself to Carina.

"Pleased to meet you," she said. "May I call you Santa?"

He grinned showing her a bright gold tooth in the front of his mouth. "All my closest friends do."

Carina liked him right away. What a wonderful match for sweet Bonnie, she thought. As if conjured by thought, Bonnie appeared. "Ms. Carina," she said. "I would be glad to give you a lift to your car if you need one. It's gotten quite a bit colder in the last half hour."

"Well, thank you," Carina began.

"I've actually invited her to dine with us at your fine establishment," Dr. Lance said. His voice didn't sound a bit sheepish about it. He sounded jovial.

Bonnie smiled and took Carina's arm. Her gaze fell to Carina's left hand as they crossed under the twinkling Christmas lights. But once again, she didn't say anything. Carina didn't know what to say.

It seemed silly to defend something that didn't exist. And

nothing existed between her and the vet. Goodness. It's just dinner, she thought. Just dinner between friends.

They crossed the street with the guys pushing the cart filled with mugs. Bonnie ran ahead to open the double doors at the side of the business, and they pushed the cart right inside. A man with a long white apron opened the huge square dishwasher and they all helped to unload and slide the trays into place.

"This is Leif," Bonnie said. "He's our chief cook aside from Elston."

Carina nodded at the stocky man. "Pleased to meet you."

"Carina is our new friend from Texas," Bonnie said. "She's renting a cabin for Christmas."

"Welcome," Leif replied, a northern European accent clipping his words.

"All right," Elston washed his hands. "Time to get cookin'. I know what the doc wants to eat, steak and baked potato with salad." He turned to me. "What can I make for our new friend?"

"Change the steak to veggies and throw them on the grill. Maybe a kabob with mushrooms added?"

"It's our specialty!" Bonnie said. "And my favorite."

Dr. Lance took my elbow again and led me through the swinging doors into the dining room. Behind me I heard the sizzle of a steak slapped on the grill.

"Don't forget the bread," Dr. Lance called over his shoulder. "I know Leif has some hot rolls around here somewhere."

Bonnie laughed as we made our way across the dining room to a cozy window booth. Flickering yellow lanterns adorned every table and the large many-paned windows framed the snowy street like a painting. Crossbow was generous with its holiday décor. Evergreen wreaths were woven through with red ribbons, and twinkly lights hung from every post as far as the eye could see.

The wrought iron lampposts lent a feeling of yesteryear to the whole village. Currier & Ives came to Carina's mind even more than Thomas Kinkade.

The smell of hops and barley infused the large room with warmth. A polished oak bar curved around the far end, and at least a dozen taps sprouted from the counter. A double row of silvery chrome vats on stilts took up the opposite wall. Craft beers of all flavors. Wow.

"What do we get?" Carina asked as Dr. Lance pulled out her chair for her.

"Samples," he replied, grinning at her across the small square table.

Carina ran her hand across the white linen tablecloths while admiring the matching linen napkins and square cork drink coasters at each place. Every coaster had a joke or trivia question printed on it. She picked up the nearest one and read aloud, "Why do hometown beers love Hobby Lobby?" She giggled and turned it over for the answer. "Because they're so crafty. Of course!"

Dr. Lance went to the bar and ordered a tray of samples for them. The bartender set them up and brought them over. "I'm Faya," she said, placing a long narrow tray of small glasses in the center of the table.

Carina smiled. "Are all these for me?"

"There are two samples of each of our beers. One for you and one for Dr. Lance. Once you've chosen your favorite, let me know." She smiled widely and made a circuit of the room on her way back to the bar.

Dr. Lance picked up one of the tiny glasses and read the label beneath it. "This one is White Oak."

Delighted, Carina picked up one on the opposite end of the tray. "Peppermint Stout." She wrinkled her nose. "For Christmas, I suppose." She sipped the beer and was surprised at how crisp it tasted. "Wow," she said. "It's delicious."

Dr. Lance tilted his shot glass toward her. "White Oak is

amazing, too." He took a drink of water from a glass Faya brought over. "Now it's time for that Chocolate Moose I saw last week. I've been wanting to try it ever since."

They both began to lift the tiny sample glasses so they could read the labels beneath. "Here it is." Carina lifted the small glass and Dr. Lance lifted his, too.

"Cheers." He held his glass toward hers.

She clinked it gently and took a tiny sip. Her eyes widened. "Oh, that's not fair. It's even better than the peppermint."

"How about Vanilla Beanie?"

Carina found it on her tray. "You first." She sipped her water.

He tilted the tiny glass and grimaced. "I thought I would love that, but *yuck*."

Carina laughed out loud at hearing the vet say yuck. She tasted it quickly and found it okay, but then she loved vanilla and always had. After another mouthful of water to clear away the vanilla, she said, "I absolutely adored the readings you gave."

Dr. Lance wiped a smidge of foam from his upper lip. "It was fun tonight." He smiled and picked up another glass to read the label.

"Does the weather always cooperate this way?"

He laughed. "Not always, but at this time of year, snow is almost always a given. Some years it's much heavier. I have to read a lot faster then."

Carina spluttered and Golden Ale dribbled down her chin. "Hah! You made me LOL." She dabbed her chin with a napkin. "And tomorrow, what happens?"

"Tomorrow we will read *The Animal's Christmas Eve* again, only this time we will have the real stable animals on the lawn."

"That's wonderful," she said. "The kids were so sweet with the little reindeer." She took a small drink. "And will you recite the poem again?"

"Oh, yes. They never let me off the hook on that one. But tomorrow night, Santa will hand out some little gifts." He smiled and his eyes twinkled. "It's my favorite part. We've been gathering the gifts all year, everything from yo-yos to scented markers to card games and Hot Wheels." He glanced down at the samples. "And every child gets a Little Golden Book."

"I hope you don't take this the wrong way," she said. "But I sort of feel like I've stepped into another dimension." She drank a bit more water. "And you seem like the father of the whole village. Like the center of it all."

The vet leaned forward. "That's very kind of you to say." He picked up another sample—they each had six—and held it up to the light. "It wasn't always that way." He looked across the table into her eyes.

Carina stopped breathing for a moment. His eyes were deep sparkling blue, but it was the kindness and humility she saw there that took her breath away. "What do you mean, it wasn't always that way?"

Dr. Lance tasted the next to the last sample from the small glass he'd been holding. "Winter," he said, tilting it toward her, ignoring her question, apparently regretting his admission. "It's a strong one."

Carina picked up her matching glass and tasted. Her nose crinkled. "Whew, it is strong. Think I'll pass on that one."

The vet laughed and tried the last sample. "Sweater Weather," he said, identifying the sample. "That's one I've never heard of before." He tasted it and smiled. "But it just may be my favorite."

"Really?" She picked it up and sipped. "Oh, my goodness. It's sweet. And smooth." She drank it down and smiled. "I'll have some more of that, too."

Dr. Lance motioned to the bartender and she hurried over. "Find any you like?" she asked.

"Carina likes Sweater Weather, and although it's a tough choice, I believe I'll go with White Oak."

Faya leaned down and gathered all the little sample glasses. "Sweater Weather is mine," she said. "Elston let me name it."

"It's very good," Carina said. "I'm not much of a beer drinker but *yum.*"

Faya smiled. "I'll bring you a glass along with Doc's White Oak. And I believe your meals are being plated now." She refilled their water glasses and carried the narrow sample tray away.

Carina watched her leave. "She's a study in economy," she mused. "Not a wasted motion. I remember my own waitress days while attending classes at UT. The first thing we were taught was to make each step count—never leave the dining area empty-handed, never return empty-handed." She laughed. "I wish I'd had my iPhone then, with its little step counter. I'll bet I got 10,000 steps per shift, easy."

She stopped talking and glanced around. Almost every table had filled with diners. Dr. Lance sat quietly, sipping his beer, and listening.

"I'm sorry," Carina said. "That was a long, long time ago." She shrugged. "I think the beer loosened my tongue." She wished it would loosen his tongue so he would tell her why he hadn't always been the village's favorite father figure.

CHAPTER 17

DAD

THE VET SET HIS GLASS DOWN. "I'M SORRY I CHANGED TOPICS SO abruptly earlier. I wasn't really trying to be evasive." He smiled, but it was a half-smile. "When we first moved here, many moons ago, my wife and I were trying to save our marriage." He let his eyes examine the tabletop. "I thought the rural setting would be ideal. She was always under so much stress in her high-pressure sales job in the city. Out here I could be the big dog in town, and she could work or not work, volunteer if she wanted, whatever she chose. But it didn't work out that way."

"I'm so sorry." Carina said. "I didn't know—"

He shook his head. "She didn't care for small town life at all. Grew bored and restless from the outset. Before I knew it she'd found a new career online. The only problem was, she needed to move back to Denver."

"Oh, that must've been tough."

He nodded. "We actually tried the long distance thing for a while, but that didn't suit her either. By the time I'd given up and decided to sell my practice and move back, it was too late. She'd found someone else."

"How awful."

The vet slid his glass back and forth on the coaster. "The worst part was my son. He was a youngster, didn't understand. And when his mother took him away to Denver, he was devastated. He loved it here. I was so thrilled when he later reconnected with a hometown girl, and then married her." He looked away, as if recalling the exact circumstance. "When she inherited the cabin, it seemed a real blessing."

Carina felt every sip of her sample beers suddenly come back to haunt her. Were her senses impaired? Surely it was a coincidence. "Dr. Lance, is your son's name Max? Max Paper?"

He laughed. "Of course. I thought you knew. He rented the cabin to you, right?"

"Well, sort of. We actually met and became friends in an online grief group, and when I mentioned how much I'd love a white Christmas, he insisted I bring my family to the cabin." Carina smiled thinking of her new friend. "It seldom snows where I'm from." She shook her head. "But he refuses to let me pay rent."

"That's Max all right. Always had the most generous soul."

"Kind of reminds me of his dad." Carina thought of how happy he'd looked, reading to the children. "He's been through a lot, hasn't he? The loss of his mom and his wife at such a young age."

Dr. Lance swallowed the rest of his beer. Something in his demeanor had changed. It was no longer easy-going country vet, now it was concerned father with an edge of sadness. She assumed it was empathy for his son's loss. "Max and I haven't been especially close the last few years. He blamed me for the divorce. His mother wasn't happy back in the city, either. And then she passed so suddenly."

"Then he found the love of his life, and lost her, too." Carina looked at his face. "So much for a young man to deal with, and yet, he seems to be getting on top of it."

"You talk to him a lot?"

"Oh, yes. Not in the last day or so, but before that we spoke almost daily." She laughed. "I just can't believe I didn't know he was your son." She studied the vet's kind face. "I never heard your last name … but now that you mention it, I can definitely see the resemblance. He's such a handsome young man. And kind."

In the muted light, it was difficult to tell for sure, but Carina was almost certain she saw color creep into the doc's cheeks. She hadn't meant anything by the handsome remark; it was just the truth.

What bothered her, more than anything, is why Max never told her his father was such an important part of the community. That seemed quite secretive, not like him at all. Could he be jealous of the time his dad gave to the village, or to the village children?

Maybe she was reading too much into it. Perhaps he'd intended to tell her when he joined them for Christmas. Alfred always said she had a tendency to analyze things to death.

"Carina?" Dr. Lance touched her hand.

She looked down at his long fingers. Her wedding ring glimmered in the firelight. "I'm sorry, I was somewhere else for a moment. Did you say something?" Carina knew she probably should, but she didn't move her hand away. His fingers were warm.

"I asked how my son is doing?"

The pain in his voice caused Carina to grasp the tips of his fingers. "Oh, he's good. He's doing fine. In fact, Match Day was last week. He learned where he will be doing his residency." She stopped short of telling him that Max would be going to Baylor Scott and White in Temple, Texas to pursue emergency medicine. Surely, he knew that much. And if he didn't, she didn't feel it was her place to tell him.

Instead, she said, "You'll see him at Christmas dinner, you know." As she uttered those words, she realized how sad it was that the vet and his son had not made holiday plans together. Hadn't Max said his father was going on a Hawaiian Christmas trip with his sister and her husband?

Faya arrived with their plates just then and saved Dr. Lance from saying yay or nay to the invitation. They both dug into their meals. The veggies were wonderful and Elston had slipped a few cubes of toasted tofu on the ends of her kabobs. "These are wonderful," she said, pulling off the first one and tasting it.

The vet smiled. "They will spoil you, those two." He glanced at Bonnie and Elston across the dining room.

Carina turned, saw that they were watching for her reaction, and gave them a hearty thumbs up which they both mirrored back at her.

"Firm believers in lots of protein," Dr. Lance said. "They feed me almost daily. Always worrying over me like a pair of mother hens." He clucked his tongue. "And watching me like a hawk."

Carina smiled. "I may never leave here." The words popped out of her mouth, and she wondered if the doc's proclivity had somehow rubbed off on her, or was it something in the water that caused everyone to say whatever crossed their mind? Oh, well, she thought. Que sera, sera and all that jazz.

After the meal, as they made their way out to his Jeep—parked at the curb—Carina thought about her offer of Christmas at the cabin. She felt compelled to ask him if Max being there would be all right. Her voice was tentative because she never wanted to interfere in other people's lives. Goodness knows she had her own things to worry over.

But in the back of her mind, a new thought surfaced. *Was I sent here to act as a go-between for Max and his dad?* She thought of her recent prayers. Prayers for purpose, for a way to get outside herself and help others.

The vet chuckled but it was a hollow sound. "He might be shocked." His voice had flattened, no longer the jolly Christmas reader. "Are you certain you have room for me at the table? I usually fly out to be with my sister and her family after the Christmas Eve reading, but they've gifted each other a trip to Hawaii this year. And while I gave it serious consideration, I finally backed out. Figured I'd just rest up a bit." His voice grew soft. "Not getting any younger, you know. Plus, those airport crowds, and an eight-hour flight—"

"Well, my goodness." Carina slid into his warm cab—he'd started it from inside the Brewery. "Of course, there's plenty of room. But Hawaii? Wouldn't that be fun?"

He nodded. "It certainly would. With the right person. At the right time. I haven't been there since I was a young man."

"Same here." She held up her hand. "Young woman, awesome vacation."

He smiled and in the reflected light of the Christmas wreath on the lamp post, it seemed genuine.

"What should I bring for Christmas dinner? And what time should I arrive?"

Carina felt the previously unknown band of worry around her heart loosening. "Bring any dessert you want and arrive around noon or one. I'm thinking of serving around two if all goes according to plan."

They drove to her Subaru, and she clicked her own remote start. "Too bad it wouldn't reach from The Brewery."

"You'd better sit here while it warms."

"Thanks," Carina replied. "Tell me more about your practice. Is it just you and Bonnie?"

"And the receptionist," he said. "And a couple of high school kids who come in after school and on weekends to help with boarded pets and those recuperating from surgeries." He laughed. "My other vet-tech is on maternity. She'll be back after New Year's."

"Wow, I'll bet the high school kids line up for those volunteer spots."

He glanced out the windshield at the snow still falling in soft feathers. "There's never a shortage. But it drove my ex-wife crazy because I never hired more full-time help." He closed his eyes. "When I would bring orphaned kittens or pups home to feed them overnight, it didn't always sit well with her."

Carina tried to understand why that would be a problem. "Didn't like having to get up and feed in the middle of the night, huh?"

"She said it disturbed her, no matter how quietly I crawled out of bed." He gripped the steering wheel tightly. "That's when I moved to the guest room. Only on those occasions when I had to bring work home, so to speak."

"That's awful!" Oops, did it again, she thought. "I mean, I can't believe she would be disturbed by that—"

"She married a veterinarian, right? What did she think life would be like?" He shrugged haplessly. "That's why she thought I should hire someone to be there overnight. She just couldn't understand why I would willingly get up in the night and go down to check on an elderly surgery patient or one that wasn't doing well."

"I think I'm beginning to see where your son gets his drive. And his compassion." She opened the door and stepped out into the cold night. The cab of the Jeep had suddenly begun to feel too small, too familiar. "Thank you for dinner, Dr. Lance, and for bringing me back to my car."

The vet leaned across the seat. "Have you still got my business card? My cell number is there. Please call me once you're back at the cabin. I won't sleep a wink until I know you're safely home."

Just like his son, she thought, as she pictured the small card in her wallet. "Yes, I've got it," she said. "I will text. Would that be all right?"

He grinned. "Please do. Bonnie says I must text more. No one calls anymore, she says. But Ms. Pinner ..."

She stopped the door, waited. "Please, call me Carina."

He nodded. "Carina, if you need anything, don't text. Just call. Anytime."

She laughed. "I will. I promise." She closed the door, got into her SUV, and cranked up the heat.

CHAPTER 18

BACK TO THE CABIN

THE DRIVE TO THE CABIN WAS BEAUTIFUL. UNEVENTFUL. THE SNOW drifting across the headlights made her feel cozy, as if a loved one had wrapped her in a favorite blankie. Sort of the way she did with the kitten.

She'd noticed Dr. Lance waiting as she backed out and made her way down Main toward the Eagle's Nest turn off. He seemed so considerate, so accommodating. How could any woman not appreciate that? His ex must have been a real shrew.

A sharp memory of the morning she'd scolded Alfred for stirring his coffee too loudly stabbed her thoughts. *Did I really raise a fuss over that?* Yes, I did. Talk about a shrew. Shame washed over her, temporarily blinding her to the beautiful drive.

She took the turn onto Paper Lane still wallowing in memories. Alfred worked hard, why hadn't she been more supportive? Is it really any wonder he might prefer to stay away? Her heart stuttered a bit at that thought. She had to admit she hadn't been easy to live with lately. But she didn't have long to contemplate her shortcomings.

A sense of urgency began to overtake her as she pulled into the drive and made the decision to park in the garage. The kitten must be so hungry by now. She'd been gone for three hours already.

Crossing the yard, grateful once more for warm boots, and well-lit porches, Carina glanced at the peaked roof of the garage. Yes. A spotlight right there would light up the whole area. Her own father had installed one on his rural property years ago. It came on at dusk and went off at dawn. Max was right. It needed something to supplement the moonlight back here.

Inside the cozy cabin, Carina pulled off her boots and coat and peeked into the kitten's basket. For the first time, two little eyes peeked back, as if looking for her. "Oh, look at you," she said. "Wide awake and ready to eat." She spoke softly and lovingly, reaching over to plug in the Christmas tree at the same time. "There now, that's better, isn't it, all those pretty lights? I wanted to leave it on for you while I was gone, but that light strand came all the way from Texas. Who knows how old it is? I certainly can't remember. Better safe than sorry."

She continued babbling to the kitten while she warmed his formula and prepared the dropper. Just then, her phone dinged in her pocket.

"Oh, shoot. Forgot to message Dr. Lance." She pulled out the device and read the text.

"I'm sure you got home safely, but I couldn't go to bed without checking." He'd inserted a smiley face emoji to end the sentence.

"Oh, I'm sorry I didn't text yet," she touched the tiny microphone icon and spoke, prompting Siri to type the message for her since her hands were full. "I arrived and came straight inside to a tiny kitten ready for his bottle." Carina placed the kitten's food on the coffee table and leaned over the basket to pick him up. "Come on little one," she whispered, wrapping him in his soft blanket. "Time for din-din."

"Glad you're safe," Dr. Lance wrote. "Thank you for a lovely evening. I'm looking forward to Christmas dinner already."

"Same here," she replied. "I'm sure Max willed be thrilled as well. He thought you'd be in Hawaii."

"Perhaps I'd better text him, give him a heads up," Dr. Lance wrote back. "Wouldn't want him to be too shocked."

"That would be nice," Carina said. "I won't mention it unless he does."

"Thank you, Carina. For the first time in a long time, I feel hopeful about my relationship with my son."

Carina squeezed a drop of formula onto the kitten's mouth, and it popped open. She put a second drop inside his mouth on his rough, pink tongue and the baby clamped down on the nipple and began to nurse.

"Oh, my goodness," she said into the microphone. "The kitten is nursing. Really nursing. For the first time. I'm not having to smear it across his little face."

Dr. Lance sent back a row of happy faces. "That kitten should be named Lucky for winding up on your porch that way."

No, Carina thought. Not exactly lucky, more like a gift from God. "I think he is a device," she texted. "If not for this little gingerbread man, I would never have come into your clinic and wound up inviting you to Christmas dinner with your son."

There was silence from the phone for several minutes. Carina rewound all she'd said as they'd chatted. I probably said too much, just like I keep accusing him of doing, *talk first, think later*.

Finally, the message came in. "Just like in *The Animals' Christmas Eve*. I don't have to be convinced animals are angelic messengers. I doubt Max would have come to the cabin alone, much less contacted me if he did."

That broke Carina's heart a little. She was reminded of the poem she'd written in her journal about how damaged hearts continue to seep blood sometimes. "Maybe this will be a turning point," she said. "I'll say a little prayer."

"Thank you. I'm not very religious. As you may have noticed. But maybe that should change."

Carina almost let that go by, and then something her mom used to say came to mind. "You know it says in the book of Matthew that if two people come together to pray, and it is in God's will, then it shall be given."

"Thank you," he wrote.

Carina hoped he didn't think she was preaching to him just because he said he wasn't a religious man. But it's what she believed, deep down in her heart, so she quickly instructed Siri to write, "Dear Lord, please help this good man mend his fences with his son, Max. They are both wonderful people."

He wrote "Amen" and followed it up with another thank you.

She quickly wished him a good night and told him she would see him at the gazebo the next day for Christmas Eve story time. She couldn't recall ever having been so bold with someone she barely knew.

He sent back a tiny Santa face and a thumbs up.

"Well," she told the kitten. "I may have driven him away. But I sure hope not. Not when he was looking forward to dining with us, and with Max." She held up the tiny bottle for a second, to get a look at the level of formula. "Look what you've done." She smiled. "Almost half gone already. You are devouring this bottle. Maybe I should call you Piglet instead of Ginger."

She gave him back the bottle amazed at how quickly he'd learned to suckle. Every time he slowed and dozed, she would take the bottle away, thinking he had finished, and he would rouse himself and make a grab at her finger. Carina laughed and smeared a bit of paste for him to lick off. That's when she suddenly realized she had never bought a litter box. *First thing tomorrow. Back to town. Should've got it today ... shoulda, woulda, coulda. How did I suddenly get so busy?*

After he finally finished, and his little head was drooping, Carina cleaned him up, snuggled him for a few minutes, and then tucked him back into his tote bag bed and his basket. Her eyelids suddenly felt made of stone. *Guess I haven't kept track of time. Or maybe it's the thin mountain air.*

It was all she could do to check the fire, brush her teeth, and slip into her pajamas. At the last second, she picked up her journal, intent on writing a couple of prayers and maybe a few paragraphs on her Christmas story. But she dozed off still holding the pen between her fingers.

When she woke at six a.m., Carina couldn't believe she'd slept all night with the lamp still on. *Oh my gosh, the baby!*

She jumped out of bed, slid her feet into waiting slippers, and hurried to the living room. The kitten slept on. It makes sense, she thought. Since he'd taken the entire bottle of formula last night, rather than just a few drops.

In the kitchen, she prepped the coffee—she hadn't even done that before bedtime—and pushed the button to brew. She couldn't remember the last time she had forgotten to get the coffee ready the night before. *'Cause you've been in such a routine ever since coming home from the hospital. You had to be.*

Yeah, yeah, she told herself. Routine, schmoutine. I've been in a rut, that's what. Now, I'm doing things on my own. She smiled and went to get dressed. She had not forgotten about the litter box. As soon as I get him fed, I'll go, she thought. They should be open by then. Maybe.

After feeding the kitten, which took less and less effort each time, Carina poured coffee into her travel mug, used the extra clicker to open the garage door, and pressed the button to honk the horn and start the Subaru.

While it warmed up, she ate a cup of microwave oatmeal with blueberries, and then pulled on her boots and coat. The snow had stopped sometime during the night, but today it had a crusted feel to it. Her boots made crunching sounds as she walked. Yesterday it had been all soft and fluffy.

Must've turned colder during the night. She blew out her breath and watched it condense in the air. *Hope it stays nice for the reading tonight. And for Aaron's flight.* He was due to arrive in Denver at 7:30 p.m. He then planned to rent a car and drive the ninety minutes to the cabin.

Carina offered to meet him at the airport, but he said he wanted to rent his own vehicle so he could drive up to the ski lodge later without inconveniencing her. *So considerate. That's my Aaron.*

In the garage, Carina looked around, checking once more for any strays that might have taken refuge in the space. It seemed weathertight. But cats were like mice. They could get into places that seemed impossible. "If anything was in here, I probably gave it a heart attack when I honked the horn that way. I'll bet it was incredibly loud."

She rolled her eyes at her own reflection in the rearview mirror. "Stop talking to yourself, old woman. The men with the butterfly nets will be following you through the Dollar Chain if you keep that up."

Carina backed out, closed the garage door, and tuned the radio to the Christmas music channel she'd found earlier. The weather felt nice and cold. Perfect. Christmassy.

Such a pleasant drive to town. The sun peeked through the pines at every curve in the road. It made the snow wink and glitter.

The local weatherman came on the radio and said the snow would begin to fall again soon, continuing off and on throughout the day with little significant accumulation in the valley. On the mountain, he said, it would be a welcome addition to the snowpack.

Within minutes, Carina found herself on Main headed toward the Dollar Chain. All the stores were decorated for Christmas. Lighted trees or happy snowmen decorated every business. And on the lamp posts the evergreen wreaths were nearly covered with snow. No need for the fake spray-on stuff here, Carina thought, reveling in the lovely lights and decorations.

Inside the store, she went directly to the pet department for the litter box and kitty litter. Then she looked at it doubtfully. He won't be able to get into that deep thing, she thought, picking out a smaller, shallower version.

There. That should do it. Then of course she had to buy a little plastic ball with a bell inside for him to bat around inside his basket, along with a fluffy stuffed kitten for him to snuggle with. *Why didn't I think of that earlier?*

Near the counter, a rack of Christmas books and coloring books caught her eye. Something for all ages, or so it seemed. *But I've already bought books for the grandkids.* Oh, seriously, Carina, she told herself, one can never have too many books. Or crayons for that matter.

She laughed all the way to the car with her impulse purchases and discounted paper with which to wrap them. *At least I got what I came for this time, just a few more things as well.*

She stowed the packages in the back seat and then climbed in behind the wheel of the Subaru just as Bonnie walked a lady and her dog to a small car. The little dog was all wrapped up in a blankie just the way The Gingerbread Man had been.

Carina waved as she backed out, but she didn't go down to the clinic to visit. She wanted to give Dr. Lance plenty of space in case she had stepped on his religious toes last night. Or non-religious, as the case might be. She laughed to herself as another classic Christmas song came on the radio. This time it was "Santa Claus is Coming to Town" by The Boss, Bruce Springsteen. It brought back good memories of dancing around the living room when the kids were small.

They'd always enjoyed Christmas music—from church carols to rock-n-roll—along with every Christmas movie known to man starting each year, the day after Thanksgiving.

I can't believe those days are gone. Time just flew by. Just like some smarty pants said it would. I wonder who first said that? She envisioned Benjamin Franklin drawing a little clock with wings in his Poor Richard's Almanac beside that quote. Sounds like something he'd dream up, she thought, smiling. One of his truisms. *Is that what he called them, or did I just make that up?*

She drove back the way she had come, stopping only when a before-unnoticed sign invited her to pop in for a fresh cup of brew. I have a ton of cooking to do, she thought. But still … she tilted her travel mug. Yep. Near empty.

Crossbow Coffee wasn't crowded, but there were a few patrons in line. Carina parked, went inside, and ordered a medium cup of fresh black coffee and a light and lovely slivered almond coffee cake that was so delicious she had to steel herself from ordering another to take back to the cabin.

Next door to Crossbow Coffee, a small clothing store beckoned. Christmas sweaters were on sale. Of course, they are, she thought. Today is Christmas Eve.

She bought one to wear to Dr. Lance's reading, and then since they were half-off, she bought another—a fleecy one—to wear on Christmas day. The sweater was decorated with bright red poinsettias on a black background, and the other, the deep green fleece, sported a crazy reindeer with lights strung from its antlers. Both made her feel happy. Retail therapy again, she thought. Jodie would be proud.

Then, since she was on a roll, she asked the cashier to break her two twenties into four ten-dollar bills. I'll pick up some funny cards, stuff them, and mail them to the kiddos, she told herself. A nice little surprise along with the other small gifts she'd collected. They won't care if the gifts arrive after the holiday. Surprises were always good.

Back in the SUV, Carina pumped up the volume on the classic song, "White Christmas" and jammed along with Bing all the way back to the cabin.

This time when she pulled into the driveway, Carina didn't bother to head around to the garage. She knew she would be going back to town in a few hours for story time. Glancing up at the sky when she stepped out of the Subaru, Carina was a bit surprised to find how overcast it had become.

She examined the weather app on her phone, but it showed no change.

Tucking her phone back into her coat pocket, Carina carried her purchases into the cabin. Bing Crosby's song had lasted almost all the way from town to the turnoff. Now it was time for something a little less sing-along.

After carrying in all her purchases and sorting them out, Carina checked on the kitten and then pulled up a classical playlist on her phone. Tchaikovsky's "Nutcracker Suite," followed by Corelli, Sibelius, Mendelssohn, and Mozart. That should do it, she thought, pressing play.

As the light music floated through the house, Carina washed her hands, tied on her Christmas apron, and preheated the oven. Then she began to assemble the ingredients for the sweet potato casserole and other side dishes that could be made ahead of time.

Once she had two casseroles in the oven, she pulled out the Christmas books and crayons she'd picked up for the kids and wrapped them in the colorful paper. She also wrapped the coffee mugs she'd bought for Max and his dad at Crossbow Coffee. One was black with thick white snowflakes and the other was white with tall pines reaching toward the sky. She'd gotten one for Alfred, too. But it was heavy denim-colored china with Crossbow, Colorado dripping down the front in melty-snow lettering.

She wrapped it, too. But she knew she'd be giving it to him at home which is why she'd made certain it was more of a Christmas souvenir. They'd always made it a point to buy each other some sort of memento when they'd traveled together. She had them tucked around all over the house.

By the time the sweet potato and broccoli rice casseroles came out of the oven, it was time to feed the kitten. Afterward, she put his new litter box together and set him down in the center of it.

He wasn't quite ready for prime time yet, so she cleaned his face and bathed his little tummy and nether region like always. That did the trick every time. For once, he stayed awake for a few minutes, exploring inside his basket.

I'll try him in the litter box again before I leave, she thought. Then she put the cooled casseroles in the fridge and went to take a quick shower.

As her hair air dried, Carina cut up and boiled a few potatoes, then mashed them with butter, a dollop of cream, and a small brick of cream cheese. They would also be easy to reheat tomorrow.

"Well," she spoke aloud, "I guess that's all the damage I can do for now." She had sampled a spoonful of the mashed potatoes and that seemed to whet her appetite.

She whipped up a quick cheese omelet and topped it with a handful of cherry tomatoes. "That should hold me until dinner." While she ate, she made a few notes in her journal. The story she'd started held little appeal now, but she wanted to jot down a few impressions of the snowy day and the quality of light outside the large picture window. She knew if she didn't write it immediately, the impressions would fade, and the words would be lost.

Finishing up the omelet and sipping her Diet Coke, Carina laid the journal aside and closed her eyes. She'd been going full steam since getting out of bed that morning. Five minutes to recharge wouldn't hurt anything.

She laid the journal on the coffee table and put her feet up. But she didn't drift off to nap as she'd hoped. Her brain said if she let herself drift, she might be down for the count.

"Oh, well," she sipped the rest of the soft drink, put the bowl of potatoes into the fridge—a tricky jigsaw-puzzle-undertaking with the other items—and washed up the sink full of dishes.

After she brushed her teeth and clipped her now-dry hair up in a couple of strong hair claws, Carina slipped on her new Christmas sweater. It was a perfect match with her favorite black jeans and ever-present boots.

"I feel like a teenager," she whispered to the ginger kitty as she peeked in to make certain he was asleep. "Not really sure if I like that feeling or not." She pulled on her jacket and strolled out into the dim afternoon. The reading would be starting in about thirty minutes, but she wasn't worried about getting a seat. She didn't want to sit close to other people. After her battle with Covid, crowds still made her nervous. All the chairs should be for the kiddos anyway.

She caught a glimpse of her face in the car window as she opened the door. Her color was high, and she felt a little nervous. But she told herself everything would be okay. By the time she attended the story time, Aaron would probably be landing. A couple hours after that, he would be here. In Crossbow. She couldn't wait.

CHAPTER 19

'TWAS THE NIGHT BEFORE ...

MAIN STREET WAS PACKED FOR THE READING. CARINA PARKED AND walked, just like the day before. The buzz of the crowd seemed muted by the falling snow.

When she reached the gazebo, she could hear Dr. Lance thanking everyone for coming, explaining that the Christmas Eve church service at St. John's down the block would be held early, immediately following the reading. "Apparently we have a bit of a squall headed our way."

The kids all cheered.

"Liable to blow Santa right on into the village," he joked. When he glanced up and saw Carina, he waved and then began the story just like the night before. Only this time, there were live actors in the nativity scene, along with a small donkey and fat, white sheep. The gazebo was full.

Carina couldn't tell if the Baby Jesus was live, or a life-like doll. She hoped it was a doll since the weather seemed to be growing colder by the moment.

Even though Dr. Lance went through the story rather quickly, it still felt every bit as magical as the night before and once again, the children almost said the poem by themselves. But this time, instead of bringing out the little reindeer for the kids to pet, a large old-fashioned sleigh appeared. It appeared to have regular rubber tires, like a flatbed trailer, hidden behind the wooden cutout runners of a sleigh.

Decked out with opulent red paint and seats, the sleigh driver, Santa in all his white-bearded-glory, looked suspiciously like Elston. As adults gathered and stacked the folding chairs and hot cocoa mugs, the kids were given turns on the sleigh. Pulled by a matched set of horses with jingle bells on their harnesses, the sleigh went up Main and down again.

Dr. Lance made certain every child got a ride. While this was going on, the nativity actors loaded the donkey and sheep into a covered stock trailer, and without adieu, they disappeared down the road pulled by an F-250 with giant tires. Everything ran like a well-oiled machine on fast forward due to the coming snow.

"That must be some weather they're expecting," Carina said as she finished her complimentary cocoa.

"Yes," Bonnie said. "It isn't certain yet. But once you've been through a few winters in the mountains you learn to prepare. Sometimes it sneaks in under the radar. Better safe than sorry, as the old saying goes."

Carina felt a bit of trepidation. "My son is flying into Denver just about now. Do you think—"

"He'll be fine," Bonnie said with a reassuring pat. "We've got a couple hours yet."

Carina trusted Bonnie. She wouldn't tell her it was okay if it was not. "Maybe I'd better skip the church service and head on back to the cabin."

"Oh, that won't be necessary," Dr. Lance said from behind her. "We've talked to Father Brown. It was his idea to move the service up. He guarantees a shortened version." He laughed. "But he promises to make up for it on Sunday."

Bonnie and Carina chuckled and helped pull the carts of chairs and the trays of mugs across the street to The Brewery. "I love how everything is so concentrated here on Main Street," Carina said. "So cozy, just like the cabin."

"I understand Max is coming to stay at the cabin when he arrives."

Carina glanced up at the vet's face as he spoke, but it was in shadow. She couldn't read his expression. "Well, I believe he said he would rent a car at the airport when he arrives. I know that's what my Aaron is doing. Boys, they just refuse to be without their own wheels." She smiled, hoping to take the sting out of the fact that Max might be coming to the cabin rather than to his dad's house.

It was actually the first time she'd heard about that. The last time she'd messaged with Max he had thought he would have his dad's empty house to himself. Maybe he had changed his mind after his dad contacted him.

They were at the back door of The Brewery now, handing off the chairs to a busboy who promised to push them back to the storage unit. "Thank you," Bonnie said. "I'll load these in the dishwasher and then we can all go on to St. John's together."

"Yes, ma'am," the teenager replied.

Dr. Lance held open the double doors so Carina and Bonnie could steer the cart of cups inside. "I'll be right back," he said. "Let me help Trey get the chairs stowed away."

"Thanks," Bonnie said.

They slid the large plastic trays into the stainless-steel dishwasher, pulled the door down to enclose them, and that was that. They heard the rush of hot water begin, so they went back outside to wait for Dr. Lance.

"Will you guys open the restaurant at all tonight?"

Bonnie shook her head. "Not now. Ordinarily we would have remained open until time for the late service, lots of folks stop in for a bite after the reading and before the service, but since everything has been moved up, we will go ahead and close. We don't want to tempt anyone to stay in town afterward, you know."

"Ready?" Dr. Lance asked as he and Trey came around the corner.

The women nodded and they all walked across the street together.

~

INSIDE THE CHURCH, CARINA GAZED ON THE CROWDED NAVE WITH dismay. She hadn't relayed her months-long hospital stay to either Dr. Lance or Bonnie, so they had no way of knowing how nervous a large group made her.

"Not really caring for the closeness in here," Dr. Lance said.

"I hear that," Trey agreed. "My folks are way down in front."

Bonnie elbowed Carina gently. "Dr. Lance had Covid a while back, doesn't really like to be immersed in crowds without a good mask. I think that's why he decided not to fly to Hawaii. Close quarters on the plane for eight hours, you know?" She pulled four N-95s out of her pocket and handed one to Carina, one to Trey, and one to the good doctor. The other, she placed on her own face. "Don't worry," she said. "These are brand new. I just opened a box today. Had a feeling we might need them."

Carina pulled it on and gave Bonnie a quick, side-arm hug. "You don't know how much this means to me."

Trey thanked her and went to sit with his parents.

"Are you ladies exhausted?" Dr. Lance asked.

What a funny question, Carina thought, shaking her head. "Not even close."

"Good. Bonnie?"

The sweet woman also shook her head.

"Excellent," he said. "Then follow me. I see an out of the way spot near the side door. There are no chairs or pews, but at least we will not be elbow-to-elbow with the masses. It's going to be a short service anyway."

"Sounds like a great plan," Carina murmured. And so they went, the three of them, and stood and sang and prayed and answered the priest when the service called for responses, and then they were all given candles to light as symbols of the birth of Jesus and the light he brought into the world.

Carina felt at home even though the three of them seemed apart from the main body of worshippers. She gazed around at the elegant atmosphere. The stained-glass windows, the altar with its beautiful gold and white cloth, even the brilliant red of the poinsettias on the altar steps, provided a festive, yet holy, air to the already magnificent church.

The lighting of the Christ candle, in the center of the advent wreath, brought a sense of quiet joy that truly surprised her. When the eucharist was brought forth, Carina realized how much she'd missed attending services.

The three of them remained in their corner, waiting their turn, until all the others had gone up to the front to take communion.

"I'm so glad we all came together," Dr. Lance said as Carina and Bonnie returned to where he waited in their corner. "And that El was able to find us over here in the corner."

Bonnie's husband grinned. "The sleigh is parked outside. There are a few children who didn't get to ride so I will make sure everyone gets a turn before I put it away."

Bonnie leaned in and whispered something in his ear.

He grinned. "Nope," he said. "I came to the early service this morning and took communion." He planted a sweet kiss on top of her hair. "I'll be home soon. No worries."

He left to make certain the horses were okay with everyone coming out of the church and starting up their vehicles, so Carina, Bonnie, and the vet strolled toward the door as the rest of the congregation were offering handshakes and Merry Christmases to one another.

"It was a lovely service," Carina said as the doctor ushered them out the side door. "Thank you for including me." She noticed the snowfall had grown quite a bit heavier although it still wasn't what she would think of as a "squall."

Dr. Lance took Carina's elbow. "You are very welcome. I noticed you don't have snow tires on the Subaru."

Carina's head popped up. "You're right, I don't." And then she thought, *and that wasn't very smart, was it? Drive to a ski resort in December without snow tires? I should win some kind of award. Stupidest human, perhaps.*

She continued mentally berating herself as they walked Bonnie back across to The Brewery where she would wait for Elston to put the sleigh and horses away.

"I have a thought," the vet said.

Carina looked at him, pressing her key fob starter at the same time.

"Why don't I ride out to the cabin with you, since both our sons are supposed to come in tonight, then I could ride back to my place with Max. I plan to use that excuse to make him stay with me … is that awful?"

Carina said, "I think that's a wonderful idea. To be honest, I'm getting a bit anxious about this weather. Everyone keeps saying it will get worse and worse." She pulled her jacket a little closer around her throat. "Is there a highway report we can look at, to find out about the road accessibility from Denver?"

Dr. Lance opened her door, then hesitated. "Would you prefer I drive out to the cabin? You can look at the weather and highway report on our local news app on my phone."

Carina handed over the keys to the Subaru. "Thank you. That sounds good." She took a deep breath and tried to relax. All the good feels from the church service began to come back as she settled into the passenger seat.

Dr. Lance was a careful driver, thank goodness, because the snow was falling much thicker and faster, like a white curtain instead of a loose feather pillow.

"At least there's no sleet to ice up the roads," he said as they made their way through town, "and this Christmas music on the radio makes it seem as if we're in a giant snow globe."

Carina watched the colorful store fronts as they passed by. "The Christmas lights are so beautiful through the falling snow. It makes me nostalgic for something. A bygone era, perhaps."

He nodded. "It makes me want to be a kid again, that's for sure."

Carina smiled. "That's why you make certain all the kids have a wonderful Christmas."

He shrugged. "It's the least I can do. I love this place."

"It is rather magical, isn't it?"

The doc agreed. "I can't imagine living anywhere else."

They drove the rest of the way in silence, only occasionally commenting on the beautiful, snow-laden branches of pines, or the way the soft snow swirled from one side of the road to the other as a gust of wind swept down from the mountain.

Even though the snow fell steadily, they had no trouble getting to the cabin.

Dr. Lance drove to the garage without asking, and then mentioned, just as Max had done, that a spotlight was needed to light the way from garage to house. "Actually," he said, "I think it would be nice to have a covered walkway from the garage right to the backdoor. It isn't that far, and it would be so nice when it rained or—like now—when it snows. Maybe even a heated walk to keep it from freezing over."

"That sounds expensive." She thought about Max saying he might give the property to his in-laws.

"Probably. I just wonder if it would add to the rental value."

Carina unlocked the back door, and they went in together,

pulling off their boots and placing them on the long runner, hanging their jackets on the colorful pegs above.

"I'll build up the fire—" he began.

"While I check on The Gingerbread Man," she finished.

They both laughed.

"Make yourself at home," she said.

By the time she'd gone to the bathroom to powder her nose and brush her hair, Dr. Lance had made up the fire and settled himself into the corner of the sofa. The Christmas tree twinkled merrily.

She heated the kitten's bottle and placed it and the tube of paste on the coffee table. Then she plucked the baby out of his bed, swaddled him in his little blanket, and carried him to the sofa.

Dr. Lance had his head down, reading her journal by the light of the fire.

Feral Story

A Time of Dying

Baby Gray used to sleep right there, on that cushioned chair by the back door. At first it would be him and his sister, Little Blackie, named after the ill-fated pony in the movie, True Grit.

Little Blackie was friendly. It made my heart smile every time I walked out on the back patio and that little feral cat came running to meet me. Pretty soon she had Baby Gray running to meet me, too. He'd only come halfway and stop, leery of all people, not just me.

But not Little Blackie. She'd run right up and bump my legs. When I put the food in the bowl in the shade of the upright cistern, she would start in right away, purring and eating at the same time.

She was fearless.

Her mother, I called her Mama Cat, was the one I'd first started feeding. I'd seen her skulking around, hunting mice and birds, thin as a rail and wild as the wind except for her round little pregnant belly hanging down.

I never intended to start feeding her until the day I saw her dark shape dash across the road followed by four little puff balls doing their best not to get left behind. *They grow fast*, I remember thinking. The last time I saw her, she was still pregnant.

The next day I began putting scraps of meat in the shade of the cistern, watching from the kitchen window.

Mama Cat found the food right away. She attacked it as if she were starving. It wasn't long before the little ones were following her to the scrap bowl, too.

At first there were four. Little Blackie, Baby Gray, Cali-the-calico, and a precious black and white Tuxedo I called Tux. No one ever said I was original.

Tux and Cali were the first to disappear. I'm certain coyotes or foxes got them, maybe even the hawks that circled overhead. Or it could have been one of the huge feral tom cats I would see from time to time. There was no way to know for sure. I just hoped my feeding them hadn't made it worse.

Was I attracting predators the way hunters attract deer to feed stands? I didn't think so, I tried to only put out the amount they could eat at one time. Besides, they had to eat something, and once I got them tamed, I could take them to the vet and have them spayed and neutered.

I couldn't stop now.

Little Blackie was half grown. She bumped my legs and practically waited by the back door for me.

Then she was gone, too.

Baby Gray slept on the cushioned deck chair a few times by himself, but he appeared so forlorn it broke my heart. When he tried to follow Mama Cat back to the tractor shed where I suspect they were born, she would hiss at him and drive him away.

I wondered if she could already be pregnant again. If so, was she simply worried about the new ones she would have? After all, Baby Gray was a tom. It probably wouldn't be long before he started the aggressive behaviors of the other feral toms. In fact, one of them was probably his father.

Damn. Life is hard. He was little more than a baby himself, now he *was all alone. He and his sister had been so close, snuggling together on the old chair, chasing birds and climbing the dead tree near the fence. I fancied I could see the bewilderment in his bright eyes when his mother hissed and showed him her teeth.*

I wanted to tame him but whatever had taken his sister had made him even more wary of me. He would come to the bowl and eat, but only if I stayed a good distance away. Maybe I'll try one of those humane traps ... get him to the vet that way.

~

DR. LANCE CLOSED THE JOURNAL AS CARINA SAT ON THE OTHER end of the sofa. "I hope you don't mind," he said. "I didn't realize it was your private journal." He patted the now-visible cover. "I saw the title and got sucked right in. It sounds like a cautionary tale from one of the pet magazines we keep in the waiting room at the clinic."

"It is *technically* my journal," Carina replied, offering the kitten his bottle, "but you're right. It's sort of the rough draft of a story. I used to enjoy writing when I was younger." Along with taking photographs, she thought. But she didn't say so, instead, she glanced out the window, thinking over the time mentioned in the journal story. "That title sounds a little pompous now. 'A Time of Dying.'"

"It's certainly eye-catching. And appropriate." When he looked up, his eyes shimmered with empathy. "Is it your home? The place you are writing about?"

She wiped a dot of milky formula from The Gingerbread Man's face. "My dad's. I stayed with him after his second stroke." She wondered how much she should tell him about Max. "I actually wrote that to share with your son." Carina waited for his reaction.

He raised shaggy eyebrows. "For Max?"

Carina nodded. "It was an assigned exercise in our grief

group. To write something that would bring out the feels as the kids say nowadays, but I intended to clean up the passive language and run it by Max before sharing with the whole group." She laughed a bit. "Some folks can be … quirky. Or maybe I have trust issues." Again, the self-effacing laugh. "Not with Max, though. We connected right away. Perhaps because he's going to be a doctor. Or maybe because he's just *genuine*. I mean, we've all suffered losses—"

"Yes, he mentioned the grief group."

"It's online," Carina replied. "I know how iffy that sounds, but it's a private group, recommended by one of my rehab therapists."

Carina expected him to ask about the need for rehab. She held the kitten's bottle in one hand while her other hand smoothed a corner of the soft blanket into a perfect triangle point on her knee, her fingers caressing the fleecy fabric.

She continued about the story. "It *was* a time of dying. Maybe *the* time of dying. First my mom, then my sister—my only sibling —and then all the kittens. I even found Baby Gray lying beside the water bowl one evening. I guess it was an illness. There wasn't a mark on him." She cleared her throat, determined to make him understand her connection with Max. "Eventually even Little Mama was killed. I walked the fields until I found her remains in the far corner of the acreage." A tear tracked down the side of her nose, unheeded.

Dr. Lance grimaced, slowly shook his head. "Nature is cruel." He shook his head. "People who abandon cats think they can care for themselves. They should read your story."

Carina nodded. "It was horrible. And then I lost my dad." She half-smiled. "But I can't really write about him, yet. Just the poor kitties. I even lost my fatcat at home, my Moochi, about six months after my hospital stay for Covid."

As if on cue, The Gingerbread Man let out a tiny mew. His bottle was done. "Time for a bit of paste," she said.

Dr. Lance rubbed the baby's head with his forefinger. "Funny how this one found you."

Carina smeared the paste on her finger and glanced out the picture window. "It was definitely a surprise." She thought about finding the tiny near-frozen kitten that first morning. "A miracle I even heard the little thing." She shook her head, then murmured, "I hope the boys are safe. The snow is coming down so much thicker. Should they have called by now?"

Dr. Lance stood and walked to the window. He was so tall he had to stoop. "Max is levelheaded. He knows the route like the back of his hand. If he thinks it isn't safe, he will find them a place to stay in Denver."

Carina tried to mirror his positive outlook, but if Max was the levelheaded one, why on earth hadn't he spoken to his dad in so long? They both seemed so *nice*. So caring. She sighed. "It's nice of Max to hang around and wait on Aaron's flight. I was certainly glad to get that text message. But are you sure they shouldn't have called by now?" She laughed at herself when she realized she'd just asked that question.

The doc turned and laid a hand on her shoulder. "The storm and the mountains make mobile phones dicey. Please, don't worry." He reclaimed his previous corner of the sofa.

"I won't," she said.

The vet raised an eyebrow again. "I think you capitulated too easily."

"Alfred says worry is my middle name." She couldn't help wondering how he was spending his Christmas Eve.

Stroking the tiny ginger kitty with one finger, Dr. Lance said, "I think you've got a baby tom here. Look at the width of that head."

"I thought so, too," Carina agreed. "Bonnie said most ginger cats are males, right?"

"Right," he said. "Will you take the little guy back to Texas when you go?"

"Oh, of course, and when he's big enough, I'll take him in for his shots and his neuter and anything else he needs."

Dr. Lance nodded. "He may need a friend, another cat to keep him company. Loneliness is a hard task master."

Carina heard the melancholy note in the vet's voice. "It certainly is. Being alone is tough … but you seem to handle it well." She hoped she wasn't assuming too much or placing a burden on a burgeoning friendship. Especially in addition to the religious talk yesterday. "In fact, you've made me see that I need to make some changes when I get back home."

He looked at her quizzically.

"I've gotten too wrapped up in myself. In my family—as odd as that sounds—I think it's time I go back to work, part time at least, and get back out into the community. I'm also going to see about delivering food to shut-ins for Meals on Wheels. They always need helpers. And I seem to need to help. I guess we all do, in one way or another."

He chuckled, but softly. "You're very astute. I think you see right through me."

Startled, Carina glanced up. His eyes were kind, as always. "I see what everyone sees when they look at you. A kind man who cares for animals and children." She smiled. "I really loved the kids' faces when you read to them. Made me miss my old classroom."

Dr. Lance stood and walked back to the window. "The kids do love it, don't they? Heaven knows I've enjoyed doing it for years, so tell me Ms. Carina Pinner, why can't I connect with my own son?"

Carina hesitated, wondering if he'd somehow read her mind. "Maybe he just needed some space to grow. Maybe he's ready now. After all, he's the one who arranged the cabin for all of us, himself included. Such an amazing gesture." When she spoke those words, she thought of Alfred, and his simple generosity.

Like the way he took care of the car for her, always making

certain it was up to date on insurance and oil changes and everything that seemed minor until someone let it lapse, the way she probably would have if left to her own devices.

He spoils me, she thought. And yet I always expect more. And now he's working long hours away from home to try and retire early so we can travel to all the places I've always longed to see. I've been so selfish, she thought. But that's another thing that will change when I get home.

She put another dot of flesh colored protein paste on her fingertip and watched as the kitten went to town. He grasped it with his tiny paws and pulled it even closer to his face, licking every bit of it off. "I hope it's okay to give him a little more," she said. "He seems very hungry this time."

Dr. Lance sat back down beside them. "He certainly does love it, and you yourself observed how quickly kittens grow."

Carina nodded. "Think I should start him on regular kitten food soon?"

"When you get back home, I think you can try mixing hot water with some milk-flavored kitten chow. While he's taking his bottle, the kitten chow will cool and get soggy, and you can mash it on the saucer with a fork. After his bottle, set him on the floor with the saucer. He will make a big mess at first, but isn't that what we all do until we figure things out?"

Carina smiled. "Yes, we do," she said. "Yes, we do."

CHAPTER 20

WAITING

The Gingerbread Man fell asleep before he'd even licked all the paste off Carina's finger.

Dr. Lance looked on indulgently. "It's so nice to have a full tummy, isn't it, little one?" He caressed the kitten's head again.

Carina smiled and took the baby to the bathroom to wet a washcloth with warm water for his "bath". Afterward, she tucked him back into his bed and went to the kitchen to wash out the bottle.

When she came back to the living room, Dr. Lance stood in front of the picture window again, hands clasped behind his back. "Snowflakes big as feathers," he said. "Thick and fast."

"Is it a blizzard?" Carina heard the tremor in her voice.

"Nothing alarming. If it turns wet and begins blowing sideways, then we'll worry." He moved over to allow her to stand beside him.

She checked her phone for the umpteenth time. "I just wish they'd send us another message."

They stood side by side for a few more seconds, watching the falling snow silence the world. "It's so beautiful," she said. "I love the way the light from the windows makes those warm squares out on the snow—"

"And the fireplace behind us, and the twinkling Christmas lights. Just like a storybook." Dr Lance rocked on his heels a bit. "I heard Andrea's folks are wanting Max to give it back to them."

"What would you do?"

He shrugged, still watching out the window.

Carina could barely discern their reflections in the glass.

"What would I do?" he echoed. "Good question. I guess it would depend on my heart. If I couldn't let it go, I wouldn't. At least not for the time being."

"Do you ever encounter her parents around town?"

The vet shook his head. "Not much. They are snowbirds nowadays. When winter comes, they head south, to Florida, I believe."

Carina leaned forward, the better to see the end of the drive where it intersected Paper Lane. "The intersection has disappeared."

Dr. Lance nodded. "So I see. I guess I should have brought the Jeep. It has a snowplow attachment on the front."

Carina turned to face him. "That's right. I remember seeing it." She laughed. "I can't believe you left it and drove mine."

He ducked his head, a soft flush of embarrassment creeping up his neck. "I can't believe it either." Then he glanced back at the window. "Truth is, I haven't been thinking as clearly as I might. It isn't often I get to squire a pretty woman around town for everyone to see."

Carina had no reply. Her own face felt warm. She dared not meet his gaze. What a bold thing to say, she thought. But what else is new? He always speaks his mind. She decided he didn't mean anything by it, especially after he said, "Besides, Elston and I were using it to clear the path for the sleigh rides and after I spoke to Max, I thought it would be a good excuse for him to have to drive me home."

Carina nodded, recalling how he'd admitted it once already. To change the subject, she said, "Is it unusual to have a snowstorm of this magnitude pop up out of nowhere? I've been watching the forecast and I didn't see this coming."

He walked to the recliner, sat down, put his feet up. "It happens from time to time. I'm just thankful we didn't have any overnight boarders at the clinic."

Carina had been so wrapped up in her own worries, she hadn't even thought about his. "What would you do?"

"I'd try to call Bonnie. If that wasn't possible, I would get there somehow. But it might be more difficult this time. Since her husband has my snowplow."

Laughter erupted from Carina's throat. "Sounds like you've been down that road before, so to speak."

He smiled and leaned back even further. "I don't worry too much. I think that always got on Max's nerves. But I believe things will work out, in time. If given the chance."

Carina sat on the sofa. "And I'm just the opposite. Worry, worry, worry."

He didn't reply. It seemed the good doctor had drifted off to sleep.

Carina leaned her own head back and took a deep breath. It felt good to be still for a moment.

HALF AN HOUR LATER, CARINA OPENED HER EYES. IT TOOK A second for her to understand where she was and who was snoring in the corner.

She smoothed her hair and sat up straighter. "I dozed off," she said. "I never thought I would, but I must have." She glanced at Dr. Lance.

He stretched and sat up a bit.

"I can't believe we fell asleep," she said. "What woke me? Was it you?"

Dr. Lance pushed the recliner's footrest down.

"It wasn't me." He covered a yawn with his fist. "Didn't *you* wake *me*?"

Carina glanced at the window just as the sound came again. "Is that an engine and ... *sleigh bells*?" She jumped up and rushed to the window. "It's your Jeep," she cried. "I see the snowplow on the front—"

The vet made his way to the window just as her hand flew to her throat. "Max is driving it. And look," she pointed to the scene, "behind the Jeep is the horse drawn sleigh. I *did* hear sleighbells." She gave a little cry. "Is that my Annabelle getting out of the passenger side? Can it be?" She got so excited she hugged Dr. Lance around his lean middle, making him laugh.

Still laughing, he said, "But who are all those little creatures piling out from under the lap blankets of the sleigh?"

Carina's mouth fell open. "My grandbabies! Oh, and there's an SUV, too. It's Heath, with Gia in the passenger seat."

Dr. Lance clapped his hands like a little kid. "Thank goodness the snow let up a little."

Tears flooded Carina's eyes. "It's *all* of my babies. Even the grown ones. There's Romy and Aaron getting out of the sleigh behind the kids. I can't believe they rode it all the way from town." She raised her hand to wave just as Aaron scooped up a handful of soft snow, fashioned a quick sphere, and flung it toward the window. It fell far short but made her smile.

She grabbed her jacket before yanking open the door and yelling, "Merry Christmas!"

Elston waved and yelled, "Ho, ho, ho!"

"Santa! What a wonderful gift you've brought. Won't you come in for something hot to drink?"

He shook his head and jerked his thumb at the snowplow

attachment on the Jeep beside him. "Santa's got to get back before the road closes again. Horses don't fly. Only reindeer can do that." He turned and waved to the kids. "Happy Christmas to all…"

"And to all a goodnight!" the kids yelled back, waving.

And then they were headed for the door.

Annabelle was the first to reach her, having come from around the Jeep on the run. "Mama!" she grasped Carina in a tight hug. "We wanted to surprise you."

Carina swiped at her streaming eyes. "You did surprise me. The best surprise *ever*." She watched as the kids realized Santa was leaving. They broke from their run toward the cabin and headed down the drive behind him, still waving, yelling goodbye.

The sleigh bells jingled merrily as Elston made a wide turn back onto Paper Lane. The snow still fell, but lighter now. Back to small feathers again, widely spaced.

Carina held Annabelle at arm's length. "How did this happen? How did you meet up with Max?"

Annabelle laughed. To Carina it sounded as tinkly as the sleighbells. "You'll have to talk to Her Royal Highness, your *other* daughter, she's the one who planned this whole scheme." She grinned and traipsed back down the steps to help unload the luggage.

The grandchildren rushed to the porch where Lance stood waiting behind Carina. Snow dusted everyone's hair. "Gan!" they cried, wrapping themselves around her. "Ganny!"

"Babies!" she exclaimed. "My sweet grandbabies. Look how you've grown. My goodness." She began trying to usher them toward the open front door, but it was useless. All four—Heather, Philly, Jake Jr., and Little Sean, the toddler—held her in their shivery embrace, hugging and squeezing, saying, "Where's Gampy? Where is he? Is Gampy inside?"

Carina peeled Little Sean off her knee and hoisted him to her hip, hugging and kissing and patting and squeezing everyone at once. "My goodness, how tall you've all become. Look at Sean.

Not even a baby anymore." She slid an arm around Heather, the oldest, and started back to the door. "Come in, everyone, come into this beautiful cabin."

The two middle children clasped her around the waist, to the best of their ability, and together the lot of them stumbled and fumbled their way into the cabin. "I could not have asked for a better Christmas," Carina said, but once again, the kids interrupted.

"Isn't Gampy here?"

Carina couldn't tell who asked that time, all the little voices going at once, but then Heather broke from her side and ran to the clothes basket near the fireplace. "You got a kitten?" She plucked the baby out of his bed and snuggled him under her chin.

"I found him on the back porch the very first morning after I arrived." She didn't have to tell Heather how to hold him, or to be careful. Romy's twelve-year-old daughter had already raised kittens and chickens and puppies and hamsters … and three little siblings. Carina smiled. "You'll make a wonderful mommy someday," she said.

"Oh, Gan," Heather ducked her blonde head. "You know I'm never having kids."

Carina laughed. "I forgot. International journalist, traveling the world with one laptop and two pair of shoes."

Heather nodded, paying no attention to anything but the fuzzy ginger kitten nestled in her arms.

The other kids turned Carina loose and tumbled through the house in search of the kitchen and bathroom, the two most important rooms in any home. She turned to find Romy, Heath, and Gia coming through the door with suitcases and backpacks. "Put them anywhere." She indicated the other side of the living room with a wave of her arm. "I can't believe you're all here."

The three of them placed the bags in a pile and turned to embrace her. "Oh, Mom," Romy said. "What a beautiful Christmas tree. And look at this place. It's absolutely amazing."

Gia echoed her sentiments while Heath simply leaned down and allowed Carina to hug him around the neck. "Dad didn't make it?" he asked quietly.

Carina shook her head, willing her silly eyes to stop leaking. "He said he can't make it," she replied. "But you all are here. Thank God, you made it safely. I thought you weren't coming." She turned to look for Annabelle who had stayed outside to help Max.

They appeared to be in deep discussion about something when Carina stuck her head out the door. She couldn't help but think what a cute couple they made. But she'd completely forgotten Dr. Lance. He stood in the overhang of the porch, quiet as a statue.

"I cannot believe this," she said, looking out at the snowbank pushed aside by the plow on his Jeep. "Did you know?"

He shook his head and that's when Carina noticed the expression on his face. "Why, Lance, are you okay? That is your Max, isn't it?" She worried there had been some mistake. "He's the one who brought all my babies to me." When there was no reply, she tried again. "Have I got it all wrong, is it not your Max?"

Once again, he shook his leonine head. "I knew Max and Aaron were coming. I didn't know about any of the others." He swiped at his own eyes. "But look at my Max. My boy. I wonder how he came up with Elston and the Jeep."

Just then, the young couple turned to the porch. "Hey, Dad," Max called. "Hope you don't mind." He gestured toward the Jeep. "I remembered you had this old thing." He looked up at the falling snow. "Thought we might need it." Chuckling under his breath, he went on, "When you didn't answer your phone, I called Bonnie to make sure everything was all right."

Lance's hand went immediately to his hip pocket. "Where is my phone?" He looked at Carina who shrugged.

From inside the house, Jake came running. "Sean knocked this off in the water, but not the potty just the sink. We were washing our hands like we're supposed to do after we use the bathroom." He held up a drippy iPhone.

Carina covered her grin. "Umm, could this be yours?"

Dr. Lance took it, gingerly, from Jake's fingers. "Guess I left it there a few minutes ago."

The boy glanced at Carina. "I hope you have some rice, Gan."

"It just so happens I bought some for the broccoli rice casserole." She ushered everyone inside and pointed the vet toward the cupboard where the rice was stored. Then she turned around to hug her last two kids. "Oh, my goodness. You two are a sight for sore eyes. Annabelle, shame on you for never calling or texting your mom back." She gave her a playful swat on the shoulder followed by a giant kiss on the cheek. "And Max. Look at you. Just like on FaceTime. I can't believe you brought the whole herd."

The lanky young doctor laughed, and Carina was almost certain he blushed just the way his dad had done earlier. "It was Romy's idea," he said. "She called to check me out and wow," he wiped a hand across his brow comically. "Did she ever check me out? She gave me a thorough investigation, got references from my professors, my mentor, even asked for my dad's number." He glanced at the ground. "I gave her the clinic number. Bonnie answered instead. Dad was in surgery."

Carina looked around, prepared to chastise the vet for not telling her. "I can't believe he didn't tell me."

Max laughed. "No, don't be mad at him. Bonnie was so happy to hear that we were all coming, she agreed not to tell him. She knew he would never keep it secret."

Carina smiled at the immense deception the kids had gone through to surprise her. She had been completely fooled.

CHAPTER 21

QUESTIONS

ANNABELLE LINKED HER ARM THROUGH HER MOTHER'S AND together they carried several suitcases up the steps and into the cabin. Max followed with a gigantic rolling bag almost three feet tall. Carina wondered about the huge case but didn't say anything. After all, four kids would require a lot of clothing. Surely the case didn't belong to Max, a young, single man living on his own. *Nice of him to help out so much,* she thought. *One thing's for certain, he won't be alone with his thoughts* this *Christmas.*

That made her think about how everything must appear to Max. This was his cabin. What must he be thinking? His first Christmas here, without his wife.

Max walked inside and stopped, looked around. Carina saw him appear to take a deep breath, his fingers tightening on the handle of the wheelie.

She pulled away from Annabelle. "Go look around," she whispered, patting her youngest on the arm.

Annabelle glanced at Max, immediately assessed the situation, then nodded almost imperceptibly.

Carina went to Max, took his arm, unclenched his fingers from the wheeled case—which Annabelle took—and led him to the sofa in front of the fireplace. "Are you okay?" she asked. "This has to be difficult."

"I'm okay," he said, not looking very okay at all. His face appeared drawn and pale.

Carina felt she should get him talking. "Is it very different from the last time you were here?" She wanted to take his hands, they looked so cold, but as close as they had been in the grief group, and on the phone, in person felt different. She barely touched his arm instead. "Is it too much?" she asked. "Was this a mistake?"

That seemed to pull him out of himself a bit. "What? Too much? Oh, no, no." He smiled at last. "This is wonderful." His voice seemed quiet, serious. "Andrea would've loved it." He patted her arm the way she had done his. "This is what she longed for, a large family, tons of kids running around, dropping phones in toilets—"

Carina didn't correct him about the toilet, she simply said, "She would have fit right in with my bunch, wouldn't she?"

"Yes," he said. "She certainly would've. It's good to see the cabin filled with so much happiness." He glanced around. "And it looks beautiful, really nice." He gave her a brief, side armed hug. "Thank you for doing this."

"Thank me? No, dear boy, thank *you*. It's your cabin, I've even dragged your dad into it." She laughed and glanced at Dr. Lance trapped in the middle of the children in the suddenly much-smaller kitchen. They were all crowded around Heather and The Gingerbread man.

"What've they got there?" Max asked.

"That's the reason I met up with your dad. It's a kitten that appeared half-starved and frozen on the back porch the first morning I was here. I guess I haven't had a chance to tell you about him yet. Would you like to see? I think he's probably had enough attention from the kiddos for a minute."

Max laughed. "Yes, let's rescue him."

Together, they went into the kitchen.

"Did you find the rice?" Carina asked Dr. Lance.

His gaze skated off her and landed on Max, gently, briefly, as if a harsh glance might be too much, as if his son might be made of glass. "Yes, Philomena—er, Philly—did. She also showed me how to pour the rice in a bowl and submerge my phone in it. Supposed to dry it out."

Carina laughed. "Yep, the kids have had almost as much experience drying out phones as they've had in raising kittens. Or so I've heard." She looked around for Romy, but she had gone upstairs with Annabelle to check out the rest of the cabin.

"Hey, kiddos," Carina opened her arms like a mother hen opening her wings to a flock of chicks, "let's make this baby his bottle and then tuck him back into his bed. You know these little ones need lots of rest to grow."

"Is his name really Gingerbread Man?" Little Sean asked. "That's a funny name for a kitty. Can't we call him Tom?"

"Tom sounds like a perfectly good name," Carina said. "And everyone needs a middle name, right?"

"Ginger Tom," Max said. "I like it."

The little boy grinned as she lured the bunch of them to the sink area to pour and heat the bottle. It was a little soon, but she didn't think it would hurt for the kitten to have an extra bedtime drink.

Max smiled and took that opportunity to move into the living room. He grasped the handle of the large, wheeled case and pulled it toward the Christmas tree where his dad now stood, gazing upon the kitchen scene.

Bits of conversation followed.

Carina couldn't hear exactly what was being said, but she caught a few words. "Need to talk ... glad you're here ... such a surprise ..." From the corner of her eye, Carina saw Max touch his dad's arm almost the same way she had touched his only a few moments earlier.

"Okay," she told the kids. "Heather will hold him, and I'll show y'all how to warm the bottle."

"We know, Gan," Philly said. "We raised a whole litter last year, just like you said. Remember?"

"That's right, of course you did." Carina continued demonstrating how to hold the tiny plastic bottle under the hot water tap, testing drops on her wrist every few seconds. "Okay," she said. "I believe it's just right. You know you always have to test it on the inside of your wrist just like you would with a real human baby." She smiled, knowing all of them had been breastfed, one of Romy's hard and fast rules.

"Oh, Mom!" Annabelle came down the stairs, speaking as she did. "What an adorable place. I'm so glad you and Max became friends."

Carina handed the bottle to Heather and made certain she knew how to squeeze a drop out and put it on the kitten's mouth to get him started. "I'm glad we did, too," she said. "And having you all here means so much." She spoke while putting a thin smear of protein paste on Jake's index finger for "Tom" to lick off.

Heath and Gia came in from the master suite. "This is amazing," he said.

"I was thinking you and Gia might be more comfortable in the guest quarters above the garage," Carina said.

Gia's face lit up. "Thank you, Mama. I appreciate that."

Carina blew her a kiss. "I remember being pregnant," she whispered. "It changes things."

Heath nodded, bobbing his head in mock exasperation. Gia elbowed him and he gave her a hug and dropped a kiss on top of her dark, shiny hair.

"I don't know how you can all look so wonderful after flying across the country and driving through a snowstorm with four kids—especially in a two-horse open *sleigh*."

"We did it for you, Mom," Romy interjected. "Plus, the kids

loved seeing the snow." She grinned. "Can you believe we arrived at the airport at the same time as Max?" Her smile turned into a sly, Cheshire cat grin.

Carina raised one eyebrow. "Funny how that worked out, o daughter of mine." She grabbed the grinning girl and hugged her and kissed her soundly—and loudly—on the cheek. "Thank you for checking him out and bringing him into the fold."

Everyone laughed. But they had all noticed Max and Lance speaking quietly near the tree. Carina also noticed that lots of gaily wrapped presents had appeared around the base of the tree. The big, wheeled suitcase stood gaping and empty. "This will be our best Christmas *ever*," she said. And then a picture of Alfred in a sparse hotel room flashed in her mind, showering her with guilt for her statement.

It was immediately followed by a second image of Alfred standing on the balcony of an apartment in downtown San Antonio, overlooking the famous River Walk, and the guilt melted away. In this picture he had a highball glass in one hand and a spatula in the other. On the grill before him, two T-bone steaks sizzled. They were his favorite. Even at Christmas.

"Gan!" Little Sean tugged at her pant leg. "My turn to hold kitty. Me."

Glad for the interruption, Carina reached down and brought the toddler up to her hip again. That last picture of Alfred had been painful. Especially the slinky laugh she imagined she'd heard in the background. "Here you go, sweetie. Let your sister finish feeding him, then we will give him a tiny bath, you and me, and tuck him back into his bed. How does that sound?"

"Can I help?" Philly asked. "I haven't held him yet."

"Me, too," Jake crowed. "Me, too."

"You got to let him lick the paste off your finger!" Philly said. "You've had a turn."

"Okay, kiddos," Carina said. "Everyone will get a turn. We

have to do this every three or four hours so there will be plenty of turns to go around."

"Thank God," Romy muttered good-naturedly.

Carina set Sean back on the floor and instructed him to follow her to the bathroom for a washcloth to bathe the kitten's belly. "Do we have to get him a bath every time he eats?"

"Yep," she said. "Being a mom is hard work."

Carina and little Sean cleaned the kitten and, with Philly and Jake's assistance, showed him the litter box—just in case—then tucked him back into his warm bed beside the fireplace.

She straightened just as Max gave his dad a brief hug. "I'd like that," she heard him say.

Dr. Lance turned to Carina, eyes moist. "Since we have the Jeep, Max and I are going back to town. He's agreed to stay with me tonight."

Carina smiled at another bit of manipulation, but since she truly believed everything happens for a reason, she had to believe this whole crazy trip had been needed to get father and son back together. *And get me out of my ongoing pity-party.* She pushed that last thought aside for later contemplation. Or a new journal topic.

Arms around her grandchildren, she smiled at the two men beside the tree. "I'll only let the two of you go if you are *certain* it's safe to drive."

They all turned to the window. The snow still fell, soft and light. "It will be fine with the plow," Dr. Lance said. "And we'll be back in plenty of time for Christmas dinner tomorrow."

Max leaned in and gave her a hug. "We haven't had time to catch up yet." He took her hands in his. "How are you doing?" His gaze bored into hers.

Carina felt the weight of his gaze and knew he was asking about her mental status. "Dear boy," she said, the words tumbling from her lips as they would have in print in their Facebook group. "This has been the best thing in the world." She glanced around at the cabin, now filled with the raucous sound of her loved ones. "You provided the best setting for me to get back to myself." She laughed at her own words. "And you brought my kiddos, too."

She turned loose of his hands and pressed her youngest grandchild to her side. "You and your father," she glanced at the kind vet, "are now members of our family."

Max shot a look at the group. "Thank you. I'm beginning to think something larger is at work here." He glanced at Dr. Lance. "Dad told me y'all have been spending time together. Perhaps you helped him see me in a new light."

Carina laughed. "I believe the good Lord is working to bring two wonderful men back together." She couldn't believe she'd been so bold, but in for a penny, as they say. "I think the world of you both."

Max laughed a little self-consciously. "I think the world of your family, too." His eye landed directly on Annabelle when he said that. But Carina didn't mention it. He wasn't at the place where teasing would be welcome. His grief was still too fresh.

Carina wouldn't be surprised if he'd taken a shine to her youngest daughter, though. Annabelle had a way about her. An inviting way that probably came from being out in the wilderness, having friends she could depend on. Life or death friends, she called them. She had high expectations and it showed.

Dr. Lance smiled. "We will see you tomorrow."

Carina nodded and opened the door. "We're all looking forward to it." She watched as the men made their way to the Jeep.

Dr. Lance got into the driver's seat and made some adjustments to the mirror and something on the dash. As soon as Max climbed into the passenger seat, Carina began to close the front door. She stopped when she noticed Dr. Lance turn left instead of turning right to leave the driveway. He waved when he went around the end of the cabin toward the garage.

Carina walked to the opposite side of the living room to peer out the other window as Dr. Lance drove the Jeep slowly down the straight-shot drive to the garage. Her pathway from when they came home from church had already been obscured by the fresh snow.

It took only two passes with the small plow attachment to reveal the driveway. He also made certain to extend the drive around the corner to the guest house stairs and then he did the same around the back of the house so the kids could step off the porch and follow the path to the guest house without wading through deep snow.

Carina pulled her phone from her pocket and sent Max a quick message. "Tell your dad thank you."

"No problem," he wrote back. "I hope it is still passable in the morning when they wake." He ended with a laughing Santa emoji.

Hard to believe tomorrow is Christmas, Carina thought, sliding the phone back into her pocket. And I haven't spoken to my husband. Should I be worried?

She turned to ask the kids' opinions on that question and was surprised to find them all plastered to the kitchen windows, watching Dr. Lance finesse the driveway.

"That was nice of him," she said. "He and his son are both so thoughtful—"

"When is the last time you spoke with Dad?" Romy interrupted, echoing Carina's own thoughts.

CHAPTER 22

STOCKINGS

"I was just about to ask you guys the same question." She waited a beat for someone to volunteer information, but no one said a word. Apparently, their dad had been completely incommunicado. "Well, to answer your question, I had a text from him saying he wasn't going to be able to make it for Christmas." Carina kept her voice low because she didn't trust how it might sound.

She saw Romy and Heath exchange glances over Gia's head. Annabelle was in the bathroom, and the kids had gathered under the tree, examining the names on the gifts.

"Where my 'tocking, Gan?" Little Sean asked, rubbing his eyes as he came to her. He glanced back at the two stockings hanging above the fireplace, hers and Aaron's.

Thinking quickly, she said, "I was interrupted in hanging them when I found this tiny kitten on my back porch."

That satisfied the tired boy, and he ran back to the kitten's basket beside the fire.

Carina hurried to her bedroom and dug out four thick socks, took them to the kitchen, and began to rummage through the cupboards. "Thank goodness I bought all this stuff yesterday," she told Romy. "I also had the cashier break a couple twenty-dollar bills into four tens. I was going to mail those, but this is even better." She took the cash out of her wallet and stuffed a bill into each kiddo's sock.

Romy laughed. "Mom's intuition. You've always had it."

Together they packed the makings for s'mores into individual sandwich bags and then stuffed them into the socks. "But how can we make them without skewers or something?" Romy asked.

"We'll find some sticks outside," Gia said. "We need to go put our bags in the guest quarters anyway. Surely we can find four clean twigs or something." She grabbed Heath by the arm. "I can't wait to see what our room looks like."

Carina continued rummaging through drawers in the kitchen. "Ah ha!" she said. "No need for twigs." She held up several kabob skewers. "These will do nicely."

Gia hesitated, halfway to the back door.

"No, no. You guys go ahead while the driveway is clear." She shooed at them with her hands as if shooing away a couple of birds.

"We'll be right back," Heath said. "Don't eat all those—"

Romy smacked him in the ribs. "Shh! It's a surprise, dummy."

Heath shot her a scathing look before grabbing a suitcase and duffle bag from the living room. He started out the kitchen door with Gia. Romy stuck her tongue out at him just as she'd always done when she was the bothersome little sister and he the over-protective big brother.

"Don't be too long," she said. "It's first come first served, as always." She smacked her lips and licked her fingertips as if they were sticky with marshmallow.

He reached back in and gave her shoulder a quick shove. "Brat," he teased.

"Sorehead," she laughed.

Carina watched her eldest and his lovely, dark-haired wife as they walked lightly through the still falling snow. Both had to stop and attempt to catch a few flakes on their tongues. Just as she'd done earlier.

Romy draped an arm around her mom's shoulders.

Carina patted the slender, hairdresser's hand. The one that could make anyone look magnificent with a pair of scissors and a blow dryer. "Thank you for checking out Max and getting everyone to come—"

Romy planted a smooch on the side of her face, knocking her glasses askew. "I needed this getaway, too. I just wasn't sure we could pull it off." She glanced out the window at Heath and Gia who had made it up the stairs to the apartment door. "Big brother sent us plane tickets, and little brother rented the SUV at the airport." She shook her head. "I have the best sibs in the world." She looked at her mom with a crooked smile. "And that Max is some guy, isn't he?"

Carina laughed, unsure if Romy meant to echo the "some pig" statement from Charlotte's Web or not. It had been one of her favorite sad books as a child. She'd always labeled her best reads by emotion instead of genre.

"You all right, honey?" The statement Romy had made about needing this getaway hadn't escaped her. She felt momentarily ashamed for falsely assuming they all thought only of themselves. She wanted to bluntly ask Romy about her husband, where he was, what had gone wrong, but she didn't have to.

"Big Sean went back home to his parents' house for a while," Romy said. "Apparently, he didn't *really* realize what he was getting into when he married me with the kids and all their schedules and what have you."

She dabbed her eyes with the pad of her thumb. "I thought he knew it was a three-ring circus, we'd been seeing each other for *months* before we married." Her voice hitched a little. "I thought he loved the chaos as much as I do. He says he just felt *thrust* into it." She looked down at her short, bitten fingernails. "Little Sean keeps asking when his daddy is coming back."

Wiping a stray tear from her daughter's cheek, Carina bit the tip of her tongue to keep from saying, *that fool knew you had three other kids when he married you. That's no excuse for running out on his family.* But that thought was quickly followed with *maybe getting to know each other over a few years would've been better than over a few months.* But she didn't let that slip out, either. Surely the girl knew her mistake by now. Someone once said if you do the same thing over and over it's no longer a mistake, it's a habit.

Carina didn't say that, either. She'd learned her lesson about speaking bluntly. Learned it the hard way when Romy was in college but not going to classes. After quitting completely to run off with her first husband, Carina had tried to tell her what a mistake she was making.

The girl wouldn't listen.

They'd ended up estranged for the better part of a year. And then the new marriage had begun to fray, and Romy had come home, pregnant and in tears.

Carina hugged her beautiful girl and took her hand. "Let's give it to God, shall we?"

Romy nodded. They'd never been regular church goers, more the Christmas and Easter sort of worshippers, but that had changed a bit after Carina had become nursemaid to her folks. Watching someone suffer and die can do that to a person. Either turn them away from their God or cause them to reach out for mercy and comfort.

Carina had chosen the latter even though, in her heart, she sometimes wondered if the personal growth and inward search had changed her *too* much in Alfred's eyes. Hadn't he been home a lot more before she'd turned nursemaid and born-again Christian?

She took a deep breath to concentrate on her girl. Why did Alfred keep creeping into every thought? Because you haven't prayed for resolution, a small inner voice said. Carina pushed the thought aside, to deal with later.

First things first.

She clasped both of Romy's hands. "Dear Heavenly Father, we thank you for your many blessings. Especially for getting us all here safely." Romy squeezed gently, to acknowledge the thought. "And we ask you, Father, to please shine your light and favor upon Sean and Romy and the children. Bring them back together if that is your will. Amen."

Romy also whispered, "Amen." She sniffled. "Thank you, Mom. I haven't been doing that enough lately."

Carina smiled and was about to remind Romy that she was the one who had brought Carina so much comfort after the unexpected death of her sister. "Just give it to God, Mom," Romy had said. And then she'd gone about creating a sweet photo collage with her aunt's favorite prayer in the center. She'd had it framed in ivory oak and it now sat upon Carina's fireplace mantle at home. And when Carina was sick with Covid, Romy and the kids had held nightly prayer sessions for her. And then Romy had listed her mother on every prayer chain in the metroplex.

She was about to remind Romy of how it had been *her* faith that had pulled Carina through many of the toughest times she'd ever known, but before she could say anything, the kids began to clamor for their s'mores. One of them had peeked into a stocking.

"Hey," Philly's tone was indignant. "How come Uncle Aaron has more in his stocking than we do?"

Carina had forgotten all about the lift tickets. "Well, sweetie," she said. "I didn't think the rest of you were coming." She glanced at Romy while chiding herself for forgetting to include the tiny Christmas aliens she'd bought in Roswell.

"Mo-om!" Philly said. "You should've told."

Romy rolled her eyes. "That would have spoiled the surprise, remember?"

Philly laughed. "Oh, yeah. That was the best part, the look on Gan's face."

Whew, Carina thought. Crisis averted. "Alright, I'm thinking of a reindeer name. One of Santa's …"

"Rudolph," they all yelled.

"No. It's not Rudolph."

"Dancer!"

"Prancer!"

"Comet!"

"Vixen!"

Carina laughed. "It was Comet!"

Jake Jr. jumped up and down. "I said Comet, that was me, I said Comet."

"Yes, you did." She began taking the sock-stockings back down. "You get to hand out the stockings. Everyone take a seat and Jake will bring yours to you." She was so thankful she'd had the inspiration to get the four ten-dollar bills and coloring books with crayons yesterday. And that their mom had the presence of mind to bring their gifts from home.

After Jake Jr. handed out the socks, and Romy made them all hold hands in a prayer acknowledging the birth of Jesus, the kids were allowed to dig in. The s'mores makings and crisp ten-dollar bills were a big hit. Heath and Gia could be heard coming in from the backyard, laughing and stamping the snow from their boots on the back porch.

"What's going on?" Heath bellowed. "Opening Christmas gifts without your Uncle Heath?" He plopped down beside Little Sean on the floor, pretending to eat his marshmallows and chocolate squares.

"Hey!" Sean yelped, grabbing his plastic baggie from his uncle.

"But it's Christmas Eve," Heath pretended to whine.

Sean appeared to think it over. "Okay … we can share."

Romy brought the skewers from the kitchen and handed them out. Little Sean took one and then also got one for his uncle. Heath hugged and kissed the stout little toddler and helped him thread the marshmallow onto the tip of the metal skewer. Gia sat down on the sofa behind them after locating a stack of Christmas napkins in the kitchen. "Pretty basket, Mom," Gia said. "Who are Terry and Cheyenne?"

"Oh, those are the cabin caretakers. They left that for me, and they really thought of everything, didn't they?"

Gia nodded and, napkin in hand, took Sean's graham cracker and chocolate square and held it ready to receive the gooey marshmallow as soon as it was warm and toasted brown. He'd looked a little worried when his aunt took the chocolate square out of the baggie, but when she smiled and laid it on the graham cracker, he decided to trust her.

All at once, there were four skewers thrust into the fireplace. Two marshmallows promptly fell off and plopped into the fire. "Oh, my," Carina said, handing each child another marshmallow. "I hope that will burn away. I never thought about the mess."

Everyone laughed. They knew how their mom hated "a mess" of any kind. Even their camping trips had to be neat, tidy affairs. "Remember when Mom would inspect our tents on our camping trips?" Aaron asked.

"Like we were in the Army or something," Romy said, rolling her eyes.

Annabelle shrugged. "I live outside a lot nowadays, with the Climbing Club, and let me tell you, I do the same thing."

Aaron laughed. "I know what you mean, it doesn't pay to get to the top of the mountain and realize your ski goggles are underneath the tangled pile of clothing you dropped on the floor of the tent the night before."

Annabelle pointed at him. "Exactly."

Carina laughed, slightly embarrassed but thrilled that at least one thing she'd taught them had been helpful. "There's just no need to be sloppy," she murmured. "In the end, someone always has to clean up."

The grandkids shared their s'mores, and their Uncle Aaron recited *The Night Before Christmas* with them, and one by one, they began to yawn.

"I wish you all could have been here earlier, when Max's dad read Christmas stories to the village kids."

"Max told us about that on the way here from the airport," Annabelle said. "We hoped we would get here in time to see it, but apparently they held it earlier than usual this year."

"Oh, that's right. Because of the heavier-than-expected snow moving in." She sipped her hot cocoa. "They also moved up the midnight service at the church. I went with Dr. Lance and his assistant, Bonnie. You may have met her; she's married to Elston." Her eyes closed as she recalled the beautiful service and the hymns and candle lighting afterward.

"Wow," Romy said. "You seem to have made yourself at home here in Crossbow."

Carina's eyes popped open. She'd been on the verge of nodding off, like the kiddos. "The people here are incredibly kind and welcoming." She thought about everyone she'd encountered thus far. "I can't think of anyone I've met who isn't."

Aaron stood, stretching. "I agree," he said. "Max is awesome, doing all this for us. And Elston is amazing as well." He grinned. "I can't wait to check out The Brewery."

"You'll love it," Carina said. "I love it and I thought I didn't even like beer."

"Hey, big bro," Romy whispered to Heath, "help me with this one?" She indicated Jake Jr. who had fallen asleep with his legs across his mom's lap.

"You bet." He scooped up the growing boy as if he weighed nothing. "Can you get the little one?"

Romy nodded, but Aaron was already there. Heather and Philly had gone up first to claim the bathroom before the boys got there.

"Night all." Romy hugged her mother. "So glad you did this. It's great to be with everyone again."

Carina hugged her children, and her grandchildren. "I believe most of the thanks belong to you and Max." She hugged Romy a second time and then went to get the coffee ready for the morning.

"Hey, Mom," Heath stood at the back door, one hand on the knob.

She looked up, the tiny coffee scoop grasped in her fingers, the fragrant scent wafting upward into the cozy kitchen. "What is it, son?" She expected him to say how much they appreciated the guest room over the garage, the way Gia had done.

Instead, he glanced at the floor. "Is there something going on between you and Dr. Lance?"

Carina dropped the coffee scoop and the precious grounds went all over the counter top and onto the floor. "Oh, dear," she swept the mess off the counter into her palm with the edge of her other hand. "Give me the broom, hon." She pointed toward the walk-in pantry.

"Sorry, Mom," he said as Gia appeared and took the broom from him. He ran a long-fingered hand through his hair, obviously embarrassed at what his words had caused.

"It's okay," she replied, seeming a little embarrassed herself. "It was just such an unexpected question."

"I know, I know. Maybe it's none of my business, but I mean, Mom ... you and Dad have never been apart on a holiday. Especially Christmas."

Carina shrugged. "He wasn't coming home for Christmas at all. Not Landon, not here. You know he's working on that big pet food account in San Antonio, said he just didn't have time for Christmas." She bent down to position the dustpan in front of Gia's broom. "But don't worry," she tried to sound reassuring. "He said he'd definitely be home to celebrate at some point."

She straightened up, pushed a lock of humidity-frizzed hair

off her forehead, and smiled sweetly. At least she hoped it was sweetly. Some folks said she should never play poker.

Gia opened the cabinet that housed the small kitchen garbage can so Carina could dump the contents of the dustpan. "Sorry, Mom," she murmured. Then she spontaneously hugged her mother-in-law and placed a quick kiss on her temple.

Carina patted her hand. "Nothing to worry about. He's just got a big fish on the line, says if he pulls them to shore—meaning if he saves them from bankruptcy—he's been promised a percentage of the company." She smacked her forehead with the back of her hand. "But there you go. I swore to him I wouldn't tell anyone about that."

Heath grinned, relief softening his handsome features. "I guess now that you've told us, you'll have to kill us. Isn't that the way it goes?"

She laughed. "That's what your Great Uncle Wally always said."

At a look from Gia, Heath explained. "He's the one who worked at the Pentagon. When I was a kid, I asked him what he did there. I had no idea what the Pentagon was, but it sounded kind of witchy—"

"Pentagram," Gia murmured.

"Right. Anyhow, he pulled me close and whispered in my ear, 'I could tell you, kid. But then I'd have to kill you.' Then he sat back in his chair, lit his pipe, and looked over my head as if he'd never uttered a word."

"What'd you do?"

Heath's cheeks reddened. "I got out of there. And didn't look back."

"I could've cheerfully killed Wally for scaring you that way," Carina said. "But I didn't know about it until years later when you refused to go with us to visit them."

Heath's eyebrows went up. "Romy told you, didn't she?"

"Yes, but not until we were on the way home. In fact, it was kind of funny. She just piped up out of the blue and said, 'I don't know why Heath is so scared of him'." Carina put the coffee in the filter and filled the tank with water. "Of course, I *made* her tell me the story then." Pushing the coffee machine back into its place in the corner, she turned to her son. "You never saw him after that, did you?"

Heath shook his head. "Nope. I always chose to stay with Gran and Gramps. Stupid, huh?" He ducked his head but glanced up at his wife through his thick sandy lashes. "Your giant hubby is a wimp at heart. Disappointed?"

She bonked him on the nose with the top of her head. "Sooo disappointed. In fact, let's call a lawyer this minute. I don't think I can stay married to someone who was frightened out of his little boy wits when he was what? Nine years old?"

Carina looped her arms around the two of them. "You guys are going to be the best parents." She nuzzled them both as if they were puppies. "Now, get. Get out of here so I can go to bed. I've got to get up early to get the turkey in the oven."

Gia glanced down at her flat tummy, her hand seeming to go there without her knowledge. "I noticed you already have a lot of the sides in the fridge, ready to reheat," she said.

Heath winked. "See what we were talking about earlier? Always prepared."

Carina tapped her temple with her forefinger. "Just think. If I tried to cook everything tomorrow, we'd be at it all day long. The oven barely holds the turkey and dressing, no way it will hold the sweet potatoes, corn casserole, and green beans amandine."

Gia clapped her hands. "But if they're done ahead of time, you can just warm them in the microwave."

"Nuke 'em," Heath said.

"That's right," Carina laughed. "Besides, I'll have to bake the bread as soon as the turkey comes out to rest." She laughed at their expressions. "Now, shoo. Go to your lavish private garage apartment. And remember, we only got here because Max and I became friends in Grief Group." She glanced back at Tom the Gingerbread Man in his little basket. "And that little furball is the reason Dr. Lance became a new friend." She smiled more gently. "Which reminds me, the Lord works in mysterious ways, doesn't He?"

"Yes, He does. You were feeling very down before you got here, weren't you?" Heath murmured.

Carina took the powerful flashlight from the counter and opened the back door (since no one else seemed intent on doing it). "I was a *little* down." She glanced out at the spitting snow. "But it's all right now. Having all my babies here is the very best medicine for the blues." She put a hand on each of them and practically shoved them out the door.

Then she pointed the light at the corner of the snow-covered porch. "The kitten was right there. Little Tom the Gingerbread Man. The first morning after I arrived."

"He does work in mysterious ways," Heath said.

"Thank God you heard him crying." Gia took the flashlight and stepped off the bottom step.

"Hey," Carina called. "Do the others know about the baby?"

Gia laughed. "Yes, they do. I wanted to make the announcement tomorrow at dinner when we were all together, but ..."

"I was afraid I let the cat out of the bag earlier," Carina said.

Heath hung his head and raised his hand. "It was me. I'm the blurter. I'm a proud dad-to-be, not gonna deny it."

Carina whooped. "Good for you ... I guess." She didn't blame them for wanting to make a big to-do, but Heath was so comical she couldn't blame him. "Goodnight, you two. Get some rest." She looked out across the snowy woods, a few lines from the famous Robert Frost poem appearing in her mind.

Whose woods are these, I think I know,
His house is in the village though ...

"You too, Mom," Heath called over his shoulder. His tone of voice said he knew that she wouldn't sleep in.

"I'll bet she's up before the sun," he whispered to Gia as they arrived at the stairs to the apartment.

"She'll have to be," Gia agreed, climbing the steps. "I heard her say the kitten has to be fed every three or four hours."

Heath groaned. "I'll go and help with the turkey first thing in the morning. I want you to sleep as late as possible."

Gia stopped on the landing and held out one arm. "Here, twist my arm when you say that. That way I won't feel so guilty when I roll back over in the morning." Her husband kissed her instead.

They entered the warm and cozy studio apartment together. Smiles on both their faces. "I have one more thing to do before we sleep," Heath said, pulling up his dad's name on his phone. "I can't understand where Dad is. He was supposed to arrive first."

CARINA CLOSED THE BACK DOOR GENTLY. SHE WAS GLAD THEY WERE so happy, and that they'd made the trip after all. She looked in on the kitten, banked the fire and adjusted the fire screen, then slowly climbed the stairs to check on all her other treasures.

Her heart felt full to overflowing as she peeked in on the children nestled in the bunk beds, their mom and aunt sharing one of the full beds—just as they had when they were girls—and even sweet Aaron, who had been granted the other full bed all on his own.

Carina would've dropped a gentle kiss on each little brow if she hadn't been afraid of waking them. Instead, she blew them all an air kiss intended to sprinkle love across their sleeping heads like feathery snowflakes or sugary gumdrop dust.

CHAPTER 23

CHRISTMAS DAY

CHRISTMAS MORNING, CARINA STOOD AT THE OVEN, A CHEERFUL red apron covering her deep green fleece top—with the silly lighted reindeer.

When Heath came in the back door, she had an oven mitt on one hand and appeared to be checking the seal on the tin foil tenting the turkey.

He hurried to her side. "The bird's already in the oven?"

She nodded. "Been in a while, just basting a bit." She closed the oven door and pulled off her mitt.

"You must've been up for hours already."

"Oh, no," she laughed. "Only a little while. Remember who you're talking to? Ms. Always Be Prepared. You boys weren't the only ones reading those scouting manuals, you know."

Her big son gave her a side hug. "At least let me help with the kitten." He started toward the basket by the fireplace.

"Oh, he ate a while ago." She motioned toward the fire which had burned down to embers. "You can build that up if you want. Not too much. We're on propane, and it will get warmer as the sun comes through those windows, anyway."

She stopped and examined the Christmas scene. "Merry Christmas, son. Isn't that the prettiest tree?"

"It sure is." Heath stacked a couple of logs on the grate. "I'm glad you're getting back to your old self, Mom." He stood and murmured. "We've missed you."

Carina tried not to show how that statement took her breath away. *Had it been so obvious?* She thought of the 'possible story' title in her journal, now stored safely beneath a thin stack of undies in the top dresser drawer.

Just then, a small voice piped up, "I'm hungee ..." Little Sean stood in patch of winter sunlight, rubbing his big blue eyes and yawning.

"Hey, big'un.'" Heath scooped him up with one arm. "Let's get a cup of coffee and see what Gan has for breakfast, shall we?" He winked at Carina and carried the toddler to the kitchen.

"Nope," Sean said, as Heath plopped him onto one of the barstools. "Gotta go bafroom." He headed back toward the stairs, not giving them a chance to tell him there was another bathroom just off Carina's bedroom.

Romy passed him coming down. "He must be headed to the bafroom." She stepped into the kitchen.

"Exactly right," Carina said. "You know, I just realized I don't have any kids' cereal or anything like that." She opened the fridge. "But I did buy extra sausage since you know I use it in the dressing for the turkey." When she straightened up, she also held two cans of biscuits in her hands.

"Yay, Mom," Heath took the biscuits and banged them against the counter to open them. "I didn't even think about not having enough food for everyone on Christmas morning."

"It's our traditional breakfast, anyway," Romy said. "We'll just make those sausage patties a little thin. No one will notice. Some of the kids will probably only eat biscuits and jelly or honey, whatever you've got."

Carina nodded. "I've got grape jelly."

"That's perfect," her daughter said. "Do you have peanut butter?"

"I do!"

She smiled. "Breakfast is served, then. We're kind of easy when it comes to food."

Heath laughed. "Y'all keep talking, I'm taking notes."

His sister thumped him on the back of the head. "I'm so glad you're finally joining the parent club."

"Me too," Carina said as she slid the large baking sheet full of raw biscuits onto the upper rack of the oven. It barely fit. She closed the oven door and turned the temperature up a few degrees. "Maybe I should have made toast."

Both kids laughed. "Wouldn't be the same, Mom. Not the same at all." Then Romy burst out laughing and said, "What am I saying? The kids will love toast and jam or peanut butter ... the biscuits and sausage are all mine." She rubbed her hands together comically.

"Not if I get to them first," Heath warned.

Just then, Carina caught a bit of movement outside the front window. "What on earth?" She stepped around Romy and hurried over for a closer look.

The big Jeep had turned into the far end of the driveway, pushing snow aside as it came. Behind the wheel, Max wore a huge grin. Dr. Lance may have been grinning, too, it was hard to tell behind his white beard and jaunty Santa hat.

Max stopped near the end of the drive. Santa stepped out of the Jeep and made his way toward the cabin through the knee-deep snow.

Carina placed one hand over her gaping mouth so she wouldn't spoil the surprise. But it was too late. As the tall red-clad man came walking up out of the falling snow, four pairs of feet came thundering down the stairs. "Santa," they cried. "Santa's coming!"

As they rushed past her, Heather leaned toward her and whispered, "I know it isn't Santa, but you know … *kids*."

Carina winked at her. "Thanks for not blabbing."

As Santa and Max made their way up onto the porch, sleepy, squiggly haired Aaron walked down the stairs and took up residence in the recliner. "Wha's all the ruckus?" he asked.

Everyone laughed as Philly yanked open the front door and yelled. "It is Santa! Santa's *here*."

The two little boys dashed out and grabbed him by the hand, pulling him inside as if he might resist.

"Ho, ho, ho," he bellowed. "Has anyone been good this year?"

All four children, and Aaron, raised their hands.

The kids push/guided Santa to the couch and Max carefully closed the door and waved at the group. The back door opened admitting Gia, who stamped her boots and then pulled them off, one at a time. "What's going on? I nearly killed myself trying to get over here. Did I hear sleigh bells?" She was obviously pretending not to notice the big man in the red suit in the center of the room.

Max pulled a row of bells from his pocket and shook them lightly. There were eight bells attached to a leather strip, perfect for hanging above a door, or on a reindeer's harness. Carina recalled the sound from last night and from the Christmas story time downtown.

As the kids jostled for position around Santa, Max slipped quietly back out to the Jeep. Carina watched as he removed four large, brightly colored plastic discs from the cargo area. He had them stacked one inside the other like giant rainbow Frisbees. One was green, one red, another purple, and the last one bright blue.

When he turned them toward her, to close the Jeep's rear gate, she could read Flexible Flyer stamped across the broad bottom of the blue one. Handles were built right into the sides of the discs, and the shallow centers were perfectly shaped for children.

While she watched Max out the window, Heather and Philly —the usual partners in crime—sorted all the tiny gifts under the tree. In no time, there were four separate piles of presents. One for each child. Behind the tree were also a few more gifts that didn't fit any of the kids' stacks.

Sean stopped studying Santa long enough to notice what they were doing. "Can we open?" He wore a look of consternation on his little face.

"I don't see why not," Romy said. "Any objections?"

Jake had no objections, but he did have a burning question. "How come Santa didn't come down the chimbley?"

Carina laughed behind her hand. I wouldn't touch that with a ten-foot pole, she thought. But she didn't have to. Heather put on her big-sister face and said, "This isn't the real Santa, silly. Only the real Santa comes down the chim*ney*. Besides, he came to our house in Texas early, remember?" She almost rolled her eyes but must have felt the weight of her mother's stare. "I mean, this is the *official* Santa's helper guy. You know. Every town has one."

Romy nodded and gave her daughter a little smile.

Another good save, Carina thought. Then she jumped up, alerted by the smell of baking bread. "The biscuits!" She hurried to the kitchen, grabbed a potholder, and flung open the oven door. "Perfect. One more minute and they would've burned."

"Are you hungee, Santa?" Little Sean asked.

Santa rubbed his strangely poofy belly. "I could eat a biscuit."

Jake piped up, "We might have some cookies, too."

Everyone laughed. Jake's face fell. "Santa always eats cookies," he mumbled.

"You know, I wouldn't mind one of each," Santa said. "If it isn't too much trouble."

"I'm just starting the sausage," Carina said. "Shall we eat first? Then open those gifts?"

Annabelle made her way to the coffee pot. "Sounds good, Mom." She pecked Carina on the cheek. "What can I do to help?"

Max came in, empty-handed, and pulled off his boots inside the front door. In the kitchen, he smiled and winked at Carina, and she got the idea the sleds were left out on the porch, a Christmas surprise from Santa.

She wanted to ask him where on earth he'd gotten them on such short notice but wasn't about to risk spilling the beans.

He wasn't looking at her anymore, anyway. His eyes were on Annabelle.

"Cold?" Annabelle asked.

Rubbing his unmittened palms together, Max nodded. "Little chilly. But thank the Lord the snow squall was only a whimper."

She held up an empty mug. "Would this help?"

Max grinned. "I thought you'd never ask."

After pouring, she held it toward him. "Cream or sugar?"

"Black, thanks." He sipped. "No time for extravagant stuff in the hospital. Take it on the run and hope it doesn't scald the tongue."

Annabelle sipped her own cup. "Just like camp. I always get it while it's hot off the fire." She looked up at her new friend. "You ever get time for weekend trips?"

Carina swallowed the drink she'd just taken from her own mug and nearly scalded *her* throat. Was this her girl, flirting? She'd never seen this side of Annabelle. *Ever.*

Without a moment's hesitation, Max replied. "I could make time."

Carina turned back to the gently frying sausage, turned it down even more, and slipped over to the family room. All the gifts were passed out and Romy appeared to be waiting on a signal from her. Second in command, Carina thought. It's always been that way between the two of us. The second mom. Funny how that worked.

Until now, she'd never even realized how much she had always depended on her eldest girl. Heath was more like his father, do anything for anyone if he was around. Trouble was, he often wasn't. He also worked like his father.

"What's the hold up?" she joked. "Don't we always let the youngest go first?"

That was the cue Little Sean had been waiting for. "He grabbed the first gift off his pile and tore into it." He wasn't disappointed with a superhero action figure.

Jake opened his next. He also got an action figure. Carina knew there would be epic battles in the snow later. The girls went next, in order of youngest first, and both were delighted by bracelets with their names on them.

There were several other small gifts for grandchildren and children as well.

Carina also had several to open. One was a pretty necklace with all the kids' and grandkids' birthstones arranged in a gold, semi-circle heart. The design left room to add more stones as needed. She thought of the little one Gia was carrying and smiled. Romy fastened the dainty gold chain around her neck.

"I love it," Carina said, holding the stones up to the light. She went on to unwrap a pretty turquoise blouse, a novel by Mitch Albom, and a desk size book of inspirational quotes. When she opened the quote book, she was surprised to read an inscription written in an unfamiliar hand.

"Thanks for all you do for others," it read. "Especially me." It was signed Max Paper.

"Oh, my goodness," she said. "I got so carried away, I forgot to look at the gift tag." She glanced at her young friend. "Thank you, Max. This means a lot." She then touched the beautiful necklace, the silky blouse, and the two books which were sitting upon her knees. "All my gifts mean so much. Almost as much as having you all here with me."

Carina felt a lump growing in her throat, so she stopped talking and her hand went to her mouth, but before she could utter an exclamation about the still sizzling sausage, Annabelle called out, "Don't worry, Mom. I'm on it."

Everyone stood and began to gather their gifts and gift wrappings. Max and his father looked at one another and Santa gave a nod. "Boys and girls," he said in a deep voice, "it seems there is one more gift Santa couldn't fit under the tree." He turned to Max. "Young man, if you don't mind ..."

Max walked to the door and pulled it open. He had placed the sleds within easy reach, but when he pulled open the door, it wasn't a sled he brought back in, it was Alfred.

"Ho, ho, ho," Alfred called, a red and white Santa hat on his head.

"Gampy!" The children crashed into him like waves on the shore. "Where have you been?" Philly cried. "You were supposed to be here before us."

Alfred hugged them and kissed them and hoisted Little Sean into the crook of his arm. "My plane was delayed because of ice. Big drop in temperature there." He waded through the children toward the kitchen. "I sent your mom a text. Didn't she get it?" He glanced up at Romy.

"Oh, I got it," she said. "And I told them about it." She grinned. "They're just scolding you because it's Christmas and Santa is already here so they don't have to be good anymore."

Everyone laughed.

"Not true," Santa said. "They still need to mind their Ps & Qs because there are four more gifts still unaccounted for."

Alfred looked at me, then at Santa. "Could it be those colorful things I saw out on the porch?"

Santa laughed. Max laughed. Carina laughed. And all the kids dashed for the door. Alfred caught Carina's eye. "I'm sorry," he mouthed. "I got here as soon as I could."

Carina felt her own ice begin to melt. Until now, she hadn't even realized how frozen she felt inside. "It's okay," she said aloud. "You're here now." She followed the children toward the porch.

Alfred stood in her path. "I've missed you." He took her in his arms, holding her only a few inches from him.

"I missed you, too," she said. "We all have." Their lips met briefly, with an old familiar promise of more to come.

A chorus of squeals arose from the front porch. "What are they?" Little Sean bellowed, obviously thrilled with whatever the colorful things were.

"They're sleds," Philly yelled. "For the hill over there!" Then she lowered her voice. "They are sleds, aren't they, Santa?"

Max and Santa both laughed and herded the kids back inside. Each one had a large Flexible Flyer. "That's exactly what they are," Alfred exclaimed. "You see, I knew you all would be here when it snowed, so I sent Santa a secret message—through Annabelle and Max—and asked him to bring sleds to all my good little grandkids." He grinned like a possum. "Just in case I couldn't get here in time."

Annabelle spoke up. "But no one goes sledding on an empty tummy!" She held aloft a platter of biscuits stuffed with thin sausage patties.

Everyone crowded around the table and onto barstools at the counter. Milk was poured, along with juice and coffee. "I'll put on another pot of coffee, Mom," Romy said around a mouthful of food.

Even Gia wolfed down a couple. "What?" she said, when Heath looked at her aghast. "Apparently, the baby isn't vegetarian."

"Definitely a boy," Heath replied. "My boy," he crowed.

Everyone laughed.

Jake looked at the empty platter. "Gan, do you have peanut butter and jelly?"

"I sure do, kiddo," she said. "Grape jelly. I hope that's all right."

"It's my favorite." His voice was serious. "Can I have it on toast?"

"I'll get it, Mom," Gia said. "It sounds pretty good to me, too." She blushed self-consciously. "I guess my days of morning sickness are over."

"Thank God," Heath muttered.

She elbowed him when she walked by.

Alfred reached out and clutched her in a brief hug. "I'm so glad you're feeling better."

She clasped his hand. "Thank you, Papa Bear."

He grinned again, obviously delighted by the nickname she'd given him when she and Heath had first married.

CHAPTER 24

ALL'S WELL THAT ENDS WELL

As soon as the milk and juice glasses were empty, the four kids scurried up the stairs to get dressed. "I can't wait," one cried.

"I'll be first!" cried Heather.

"Not if I get there before you," said another.

"Get out of the way, Sean" Jake cried. "*Hurry.*"

Philly chimed in, "All of you better move, 'cause I'm coming through." She came thundering down, clothes askew, wearing two different socks. "I'm ready. Let me put my boots on." An entire row of boots was lined up on the waterproof runner along the wall.

All the commotion woke the kitten and before Carina could get there, Alfred had plucked the baby out of its nest and was nuzzling him under his chin. "Aren't you a tiny thing?" he asked the kitten.

Carina watched him, questions running through her mind. Why hadn't he called or texted? Was the job finished? Was it done? And on top of all that, how had he known to call Max?

In a way, it reminded her of her twenty-first birthday. They had only been married a few months, still in the bright, shiny, honeymoon phase, and Alfred had rented the entire community swimming pool and invited everyone they knew. And somehow, they'd all kept it a complete secret. To say she'd been stunned would be an understatement.

She wondered if it could be that simple this time? But she had no time to ponder, the other kids had made it down the stairs without killing each other and they were all on the floor, pulling on their boots. Philly finished first, grabbed the purple sled and headed out the door.

"Hang on there, kiddo," Romy called from the kitchen. She and Gia had cleaned up the table while Annabelle washed the meager dishes. Aaron, the last one to finish his biscuits and sausage, took his plate to the sink and began to dry the dishes on the drainboard.

Heath headed to the door where Philly waited. "I got her, Sis," he said. "We'll get this party started." He turned back to the room. "C'mon, troops. Grab your coats and don't forget your gloves." And with that, he was out the door.

Max grinned and went out behind him. Then he stuck his head back in the door. "Santa left a couple more sleds out here. They're a little bit bigger."

Annabelle dried her hands, grabbed her coat, and pulled on her boots. "C'mon little Sean, I'll help you." He was struggling with his jacket zipper. "Hold on, Uncle Aaron's coming, too."

Before long, the only ones left in the cabin were Carina, Alfred, Gia, and Santa.

"Whew," Dr. Lance said, pulling off his long, white beard. "That thing's a little itchy."

"Doc," Alfred said, "I sure want to thank you for getting those flying discs." He chuckled. "I don't know how you pulled it off on Christmas morning."

Carina quickly heated a bottle of formula for the kitten and carried it to Alfred. He handed her the mewing baby with a smile. "I've got to get out there," he said. "You don't mind?"

"Of course not," she said. "I'll be out as soon as I get this little one fed and all his tires rotated."

"I'm coming, too, Papa Bear," Gia said. She pulled on her own coat and gloves. "I can't wait to see those kids fly." Giggling, she continued, "Maybe Max will let me try one, too."

When they were gone, Carina sat down in the recliner, the kitten still cuddled in the crook of her arm, nursing from the bottle as if he'd always been doing it. "It didn't take this one long to figure out what he needed." She glanced at her red-clad friend. "How in the world did all this come about?"

Dr. Lance laughed. It wasn't quite as deep as his Santa laugh, but almost. "Apparently Max and Annabelle have been texting for a couple of days." He wagged his head comically. "They seemed to have hit it off even before they met up at the airport."

"Hmm," Carina said, not sure how that happened. "But Alfred? The discs?"

"Well, it seems your children were quite worried when they got here and found me and not your husband." He smiled. "Of course, even Max didn't know about our friendship. But apparently Romy did some checking and they all put their heads together and once you mentioned the kitten and the kindly vet named Dr. Lance, Max figured things out."

Carina laughed. "I didn't know you were Max's dad at first." She thought back to that first harried trip to town with tiny Gingerbread in her tote bag. "So, what'd they do when Max found out?"

"Someone called Alfred and read him the riot act. That's what he said, anyway." He chuckled again. "Later, he told me privately that he'd been intending to surprise you like he'd done on your twenty-first birthday." He shrugged. "I didn't know what he meant and he swore me to secrecy. 'Let the kids think they got one over on their old dad', he said."

"That sounds like Alfred," I agreed. "He threw me a huge surprise party the first year we were married. It was amazing.

But I'm still confused," she said. "You mean they called him in San Antonio as soon as they got here last night? They really thought you and I were, you know—"

Dr. Lance nodded. "Alfred was supposed to fly into Denver yesterday, hours before the kids did. But his plane was delayed twice, and he couldn't even get a call through to anyone because after the kids landed, he was finally in the air. So, when the kids got here and found me and not him …" he made a shocked face. "When he did get enough bars to call, he had several messages from the kids." He laughed. "That's when he quizzed me quite thoroughly. Which Max had already done."

He chuckled again. "By the end of the conversation, Alfred was asking me if I could find four little sleds. He sounded like a kid himself, looking forward to a snow day off from school."

Carina shook her head. "What a *mess* I created. Here I thought no one was thinking of me at all, and they were all busting their butts trying to get here to surprise me." She felt a little ashamed even though everything had worked out so well. "But come to think of it, how *did* you find those sleds?"

Eyes twinkling, he smiled. "It pays to be the best vet in town. Carl Melucca had them in his shop. I remembered seeing them yesterday when I went to pick up new ski boots for Max." He hesitated. "You know, just in case he wants to ski while he's here."

Carina squeezed a bit of paste onto her finger for the Gingerbread Man. "Is that the same shop where I bought Aaron's lift tickets? The one where the owner lives upstairs?"

He nodded. "Good people, Carl and Carol."

"That reminds me," Carina said. "Did you and Max have any time to talk, or did my problems take precedence?"

Dr. Lance rubbed his chin and cheeks where the beard had irritated his skin. "We did. After we left here last night, we both admitted we'd been stupid and prideful over the years." Tears filled his eyes but did not fall. "I told him how sorry I was about Andrea. Of course, I'd told him at her funeral, but I knew he didn't hear me then. He told me how numb he'd been. How lost." He looked at Carina. "Until he found you."

"Well, not me, really. It was the group. The grief group, you know." She dried the kitty's chin and placed him in his shallow kitty litter box to see if he could use it.

He crawled around a bit, acted like he might dig, then let out a tiny mew. "I think he may get the hang of it," she said.

The tiny thing gave up and tried to climb out. Carina got up and warmed a washcloth under the tap, picked up the baby and sat back down. She laid him on his back on a thick towel and bathed him with the warm water. "There you go, that's a good boy." Afterward, she dried him gently and tucked him back into his warm bed in the laundry basket.

"You're very good at that," Dr. Lance said. "Nurturing comes naturally to you. That's why you connected with Max." He closed his mouth as if done, then decided to continue. "I feel that's how you and I connected, too."

She nodded, but said, "You're the one who cares for everyone in this town, all your animals, the employees at the clinic." Carina pulled on her boots as she spoke. "I've seen you interacting with everyone from Bonnie and Elston to the girl at the grocery store to the children at story time. If anyone's a natural, it's you." She stretched to the back of the rack for her coat and gloves. "I think you and Max are a lot alike. Especially that stubborn streak, my goodness." A giggle escaped her lips. "I'm glad we are all in a better place now." She looked him up and down as he stood and reached for his beard.

"So, Santa," she said. "Do you need a jacket over all that padding?" She poked at his spongy belly. "Or will you be alright to fly like that?"

He reared back, held his belly, and "ho ho ho'd" again. "I'll be fine," he said. "And for the record, I'm really glad you and your whole family came to Crossbow." He smiled the kindly smile that had first warmed her heart. "I hope we can make this an annual thing."

Carina grinned. "I love the way you always say what's on your mind, and for the record, I think that would be fantastic. And in case I don't get to say it later, I want you to know how much I appreciate everything you've done for me. For Alfred and me. And the kids." She waved her hands. "For *all* of us."

He placed one palm on her back and pushed her gently toward the door. "That goes for me, too, friend. Me, too."

Together, they stepped out into the gently falling snow. On the shallow hill beside the cabin, shouts of glee rang out, only slightly muffled. Carina pulled out her iPhone and hit record. "Now this is what I call Christmas."

Santa hopped off the bottom step and turned to hold his hand out so she wouldn't slip. "Watch your step," he said.

Carina pushed stop on the recording and slid the phone back into her pocket. He's right, she thought. I don't want to miss this while trying to record a memory. Now's the time for making memories—

She watched as Alfred dragged little Sean's sled back up the side of the hill. "C'mon, buddy," he called. "Let's go again!" The other kids and grandkids were flying down and climbing back up one by one. Whoops and shrieks accompanied the sledders.

"This is the best place for a winter vacation," Carina said.

"It sure is," Dr. Lance agreed. "I can't believe Max offered it back to Andrea's parents."

"I'm not completely surprised," Carina said. "He felt so much guilt about keeping it when it had belonged to her grandfather."

"But he's put so work much into it now. It was nothing but a sha—"

A snowball came flying out of nowhere and whapped Santa in the belly. "Oh, you've asked for it now," he yelled.

"Ho ho ho," Carina said. "Merry Christmas, Santa!"

He took off after Max, the suspected snowball sneak. "I'll get you for that." He stooped along the way and scooped up a huge handful of snow.

Carina looked up at the sky. The snow was not thick, but it was steady, the flakes large and fluffy again. The Jeep's tracks on the drive were growing shallower and shallower.

Alfred left the hill after handing Little Sean off to his Uncle Heath. He made his way down to where Carina stood, his footfalls silent in the powder. "What are you thinking, my pretty wife?" He slipped off his glove and stuck his hand in the deep pocket of her coat.

She pulled off her own glove and slid it in the pocket, too. Their fingers wove together the same as they'd done for decades. She felt the familiar shape of his long, strong fingers, every callus from his golf habit, even the ridges in the grown-back thumbnail he had lost after he smashed it while attempting to build her a greenhouse last year.

His voice was warm in her ear. "I'm so sorry my surprise fell apart. If I'd just sent you a message before I got on that first plane in San Antonio."

"Who knows what might have happened?" she said. "Anyway, all's well that ends well."

He leaned into her back, pressing his chin over her shoulder. "Still love me?"

"Oh, you know I do," she said. "I'm a little angry though. And a bit confused as to why you've been so out of touch. You felt so far away."

He pulled her back against his body. "I'm an old fool," he said. "I have no excuse other than tunnel vision."

Carina felt herself begin to relax at last. "I thought you'd found someone else to spend Christmas with."

"Stupid, stupid, me." He turned her around to face him, the snowflakes caught up in his thick dark lashes. "May I ask you a question?"

"Of cour—"

He knelt on one knee in front of her, and somehow, Carina felt the years slip away as his fingers slipped out of hers. "What on earth?"

Alfred reached into his own coat pocket and produced a black velvet jewel box. Slowly, his fingers pried up the hinged top. The lining was emerald colored satin. "Look how the dew sparkles like a handful of diamonds flung out across the valley," he whispered. "That beautiful green grass could be the lining in a fancy lady's jewel box—"

"Oh, Alfred," she picked up a dainty gold ring with a perfectly huge cushion cut diamond. "A jewel box full of diamond dew."

"You never let me buy you one before. Not in all the years we've been married." He cleared his throat, "But now that we own part of a large—and totally *organic*—pet food company, I thought it was time." He grinned that hopeful grin Carina had fallen in love with so many years ago.

"Super Al strikes again," he joked. "That diamond represents our first dividend check. No more buying on time for us. But more importantly, it represents the question I want to ask you."

"Your knee is getting soaked," she mumbled.

He laughed, the corners of his brown eyes crinkling the way they always did when he was happy. "My darling little pragmatist," he said. "Will you marry me? Will you marry me all over again, Carina Pinner?"

Carina pulled him to his feet and kissed him soundly. "Of course I will," she whispered. "If we can have a destination wedding this time."

He held her away from him and gazed into her face. "Only if that destination is Vicenza, Italy."

She smiled and pulled him in for another kiss. "You read my mind."

Joyful yelling broke out all along the small hill. "Yay, Gan! Yay, Gampy!" Even the adults clapped and cheered.

Carina felt her face flame, but it was all right. There was

plenty of snow to cool her cheeks. She held her diamond up to the winter light. "I swear Alfred Pinner, the things I have to go through to get a Christmas gift from you." She thought of the unfinished story in her journal. *Write myself a Christmas, indeed. No need for that, not with this family around.*

Alfred kissed her burning cheek. "Penny for your thoughts?"

Looking into his eyes, she said, "I owe you a big congratulations on your business deal." She took his hand and stuck it back inside her pocket. "I haven't been very supportive of your work lately."

His fingers clasped hers. "You've been through a lot the past few years. I just wanted to get to retirement sooner so we can be together all the time."

Carina squeezed his fingers. "Thank you, Super Al." She kissed him a second time. "Merry Christmas to us."

PLEASE REVIEW

We hope you enjoyed *A Crossbow Christmas* by Ann Swann. If you did, we would ask that you please rate and review this title. Every review helps our authors.

Rate and Review: A Crossbow Christmas

MEET THE AUTHOR

Ann Swann was born in West Texas. She grew up much like Stevie-girl in *The Phantom Pilot* series, though she never got up the nerve to enter the haunted house. Ann has done everything from answering 911 Emergency calls to teaching elementary school. She lives in Texas with her husband, Dude, and several rescue pets. When she's not writing, Ann is reading. Her to-be-read list has grown so large it has taken on a life of its own. She calls it Herman.

OTHER TITLES FROM

5 PRINCE PUBLISHING

www.5princebooks.com

Kennedy Devereaux *Bernadette Marie*
The Seven Spires *Russell Archey*
At Last *Bernadette Marie*
Masterpiece *Bernadette Marie*
A Tropical Christmas *Bernadette Marie*
Corporate Christmas *Bernadette Marie*
Faith Through Falling Snow *Sandy Sinnett*
Walker Defense *Bernadette Marie*
Clash of the Cheerleaders *April Marcom*
Stevie-Girl and the Phantom of Forever *Ann Swann*
The Last Goodbye *Bernadette Marie*
The Gingerbread Curse *April Marcom*
Stevie-Girl and the Phantom of Crybaby Bridge *Ann Swann*

PUBLISHER ACKNOWLEDGEMENTS

The team at 5 Prince Publishing would like to give special thanks to the following people for helping make A Crossbow Christmas the best that it can be:

Bernadette Soehner, Cate Byers, Marianne Nowicki, Sophie Jefferson, Cayla Rusielewicz, Laura Chambers, and Lindsey Haggerty. We would also like to thank our Brand Ambassadors, touring companies, bloggers, and influencers that help to promote the work of Ann Swann.